SMOKED OUT

DAVID WOLF BOOK 6

JEFF CARSON

CROSS ATLANTIC PUBLISHING

CHAPTER 1

TWO THUMPS RIPPED Wolf out of his sleep.

Or so he thought. The silence in his ranch house living room was absolute save the ticking clock. The walls flickered in the darkened space as muzzle blasts puffed out of an actor's revolver on the muted television.

With a slow breath, he tried to blank out the throbbing in his limbs. Every time he woke, the pain seemed to have multiplied anew from the previous conscious moment; of course, being drugged up on Percocet and a smattering of other pills, adding doses of Scotch to the cocktail of medication, made it hard to remember those previous conscious moments.

This must be what it's like to have Alzheimer's. How many times had he repeated that thought in the past few days? What day was it?

He craned his neck as crunching footsteps approached his house outside, and then a knock on the door echoed in his skull, making him cringe.

He cracked his lips and peeled his tongue from the top of his mouth. "Come in."

There was no response.

"Come in!" Pain shot through his pelvis.

The knob turned and the door opened, letting in a burst of light that assaulted his eyeballs.

"Mr. Wolf?"

"Yeah."

"My name is Special Agent Cumberland with the FBI."

Two men were silhouetted in his open doorway, holding square ID wallets in his direction. He lay back and closed his eyes, staring at their after-image burned into his retinas. "I'll have to take your word for that. Come in."

"This is the Assistant Special Agent in Charge of the Denver field office, Steven Frye. We're here to ask you a few questions."

Wolf reached over and grabbed the handle of the oversized plastic cup of water and sucked from the straw. He was vaguely surprised that it was so full, cold, and rattling with ice. He drew a blank trying to remember who had filled it. It could have been any number of people who came in and out of his house as of late. Probably the big nurse.

"Open those shades," one of the agents said.

His living room brightened and Wolf tried to straighten in his reclined hospital bed, sending another bolt of pain from his pelvis up his spine. He broke into a sweat and pulled off his sheet, letting the relatively cool air caress his damp gown.

Fumbling at his sides for the bed controls, he found the plastic box next to his leg cast and pushed the incline button.

As the bed whirred, one of the agents stepped in front of the television. He was tall and wide, and filled out his suit with muscle underneath. Holding mirrored sunglasses in one hand, his badge wallet hung in his other.

"Let me see those badges and IDs again."

The big agent glanced at his partner and handed it over.

The badges were real, and the ID cards looked genuine enough. Cumberland was the tall guy in front of him, and ASAC Frye was the other man to his left that he'd yet to look at properly.

Both men had military cuts in their pictures and no-nonsense blank facial expressions. They wore white dress shirts and black ties cinched around muscular necks.

When Wolf looked up, the two men were identical in dress and presentation to their IDs. But from each other they were different in every way. Cumberland was tall and imposing, while Frye was short and wiry. It looked like Cumberland had to endure a grueling physical routine to hold his shape, while Frye had to eat to hold his.

He handed the wallets back. "What questions?"

Cumberland tilted his chin up. "We need to ask you about the night Sarah Muller and Carter Willis were murdered. Straighten up a few things."

Though he spent most waking moments thinking about Sarah and her gut-wrenching demise by the hand of an unknown coward, the mention of her by these agents startled him to the core. "Straighten up a few things? What's there to straighten up?"

Cumberland clenched his fists and spread his hands while gazing around Wolf's living room.

It was a reflexive move for the big man, Wolf thought, like the agent was trying to contain anger.

Agent Frye cleared his throat. "What were you doing the night of Sarah Muller and Carter Willis's deaths?"

Wolf took a deep breath, suppressing upwelling rage at the direction the conversation had steered. "I was out having a drink."

"With a woman who was a suspect in your murder investigation up at Cold Lake, correct?" Frye asked.

"At the time, she was a person of interest."

"Until what time were you two having a drink?"

"I don't know. Nine-thirty? Ten?"

"You're not too sure about this because?"

"I left under extenuating circumstances."

Frye blew air from his mouth. "And I guess what you mean by that is you were in a fight with a man named Carter Willis, knocked unconscious, and dragged out of there by this woman of interest?"

"Something like that."

Cumberland squeezed his hands into fists again.

"Have you heard that said woman of interest, Miss Kimber Grey, aka Rachel Kipling, has just committed suicide at County Hospital?"

"No, I haven't."

"Ah. Well she has. So, there goes your alibi right there."

"Actually, you don't have your facts straight. I don't think I was having drinks with Rachel that night. I think it was her twin sister, Hannah Kipling, whom I pulled off a cliff and killed. So, actually, my alibi was long gone before Rachel offed herself."

Frye smiled without teeth. "So, you have no alibi for your whereabouts for the rest of that night. We talked to the bartender at the Pony Tavern. You were dragged out of there at closer to nine p.m., so you had the whole night ahead of you to recover from your fight and take care of whatever you needed to."

Wolf ignored the bait.

"You've got motive like nobody else," Frye continued.

"What's this guy here for? To stand and flex? You mind moving away from the TV there, Hulk?"

Cumberland's face darkened, and then he turned and poked the off button.

The flat screen squeaked as it rocked back and forth on its stand.

Frye smiled again, this time displaying teeth that seemed to glow. Clearly a fan of whitening agents. "We've been checking on your recent movements, specifically before the murders of your ex-wife and Carter Willis. Turns out you and Carter had a little run-in at Antler Creek Lodge, the restaurant at the top of Rocky Points Ski Resort?"

"Is that a question?"

"And from what we've been able to gather, it looks like Carter Willis and your ex-wife hugged at that encounter, and you overreacted, causing a scene."

"I reacted the appropriate amount."

"Out of jealousy?"

"The guy was a sleaze ball. He was groping my date in front of me."

Frye nodded. "I'm just going to cut to the chase, maybe save us all some time here. Did you kill Carter Willis and your ex-wife, Mr. Wolf?"

"No."

"Because it looks like you did."

"Can't arrest someone for looking like they might have murdered someone. Listen, I've got some *Rifleman* to catch up on, so if you guys don't mind leaving and lifting your legs on some other tree? Thanks."

"What are these?" Frye slapped a manila folder on the plaster cast that covered Wolf's lap.

Wolf stared at it but didn't move.

Frye opened it and tipped out a stack of photographs.

They were photos of his deputy, Tom Rachette, and the girl they'd come to know as Gail Olson. They were familiar—Gail Olson handing Rachette a bag, Rachette hugging the woman, Rachette putting the bag in his car, Rachette and Gail driving their separate ways.

They were an innocuous set of photographs under normal circumstances, but Wolf knew Gail Olson had been caught months earlier by the Ashland PD with marijuana and money in her car, lots of both, and these photos were supposed to implicate Wolf and his department in the smuggling of drugs.

When Wolf kept silent, Frye picked up a photo and studied it. "Sheriff Will MacLean of Byron County told us that he brought these photos to you. He knew all about Gail Olson's past and mentioned that he might make these photos public. He said you freaked out and dropped out of the race. He's done right by giving up the pictures to us now."

"Yes," Wolf said, "these photos were a blackmail attempt by Sheriff MacLean, who set up Gail Olson to make this fake drop while he took these pictures to make my deputy and my department look bad."

Frye straightened with a confused look. "MacLean set the whole thing up, which you figured out, and yet you dropped out of the race? So the blackmail attempt worked? I'm confused. You say it was a set-up, but you dropped out of the race to keep these photos under wraps."

"I dropped out of the race because I didn't want the job."

"And why's that?"

"I learned I didn't fit the job description. MacLean did perfectly."

Frye laughed. "That's an interesting angle."

"What's that supposed to mean?"

"It means that's not what we heard."

Wolf leaned back. "Heard about what?"

Frye smirked and walked away from the hospital bed. He picked up a sheet of paper and studied it, set it down, and moved on.

"Hey, why don't you take a look around?"

"Thanks, I will," Frye said, his voice coming from inside Wolf's bedroom.

Cumberland stood motionless, gazing at Wolf.

Engines revved and tires rumbled on the drive out front, getting louder as they approached.

Frye appeared next to Wolf and gestured to the window. "The rest of our crew."

"Why?"

Frye stepped to the window and forked open the blinds with his fingers. "Did you kill Gail Olson, Sheriff Wolf?"

Wolf frowned. "What? No."

Frye twisted and stared at him.

Wolf looked at Frye and Cumberland in turn. "Gail Olson's been murdered?"

Both agents held their stares.

Frye blinked first. "She's been missing since the night of Carter Willis and Sarah Muller's deaths. Vanished."

The vehicles outside came to squeaking stops and car doors opened and closed. Chattering agents and squawks of radio static filled the silence.

"You guys seriously think I shot my ex-wife, Carter Willis, and Gail Olson?" Wolf tried to counteract his escalating blood pressure with deep breathing, but it wasn't working.

Frye gestured toward Wolf's bedroom. "Could have been with that Walther PPK sitting in your nightstand drawer."

"The bullets that killed my ex-wife and Carter Willis were

nine millimeter parabellum. Since a blown-off right hand isn't one of my current injuries, clearly, I didn't use the PPK to fire those rounds. You got a warrant inside that empty head of yours? If not, then get the hell out of my house."

"And your department-issue Glock 17?" Cumberland asked.

"My deputies already checked to see if my piece was fired the day we discovered the bodies."

"We discovered the bodies?" Frye asked. "They. Your deputies discovered the bodies. You were supposedly here with a psychotic serial murderer at the time, doing hell-knows-what kind of sick things in that bedroom of yours—or at least, you say you were here. And when your deputy checked your weapon? We heard about that visual check and sniff. That's not going to cut it. We'll need to do some ballistics." Frye slapped a folded sheet of paper on his bed. "And here's our warrant. We're going to take a look around now. You just sit here and make yourself comfortable while we do." Frye pulled a radio from his belt. "All right, let's move."

Calls and responses echoed outside and the front door blew open. Two male agents entered in full stride.

"Go ahead, make my day." Wolf leaned back, his confident words sounding not so confident to his ears. Because the truth was, he remembered little of that fateful night a few weeks ago, when Sarah and Carter Willis were shot dead and left in a BMW sedan.

There were still unanswered questions about that night— as in *all* of the questions.

"Agent Frye."

Frye paused in mid-conversation with an agent and stepped close to Wolf. "What?"

"Carter Willis."

"What about him?"

"I've been looking into him. Who the hell is he? Aren't you guys worried about that? He's not in any of the databases, no public record, nothing. He doesn't exist. He's a ghost. And you guys are worried about me?"

"That's not your concern."

"Not my concern? He was found dead with my wife."

"Your ex-wife." Frye squinted and tilted his head. "Is that all, Mr. Wolf?"

Wolf leaned back and closed his eyes. "Is Special Agent Luke here?"

Nobody answered. When Wolf cracked his eyes open, Agent Frye was gone.

Wolf looked on his bedside roll-table for his cell phone but it, too, was gone. A young-looking FBI agent was dropping it in a plastic bag.

"Is Special Agent Luke here?" Wolf asked the agent.

The agent kept silent, but after a quick glance around the room he nodded.

"Tell her to come talk to me."

The agent ignored him and stepped away.

Wolf sat back and pulled up his bed sheet, feeling exposed in more ways than one. There was nothing he could do but breathe and remain calm.

He leaned back and racked his brain again, like he'd done in every waking moment between pill and Scotch-induced sleeps the past couple of weeks.

He'd relived every memory from the night of Sarah and Carter's deaths countless times, but the problem was that the memories were few. Wolf had been having drinks with a woman he'd thought to be Kimber Grey when Carter Willis had come into the bar with two of his cronies. It had been only a few minutes until Carter Willis had approached Wolf, leaned close, and told him his ex-wife was an *unforgettable piece of ass*. He remembered that clear enough. And then Wolf had attacked him without hesitation.

Wolf had gotten some good shots in, and taken a few, too. But the lights had gone out when he'd taken a pool cue to the head from one of the two men with Carter.

From that blackout moment onward, Wolf had been at the mercy of a woman who had murdered an unknown number of young men, mutilated their bodies, and dumped them into Cold Lake, south of town. The rest of that night had been erased from his mind, if it had ever been there to begin with. He'd had more than a few whiskies at the Pony Tavern before the action ensued.

Then there were the memories of the past few weeks since his plummet off a cliff. Those were chopped and jumbled, and remembering anything in any order was like trying to put together a thousand-piece puzzle with the pieces turned upside down.

"David." The voice in his ear was feminine and full of concern.

Wolf opened his eyes.

"You look like shit," Special Agent Kristen Luke said.

Luke's brown hair was pulled back in a tight ponytail, her face chiseled, yet soft. Her wide cinnamon-bark eyes were bleary but still as stunning as ever.

"You look good," Wolf said.

She darted a glance toward the nearest agent and waited for him to move on. "I'm sorry I haven't gotten back to you. I can't really ... *talk* to you."

He nodded. "Deputy Baine has proof that MacLean was behind those photographs with Rachette and Gail Olson—a video interview Baine conducted with Gail. Which makes me think MacLean might be behind her disappearance. Get to Baine, and get that video file he has."

"Of course I ..." she stopped talking and stepped away.

A few seconds later she came close, this time avoiding eye contact with him. "Go ahead."

"MacLean also said he had photos of me and Hannah Kipling here at the house that night. Those photos might be my alibi."

She walked away as if he'd said nothing.

Agent Frye appeared next to Wolf, his eyes trailing Luke. "She tells me you're innocent."

"She's a smart agent."

"So am I. That's how I became ASAC. And I know that when emotions get involved, investigations go sloppy. So I'm not listening to a thing she says."

Wolf closed his eyes. "Let me know what you find. I'm confident I'll see you again soon, and you can apologize to me then, okay?"

When Wolf opened his eyes, Agent Frye had gone, back to the bustle of agents ransacking his home.

CHAPTER 2

THREE MONTHS LATER—TUESDAY, September 9th

The Sluice–Byron Sheriff's Department SUV rocked back and forth as it passed through the headgate of Wolf's ranch.

Shiny new turret lights topped the spotless rust-brown vehicle, and as it slowed into the circle drive the logo stamped on the door came into view. It was key-shaped—Sluice County represented by the jagged blade, and Byron making up the boxy bow at the bottom.

Wolf was still not used to the new look.

He put his hands in his jacket pockets and tucked his chin under his collar. The September morning air was chilled and smelled like wood smoke, pine, and wet earth.

Peaks that had been bare rock all summer were dusted today with lace yarmulkes of snow from last night's monsoon storm that had dumped hours of roof-rattling rain.

A pinprick reflection sparkled in sunlight halfway up the mountain slope.

Wolf dismissed the anomaly and focused on his approaching visitors.

The SUV splashed through a puddle and rocked to a stop.

The passenger-side door opened and Deputy Heather Patterson approached with quick strides.

"How are you feeling?" she asked.

"Hello to you, too. Like a new man, thanks." Wolf smiled against her look of concern. "Aren't you going to close your door?"

She walked back and shut it.

Wolf stepped forward onto the muddy drive and shook her hand.

As always, Wolf's hand dwarfed the much shorter deputy's, but, as always, her grip sent electricity up his arm.

Patterson was like that, tiny in stature but large in presence, and that's why Wolf had hired her on the spot after meeting her once, and had never regretted the decision in the years since.

Her granite physique told she worked out seven days a week, every week, every month, every year. Her tanned, freckled skin told of her willingness to be out doing the job. One look at her hardened blue eyes told of her intelligence. And one look at her smile told anyone with a brain that she was a real catch.

Scott Reed, a snowcat operator for the Rocky Points Ski Resort, was a lucky man to have caught Patterson. She and Wolf were on strict professional terms, though if he'd had to stretch their relationship to something more, he would have said he looked on her as the daughter he'd never had. A daughter who carried a pistol and had a fifth-degree black belt in Kenpo karate.

Patterson eyed him suspiciously for a second and then turned at the sound of the SUV door slamming shut behind her.

Deputy Baine stepped around the vehicle, shoving a phone in his pocket. "Sorry. Had to send a message to Andrea."

Wolf nodded and shook the deputy's hand. "How's Andrea doing?"

"Great, great." Baine shook his head and sagged his shoulders, his posture all apology.

"It's not your fault," Wolf said. "Forget about it."

"Shit. I just can't believe it. It was frickin' locked. The drawer was locked."

Patterson looked between them. "What are you guys talking about?"

Wolf waved a dismissive hand. "How're things at the department?"

Patterson and Baine gave each other meaningful glances.

"Interesting," Patterson said. "There's a definite division between the two groups of personnel. MacLean hasn't been exactly present during the whole change-management process."

Baine snorted. "He's got every Sluice deputy paired up with a Byron deputy. I've got a douche bag who reminds me of regulations all day, and Patterson, well you've heard about Patterson."

Wolf nodded. "Undersheriff Lancaster. Nice draw you got there."

Patterson looked at her watch. "I figure we've got about fifteen minutes. Then we've gotta run."

"Let's take a walk." Wolf walked toward the red barn that sat on the north side of his one-story house. Patterson and Baine followed close behind.

He led them past the old roll doors, past the work-shed entrance, and out into the woods along a path that had been there since the days of Wolf's first memories.

"So what's up?" Patterson finally said when they'd walked a hundred feet. "You sounded a little skittish on the phone this morning."

"Maybe. Maybe not. I just want to show you guys something, get the latest news."

"The news is, the FBI has been talking to me," Patterson said.

"Me too," Baine said.

Wolf kept walking.

"Sir, you don't seem surprised that the FBI are talking to us."

"You don't need to call me sir anymore, Patterson. I'm not your boss."

"Whatever, sir. The FBI? You don't seem surprised."

He glanced at Baine. "I'm sure that ever since you were supposed to produce that digital file of you interviewing Gail Olson and couldn't, you've made yourself pretty well known."

"Wolf,"—Baine crunched to a halt—"you know that wasn't my fault, right? I swear it was in the top drawer of my desk. And I erased the YouTube file because I didn't want random people watching it. I should have just changed the settings and kept it there. Someone frickin'—"

"Relax. I'm not saying it was your fault. Someone clearly removed the file from your desk. Someone who knew about it, and had something to gain by getting it. Someone like Sheriff Will MacLean. I'm just offering up reasons why the FBI is all over you now."

Baine nodded and looked at his feet.

"What interview file?" Patterson asked. "An interview with Gail Olson? Because they've been asking me about her."

Wolf turned and started walking again. "Ignorance is your best defense in all of this, Patterson."

She huffed and followed him.

"Yeah, Patterson. You're ignorant. So that's going to—ah!"

Wolf smiled at the sound of Patterson's hands thumping against Baine's chest.

"Shhhh ... damn."

Wolf veered off the trail into the woods. "Follow me. Gonna make it, Baine?"

"Yeah. Shit, Patterson. Joke much?"

A few minutes later, Wolf reached a rise in the forest floor and paused.

Ahead was a small hill by any Coloradan's standards—it always had been—but recently it was looking like a mountain to Wolf. His body ached already, and he'd only been up from bed and moving around for an hour.

For over a month now, he'd been climbing up and down the smaller hills and mountains behind his property, taking in the clean air and building his strength, but it seemed to be an exercise in futility rather than exercise for his body.

The muscles in front of his right hip were knotted painfully, a side effect of his healing broken pelvis after the fall.

His right femur, having been cracked diagonally, jarred sharply with every step, and in between paces was a dull ache that registered at least a seven out of ten.

The three compression-cracked vertebrae in his lower back were almost fully healed according to the doctor, but there was a nagging stiffness now, and he was far from confident that the occasional arcing pain up his spine would stop in his lifetime.

His ruptured spleen? That had healed and he was still the proud owner of the organ. He wondered why the doctors hadn't simply taken it out, but in the end, he'd kept it. Score one for Wolf.

Tack on the other dozen or so minor to major injuries in

various stages of healing, and Wolf figured he'd been telling the truth to Patterson earlier about feeling "like a new man."

Despite the pain, Wolf led at a good pace up the hill, and Patterson and Baine followed.

A few minutes later, flushed with sweat and suppressing a maniacal urge to cough, Wolf reached the clearing of the trees and crested the hill.

"Wow, it's beautiful up here." Patterson whistled and turned full-circle.

"Damn straight." Teeth bared, Baine wheezed with his hands on his hips.

Wolf nodded and cleared his throat, noting the way Patterson's lungs pulled in air as if she were in a deep sleep.

The valley to the north extended up to the miniature-looking buildings of Rocky Points. Even from such a distance, the glass-ensconced Sluice—Byron County building—now home to the new Sheriff's Department, numerous holding cells, and various government offices—stuck out like a beacon as the sun reflected off its windows.

"See that there?" Wolf pointed to the pinpoint reflection on the side of a mountain to the west.

Patterson followed his finger and then stepped close to his arm. "That reflection?"

"Yep."

"What's that?"

"FBI surveillance team." Wolf gestured around them. "They have a couple of guys up there watching me twenty-four seven. Me and Rachette spotted them a few days ago, taking this same walk. There're two more men down south on that bluff, two to the north along that ridge, and a couple of goons in that unmarked you passed on the way to my house."

"Yeah, we saw them parked a half-mile or so down," Patterson said.

Wolf waved to the reflection and scratched his nose with his middle finger.

Patterson looked uneasy. "You think they're listening to us?"

He shrugged. "The guys to the north are within parabolic mic range to hear us crisp and clear, as if we were standing right next to them. The fact that they're out there sitting on their asses, listening to us, rather than looking for the killer of my ex-wife, shows they might be too stupid to realize they can use a parabolic mic to listen in." He turned to her and Baine. "It's a toss-up."

She blinked. "I ... uh ..."

Baine straightened and backed up a step, looking like his space had just been violated.

"They asked you about Gail Olson?" Wolf asked Patterson.

She blinked some more. "What?"

"The FBI. Don't worry. We have nothing to hide. What did they ask you?"

"They kept asking about those photos that Sheriff MacLean gave us of her and Rachette. Then they wanted to know what I was doing the night Sarah was shot. Frickin' bastards. I saw they were interrogating Rachette before me. I don't get it. What are they saying? That we did this?"

"What did they want to know about the photos?" Wolf asked.

"They wanted to know if and how I knew Gail Olson." She turned to the woods and raised her voice. "Which I didn't! I never saw that girl in my life before I saw those pictures, which Sheriff MacLean gave to me." She turned back to Wolf and straightened her jacket. "I don't know, it's like they were trying to get a confession out of me or something. I ended up taking the fifth. My father used to say that it's never, ever, a good idea to talk to a law-enforcement officer. I'm beginning to realize why when I talk to these feds. They seem to be grasping for anything, and groping us in the process."

"And you?"

Baine was staring across the valley, lost in thought.

"Baine."

He flinched and turned to Wolf. "What?"

"What have the FBI been asking you?"

Baine wiped his nose with his thumb. "You know, what you were doing the night of Sarah and Willis's deaths. That kind of stuff."

Wolf nodded in thought. "And Gail Olson?"

"Yeah, and Gail Olson."

"Did you tell them about the video we had?"

Baine exhaled. "Yeah, of course I did. I told them I'd interviewed her but I couldn't find the file. Then they asked me about what she said, so I took the fifth, too. I don't know what the hell is going on around here. I don't want to say anything that implicates you or me. And I don't think we should talk about it now."

Wolf eyed the reflection again. "What's changed?"

"What do you mean?" Baine asked.

"They've been out there for three days. What changed three days ago?"

"The FBI talked to me a little over a week ago," Patterson said. "Not in the last few days. I'm not sure what this is about. They asked me if you knew Gail Olson and I said no. That's all they said about you. We'll check."

Baine eyed the reflection on the mountain across the valley, then back down into the forest the way they'd hiked up.

"All right," Wolf said. "Let's get you two back."

Patterson and Baine followed in silence.

As they reached the trail at the base of the hill, Patterson came next to Wolf and lowered her voice. "Sir, I wanted to talk to you about Carter Willis."

"You find anything on him?" Wolf pounced at the utterance of the man's name.

She glanced back at Baine.

"Don't worry, I'm not listening." Baine held back a few steps.

"Thanks." She exhaled and slid Wolf an uneasy glance. "No. I haven't gotten anywhere with Carter Willis's identity. Lorber can't find anything with his contacts, and Kristen Luke is dodging me as much as she's dodging you. I've checked with a CBI guy I know, and he came up empty, too. Said the guy's made up. I checked with the company who issued his car insurance, and they had no record of even having him as a customer. Not even online. The card was a forgery. The registration on his car? Same deal. Not registered with the state."

Wolf nodded impatiently. They'd already gone over all this and Patterson knew it. Wolf was asking whether she had anything new, not to rehash what they already knew.

But people didn't know how to act with Wolf as of late, because the truth was that Wolf had also sustained a second-degree concussion in the fall, and his memory was holier than Swiss cheese.

The head injury had also damaged his left inner ear, causing intermittent tinnitus and a sensation of it having been stuffed with foam. Vertigo and nausea were never far behind. This, coupled with his other injuries, acted as an off-switch for his body.

His left ear was beginning to ring.

"What did you want to tell me ... that we haven't already talked about?" Wolf asked, making his point.

"Remember I said I saw Carter and Sarah at the bar that night, when I was with Scott and his family?"

Wolf swallowed. He remembered quite well. "Yeah."

"I stopped when I saw Sarah to say hi, and Carter had his hand on her thigh underneath the table."

The ringing instantly doubled in volume.

Wolf nodded, keeping an even stride. "All right."

"I never told you, and it's been eating at me recently, because I realize it might be some kind of clue. Shit, I'm so sorry." She looked down at the ground.

Wolf walked in silence for a few steps and then put a hand on Patterson's shoulder.

She looked up with glassy eyes.

"Don't worry about it, all right?"

She nodded. "I'm sorry. I even told the FBI about it, but I didn't tell you, and then I waited and waited, and then it got harder to tell you."

"I'm glad you told me. It could be important. It was already suspicious that she was wearing her nightgown in the car when they were shot. It suggests that either she and Carter were intimate, or she was pulled out of the house without warning. With what you just told me, it's looking like they were definitely intimate. That's a clue." He turned to the trees and shook his head, trying to shake the deafening sound. "I've gotta get back to work. I can't do anything from here but think in circles."

Patterson looked up at him. "My aunt says you're a wreck and need more rest. From where I'm standing, it looks like she's right."

He felt light in the chest and sweat broke out on his forehead. "I'm ..."

"What?"

"Nothing." Wolf was starting to get the sparkly vision again, a sign that he needed to lie down, and fast. He limped onward toward the trail. "A couple of months ago the FBI came up empty with the search of my house. The ballistics didn't match. They've got nothing. So I don't know what they're up to."

The red barn came into view between the trees.

"So what do you want us to do?" Patterson said loudly, as if to include Baine back in the conversation.

Wolf lumbered forward, barely hearing himself as he spoke. "I want you to keep trying with Luke. The FBI knows something we don't and we need to know what that is. She's still our best inside man."

"Yeah, one who clearly wants nothing to do with us," Patterson said.

"Baine, keep your eyes and ears open on MacLean, I guess. And if either of you can figure out what's going on with this surveillance, I'd appreciate knowing."

"I can check on it," Baine said.

Wolf nodded. His good leg buckled and he stumbled before standing straight.

"My God, are you okay?" Patterson ducked under his arm and locked her own around his waist. Baine grabbed under his other armpit.

"It's all right." Wolf blinked away the stars again. "I've just gotta lie down."

"Let's go," Patterson said with determination.

His feet left the ground as the two deputies whisked him up the trail, around the barn, and to the front of his house.

"Kitchen entrance?" Patterson asked.

"Yeah."

Both Patterson and Baine's phones chimed from their pockets.

"Shit. You get that," Patterson said.

"What? Are you sure?"

"Do it."

Baine let go of Wolf and fished for his phone.

Patterson leaned to the side, digging her hip into Wolf's leg.

He winced from the pressure on his femur as his legs touched down.

"Sorry. You okay?"

Wolf nodded.

Patterson wrestled him through the door, into the kitchen, on through the family room, and into his bedroom.

He collapsed onto the unmade sheets and rolled to his back. "Thanks."

The ceiling spun, but the sustained ringing seemed to diminish.

"Yeah." She pulled off his shoes. "What can I get you?"

He swallowed, and it felt like a piece of cotton was stuck in his throat. "Luke probably can't talk to us. I bet she's being watched just as closely as I am right now. Her SAC probably warned her to stay away from all this. She's emotionally attached to me, and he knows it."

Patterson grabbed the empty cup of water from Wolf's nightstand, filled it in the bathroom, came back in, and held it out to him.

He gulped the water down and leaned against the headboard. "Thanks."

"Yeah. Geez, you *are* a wreck. What else? What else can I get you?"

"Patterson?" Baine called from the kitchen entrance.

"Yeah!" Patterson's eyes stayed on Wolf's. "What do you need?"

"Nothing. Go. Don't worry about me."

"We have to go! MacLean's calling us in for a meeting."

Patterson glanced at her watch. "Yeah, all right. I'll be right there."

Wolf smiled and nodded.

"I'll be back," Patterson vowed and left the room.

"Bye, Arnold."

"What?" She appeared again at the doorway with a scowl. "Arnold? Are you okay?" She rolled her eyes. "Oh yeah, I get it. Bye."

Wolf closed his eyes and went to sleep.

CHAPTER 3

"THEY'RE ALL DEAD, and it's your fault!"

Wolf opened his eyes and rolled to his side, struggling to catch his breath. The accusation seemed to echo in the room, like he was in a deep canyon.

He sat up and rubbed his temples, seeing the fictitious fireball against his eyelids once again.

For over fifteen years, since his days in the army, he'd battled a recurring nightmare that spawned from one of his worst memories—a recall of one of his worst deeds—a single shot he'd been forced to take in Sri Lanka to save twenty-three lives. It had killed an eight-year-old boy who had been running toward a Chinook helicopter, a suicide bomb strapped to his back and a detonator switch in his hand. The boy had been conned into doing it by a group of men who watched from the trees. .

Before the stock had finished its recoil against his muscled shoulder, before the boy was through feeling the pain of Wolf's first bullet, Wolf had already begun to focus his efforts on coming back home—back to his son, who was two years old and thousands of miles away at that instant. Back to his son, who at the time was essentially a fatherless child, impressionable, vulnerable to any bad man who walked in off the street while Wolf was around the world fighting against men with putrid values.

The shot had been a seminal moment in his life, like when Jack had been born, or when he and Sarah had exchanged vows, or when they'd divorced, or when Sarah had been shot in the head and taken before she and Jack and Wolf had had a chance to be normal again.

The dream always returned during times of stress. But now it had morphed into a fiction. In this dream, the boy reached the Chinook helicopter. He depressed the thumb button. The people were all dead in a searing fireball, and it was all Wolf's fault because he'd frozen and watched it happen, unable to pull the trigger.

He got up and went to the bathroom to splash some water on his face.

His reflection was the skinniest version of Wolf he could remember. His complexion was so pale it was almost blue; his eyes were ringed with dark circles bordered with yellow, the crow's feet next to them deep, his lips thin and dry.

There was a new streak of gray in his otherwise dark hair coming in above his ear. A matching splash of silver painted his inch-long beard.

He looked like a prisoner, he thought. He'd never had the misfortune of being captured in war, but he'd rescued people who had, and this is what they looked like.

For twenty minutes, he bathed and shaved, and in the end looked a little better, though not much.

His phone chimed on his nightstand and he went out and picked it up.

Nate Watson. He got excited, knowing exactly why he was calling.

"What's up?" Wolf answered.

"Hey, I've got him here. We're going to the river."

"Where?"

"I'll park at the Westfield Oxbow lot. I'll bring him and Brian south."

"Okay, I'll leave now." He picked up his watch and then checked out his window. The rear of the house was in shadow and the tops of the trees were blazing in bright light. *Four p.m.?* He'd slept all day.

"See you there."

Wolf slipped on the same clothes from the morning, grabbed his keys, got in his Toyota truck, and drove.

He sped down the dirt driveway, through the headgate, and took a right to follow the river north.

A mile up, he mashed the accelerator and passed the unmarked Crown Victoria, contemplating whether to stay close or give it a wide berth on the way by. He swung the wheel and passed with plenty of space to spare—no sense endangering the innocent agents inside the vehicle. They were only acting on orders.

He was satisfied, though, watching the rearview as the FBI vehicle disappeared in a storm of dust.

He reached the end of the county road, hung a left, crossed the Chautauqua river, and went north on highway 734 toward town, keeping his speed up as he did so. As he finally slowed and made his way along Main Street in town, he saw that the FBI unmarked had caught up and now tailed him ten car lengths back.

Wolf passed through town and kept going north. The highway meandered along the right side of the Chautauqua, whose sliding waters bisected the town of Rocky Points, flowing north and then west, ultimately pouring into the Colorado River a hundred miles away.

Once out of town, Wolf cruised at sixty. Slowing at the Westfield Oxbow sign, he pulled into the dirt parking lot and parked next to Nate's SUV.

Wolf and Nate had become best friends growing up by playing together in the same offensive backfield on the same football team each year from elementary school until college.

Whereas Wolf had gone off to Colorado State on a full-ride scholarship as quarterback, Nate had gone on to Golden and attended the Colorado School of Mines. Nate followed his strengths, abandoning his post at running back and honing his sharp mind instead. Eventually he'd become the owner of one of the premier geological-services companies in the western United States.

Nate's large, top-of-the-line American SUV, coupled with his sprawling house in the woods, told of the continued success of his business.

As Wolf got out of his SUV, a car on the highway leaned on the horn and sped past the FBI unmarked rolling into the lot.

The agent pulled to the opposite side of the clearing and parked. When the car shut off, they climbed out and one of them grabbed a pack of cigarettes from his pocket and lit one while the other leaned against the trunk.

"I'd appreciate it if you two stayed here," Wolf said.

Both gazed at him with an air of superiority.

The last thing Wolf wanted was a couple of suits to mess up this situation, but there was nothing he could do about it, so he walked toward the river.

The Westfield Oxbow was a bend in the Chautauqua River a few miles north of town with shores blanketed in low bushes and frequented by local and out of town fishermen.

As Wolf walked through the foliage into a clearing, he saw Nate standing with his son, Brian, a dog, and another young man.

Wolf's pulse quickened at the sight of his son.

Brian, Nate's son, was fourteen years old like Jack, but he'd yet to enter a growth spurt yet. Built like a running back, Nate was average height and his son Brian was a few inches beneath him.

On the other hand, Jack had reached Wolf's height of six foot three and surpassed it by an inch as of this summer. At least, that's what Sarah's mother had told him the last time they'd spoken on the phone.

Jack looked as awkward as ever, stooping a little with his shorter companions, as if ashamed of his height. His hair was shaggy and blew in the late-afternoon breeze.

The FBI agents watched with interest, but stayed put. One of them looked away as if respectfully giving Wolf his space. *Must have kids.* The other smiled as he blew out a drag. *Must not.*

He pushed through the weeds and grasses, the image of Jack, Brian, and Nate flitting in and out behind branches swaying on the wind.

He reached the shoreline and a game trail that led toward them, so he followed it.

"Hey, Dave." Brian spotted Wolf first and called out to him.

Jack twisted around and glared at Wolf, then at Nate.

Nate took the dagger stare and raised his chin, which seemed to worsen Jack's sense of being betrayed, because he dropped his fishing pole and walked into the bushes in the direction of the parking lot.

"Jack." Wolf followed after him.

No answer. Jack picked up his pace, his head bobbing and weaving between the bushes at breakneck speed.

Wolf struggled to keep up, his right femur throbbing, his hip tightening with each step. "Jack, please. Stop."

His son slowed for an instant and leaned his head back as if pleading to the sky, as if finally resigned to talking to his father.

Wolf slowed and approached timidly, not believing his luck. For three months, Jack had ignored his calls, screening them, avoiding him at all costs, pretending he didn't exist. Finally, he had a chance to plead his case.

But Jack changed his mind and marched forward again, this time at a faster pace.

"Please! I need to talk to you!"

He clenched his teeth and jogged after him, swerving around a bush and then another. His legs ripped through the weeds, and a branch swayed in the wind and hit him in the face.

With eyes wide open, a leaf hit one of his eyeballs and he wrenched his head back at the sudden pain. The movement sent a lightning bolt from his previously broken vertebrae up his spine and he fell over onto a pile of rocks.

He lay still on the cool ground, panting and gritting his teeth. Blood pounded in his neck as he rolled over and gazed at the bushes swaying above.

"Shit." With ginger movements, he got to his knees.

"Are you all right?"

Jack was there with a lanky hand extended.

Wolf paused and looked up at his son's face.

Jack's hand was extended, but his forest-green eyes showed little concern.

"Yeah." Wolf grabbed his hand, and Jack yanked him to his feet. "Easy."

His son turned and walked away again.

"Why won't you talk to me, Jack?"

Jack stopped and presented his profile, then faced him. His son's eyes were wild, glowing with anger. "Are you serious? You're pretending you don't know?"

Wolf lifted his chin. "I think I have an idea, but you're gonna have to tell me. Why the hell are you so mad at me?"

"Because Mom is dead because of you. That's why, Dad. Because you should have been there with her that night instead of screwing some slut at your house."

The words lashed him harder than any branch could. "I was knocked out that night, son. I ... I don't remember a thing. That woman brought me home, and then the next thing I knew I'd woken up."

"I guess you shouldn't have gone out drinking with her then. I guess you should have answered Mom's calls. She was in trouble, and she called you for help, and you ignored her to go out partying with your slut friend."

"Jack, listen—"

"And now she's dead." He raised his hands and dropped them. His breath started and his eyes welled. "Buried in the ground. So, what the hell do you want to talk about?"

Wolf swallowed. "I just want us to talk. I want to be your father again. I want us to help each other through this."

Jack turned around and walked.

"Jack, we have to talk about all this." *You can't blame me*, he thought. *I can't take it.*

Jack called over his shoulder. "Tell Nate I'm walking back to town."

With that, his son ran at speed toward the river and disappeared into the brush.

Wolf stopped and let tears flow from his eyes, not sure whether they were from the new lacerations from the bush or because he was letting out pent-up emotions.

"Hey."

He turned at the sound of Nate's voice.

"You all right?" Brian was close behind him, looking afraid to speak.

Wolf nodded. "Jack's walking back into town."

"Yeah, I heard."

Wolf nodded again, and then wiped his eyes.

"Listen, you wanna go for some food? Get a beer? I can drop Brian off at home and we'll go."

Wolf turned and finished drying his face on his sleeve. "No thanks. I've gotta get back home."

Dark clouds, pulsing with flashes of lightning, loomed behind the green slopes of the Ski Resort. Jack had disappeared completely in the brush.

"Can you make sure he gets back all right?"

"Of course," Nate said. "We'll go pick him up at the next turnoff."

Wolf walked back to the parking lot, ignoring the discomfort in his hip and leg.

He embraced the pain. He welcomed it.

Because he deserved it. More than any other man on the planet.

Check that; there was at least one other person out there as deserving, and bad health or not, it was about time Wolf figured out who they were and started giving them their share.

CHAPTER 4

CLAYTON POPE STARED at the sniveling woman and chewed his stale piece of peppermint gum. He looked at the clock on the wall of the palatial Park Hill house living room and then at the woman again.

There was a chuff of an engine expelling air outside and a squeak, and then the sound of boisterous kids offloading a school bus.

"Oh God, oh God, oh God." The woman sobbed uncontrollably, her hands shaking. Her face had turned white, almost as pale as Pope's skin, but not quite. Not many people had the lack of pigment to reach Pope's normal milky shade of ivory, no matter how freaked out they happened to be.

"Hey."

She ignored him, staring at her front door.

"Hey." Pope stood from the silk-upholstered chair, stepped to the woman on the couch, and pressed the suppressor against her temple.

She sucked in a breath and froze. "Please, don't hurt them."

"If you make a noise when that door opens, or tell your

kids to do anything other than come in and sit down, I plaster your brains on that disgusting thing you call a couch, in front of your kids, and then I do the same to your kids. Got that?"

"Oh God, oh God, oh ..."

There was the patter of footsteps coming up to the front door and then it flew open.

"Mom!" A boy, no more than ten years old, elbowed his way in front of his little sister, dropped his backpack against the wall and then froze.

Pope stood straight with a gentle smile, his pistol held out of sight against his leg. "You must be Gabriel."

"Gabe," the kid corrected him. "Who's this?"

Pope felt his smile waver, and then he felt his leather glove shudder as he squeezed the handle of the pistol.

"Honey, that's not how we treat guests. This is Mr. ..." The woman trailed off.

"Johnson," Pope said, his smile returning. "I'm Bob Johnson. I'm a good friend of your dad's."

Eyes narrowing with suspicion, Gabe stood rooted to the spot in the entryway, looking between Pope and his mother, like a spoiled little shit who didn't like his routine being messed with. Mom was probably supposed to be making his mac and cheese right now, or whatever it was that mothers did for their sons.

The kid's little sister walked to her mother on the couch, all the while keeping her wide eyes on Pope.

Pope blushed at the little girl's stare and felt his upper lip skin prickle with sweat under the silicone-based stage glue. She saw right through his gentle façade; she looked at his glove and then seemed to study his facial features, as if she knew he was wearing a disguise.

Damn it.

The woman had to have seen it, too. But she had been placating him, doing a fine job of acting like she'd seen nothing out of the ordinary, like she hadn't known his mustache was fake, his skin slathered in makeup, or he wore colored contacts.

He silently cursed his choice of makeup. It was too dark and didn't match his true snow-white complexion, which made his eyelashes and eyebrows look unnatural. And the mustache itched fiercely, something to do with the way he'd shaved before he'd stuck it on.

The disguise was still doing its job, he assured himself. He looked like a completely different man, with stuffed clothing to give him a heavier build, and with long sleeves to hide his most distinguishing mark. There would be no need to kill innocent people today.

He felt a surge of confidence and smiled anew.

"What's your name?" Pope's voice was scratchy.

"Emma."

He nodded. "That's a pretty name."

One of the woman's eyelids twitched uncontrollably as she stared at him and pulled her child close.

The sound of running footsteps outside the rear door broke the silence, and Pope saw the lawyer slam into the back door and twist the locked doorknob to no avail.

"Daddy's here." Gabe jogged past them and twisted the lock. He pulled it open and the lawyer's keys landed on the polished hardwood floor inside.

The lawyer, who Pope now knew as Jeffrey Lethbridge, Esquire, knelt and gripped his son's arms, clearly relieved and, at the same time, horrified to see his son.

"Hi Jeffrey," Pope called out before he got any ideas.

Lethbridge's face dropped as he took in Pope standing over his wife and daughter.

"Come on in. Join us on the couch." Pope's mustache popped off and he smoothed it with a gloved finger.

"Please, I have everything right here." Lethbridge held out a manila envelope. "This is everything they gave me. Take it and let us go. Leave. Please."

"Close the door and come sit on the couch."

The little boy's jaw dropped at their interaction, and Pope's new tone of voice.

The lawyer ushered his son to the couch and held out the envelope. "Sit down. Go."

Pope snatched the envelope, careful to display his pistol now.

"He has a gun," Gabe said.

"I know. Don't worry. Just keep quiet. Let Daddy talk to him, okay?"

Pope waved Lethbridge to the couch and walked to a triangular table next to one of the overpriced, overstuffed chairs. He swiped a stained-glass lamp onto the floor and emptied the contents of the folder onto the table.

Without looking, he pointed his pistol at the boy. "Take your gun out of your pants and put it on the coffee table."

"Okay, okay. Please." Lethbridge leaned forward, put a pistol on the coffee table, and sat back down. "I ... I ..."

"Shut up and keep still."

Pope lowered his gun and sifted through the contents now strewn on the table. He made no move for the lawyer's snub-nosed revolver because there was no need. Pope was too fast, legendary in his time as a marine.

He'd only recently learned that his .22 rapid-fire pistol competition-record score of 588 out of 600 had been bested by two points.

It was news he would never admit to caring about, but it had devastated him. After his Other Than Honorable administrative discharge, the only proof that he ever existed as a marine, that any of it had been worth anything, had been that engraved record plaque in San Diego.

He clenched a fist to steady his shaking hand.

The family stared at him, not moving except to breathe.

Swallowing, Pope fought to ignore the irony of the situation, but it was impossible.

What this family was unaware of was that Pope had been expeditiously swept out of the marines for killing a family of four in Afghanistan, and now here he was staring at a family of four. A boy, a girl, a mother, and a father, just as it had been back then.

It was disturbing how life came full circle sometimes. Back then he'd done the right and honorable thing. He'd saved countless lives by wiping out that terrorist and his seed with their ignition-plate factory in their tiny hut. American soldiers had already died because of that family, and would've continued to die if it hadn't been for him. Forget what his battalion commander and the rest of the brass thought in the end.

He wiped his forehead and painted his sleeve with a swath of brown.

Coming here, he'd known that this exact moment would probably arise, when he'd have to battle the demons that screamed in his brain, and that he'd have to move on from the present moment.

I'm disguised.

He was doing the right and honorable thing today, too. These people didn't deserve to die.

Sweat dripped off his chin and his mustache flapped off his lip again and almost peeled clean off before he caught it and pressed it home.

The family shuddered and averted their eyes.

Shit. Snapping out of his waking nightmare, Pope pressed the mustache to his lip again and examined the envelope contents on the table.

"What the hell is this?" he asked.

"It's exactly what you asked for. It's the documents I was supposed to leak upon the agents' deaths. One receipt and a rental agreement. And one letter of instruction written to me. The receipt and rental agreement are for a long-term storage unit in Gunnison, Colorado. Up in the mountains."

"I know where Gunnison is." Pope picked up the letter of instruction and read it.

Upon the deaths of Special Agent Terrence Tedescu and Special Agent Paul Smith, please proceed to the attached storage unit in Gunnison, Colorado, to obtain information regarding an urgent matter of domestic and national security.

Signed,
Special Agent Terrence Tedescu
Special Agent Paul Smith

Pope shook his head and chuckled. "Matter of domestic and national security."

He picked up the storage-unit rental agreement and shook it by the corner. A key slid out from between the pages and clanked on the table.

It was a small padlock key with a logo stamped into it, attached to a magnetic fob with #62 written on it. He put it in his pocket and then turned to the family.

Lethbridge and his wife sat with their children pulled close together between them.

"I'm not going to hurt you or the kids," he said to the woman.

He pointed his pistol and motioned Lethbridge to stand up.

"No, please." The woman looked over at Lethbridge.

With a deft movement, Pope tucked his pistol into the back of his pants and picked up the papers, folded them, and shoved them into his pants pocket, all the while keeping a sharp eye on Lethbridge.

Lethbridge seemed incapable of keeping his eyes off his revolver, which sat on the edge of the coffee table nearest Pope.

"Don't think about it."

Lethbridge nodded, clearly still thinking about it.

Pope was sweating like a pig with the padded clothing. Without thinking, he pulled up his sleeves to the elbows, letting the climate-controlled air of the house cool his arms.

"All right. Here's what's going to happen. You're going to …" Pope looked down at the three occupants of the couch. They were all staring at his arm.

With lightning speed, Pope pulled down his sleeves, a movement that only worsened the situation, because they'd already seen the tattoo, and if they hadn't grasped the significance of seeing it before, then they surely did now, because the tattoo might as well have been a nametag—a billboard with a headshot and phone number painted in dayglow, like the ambulance-chasing lawyers overlooking Colorado Boulevard outside.

The demons cackled in his head. They'd won. They'd

somehow duped him into this, made him drop his guard, even after so much preparation, and now he had no choice.

Pope had never had children, had never even had sex, but he was a good enough man to know that it was inhumane to let parents watch their children die. So he shot the parents first.

CHAPTER 5

W OLF SAT on his back deck and chewed his last bite of steak.

Out in the meadow, a bull elk circled his harem of females, letting out vocalizations that echoed through the misted landscape.

The beauty of the evening was lost on him. He was elsewhere in place and time, standing over someone, feeling what it would be like to have finished bringing justice to the person who had shot and killed Sarah.

As he stared down at the nameless, faceless, lifeless, man in his mind's eye, he felt nothing. No sense of satisfaction or fulfillment.

Perhaps a simple sense of completion of a chore, a task that if otherwise not done would be too much to live with. Like neglecting to clean up after a dog in the backyard. One could live with it so long, but in the end, the smell would overpower everything else, making enjoyment of anything impossible, making movement impossible, and sooner or later the scooper had to come out.

Wolf pushed his plate forward and leaned back. A low

cloud, heavy with moisture, obscured the mountain behind his house.

Standing up, he stretched his arms overhead and felt a twinge in his back that failed to materialize into any real pain, but added hesitation to his step and to his resolve.

Screw it, he thought. Metaphorically speaking, he needed to walk his ass up that mountain, up through the cloud to see what was on the other side, his broken body be damned.

Clenching his jaw, he made a resolution. Tomorrow he was going to get busy, and if the FBI wanted to tag along, then they could tag along.

CHAPTER 6

SPECIAL AGENT KRISTEN LUKE of the FBI looked over the Denver County police officer's shoulder and saw one of the dead bodies inside the house light up from a camera flash.

She blinked, and knew that image would stick with her a long time.

The Denver police officer stepped aside and shifted from foot to foot. "I've seen some gruesome killings in my time, but this takes the frickin' cake. You wanna go in and look? Fine, go right ahead."

Special Agent Tedescu, Luke's interim partner for the past three months, stepped inside as if being pulled by a tractor beam.

The flashing turret lights of countless police cars lit up the early-morning darkness, abusing her eyes. A group of officers stood with folded arms on the front lawn, watching her every move.

She checked her watch and turned back to the doorway. It was 5:20 a.m. Too early to be seeing stuff like this.

With a sigh, she followed Tedescu into the house.

He was already all the way across the room and staring down at the carnage.

She stepped next to him, giving a cursory glance at the executed family, leaning in macabre poses, their skin slathered in dried blood. It was sickening.

"Why the hell are we here?"

Tedescu was an amiable enough guy, and Luke had grown to like him in the short time they'd been working together since his partner's death. Tedescu was quick witted, surly, a straight shooter, and not too bad on the eyes, either, not that she'd entertain the idea of dating a man from work ever again.

A family man with two kids of his own, Tedescu had a soft spot for children, which made his standing there like a statue, staring at this, all the more vexing.

"Hey, Tedescu, you gonna tell me what's going on or what? Did you know this family?"

Tedescu ignored her and homed in on a torn envelope on a triangular table. He stepped to it, tilting his head, and Luke noticed him take a sharp inhale; then, as if catching himself, he tried to pull off an air of indifference.

But she'd seen it. Something on that table had him spooked, so she edged closer. The basic manila folder had no writing on it. The brass tines were pushed together and the flap was open, though ripped on one side as if wrenched open hastily.

"You guys get any prints?" Luke asked a female CSU officer.

She shrugged. "Plenty of them. All from the family, though."

Luke nodded and then did a double take at Tedescu.

He was staring hard at her.

"What? Jesus, Terry, you gonna speak or what?"

The CSU officer eyed them and then snapped off a few more pictures.

Tedescu finally blinked and shook his head. "Let's go."

"Good idea."

Luke followed him out the door, never looking back. She had a strong stomach, but not when it came to stuff like that.

When they got outside, it was sprinkling rain in the pre-dawn hours and she felt grateful for it, like it was washing her. Not fast enough, though. She needed a downpour.

She was suddenly enraged at Tedescu for bringing her in there. She could have gone her whole life without seeing that. She agreed with the DPD that they had it all under control. There was no need for them to be there.

She sucked in a breath and leaned her head back, feeling the drops hit her face.

Tedescu stopped without warning on the front walkway and she ran into his back.

"Damn it, Terry. You'd better start talking or I'm gonna start throwing punches."

A couple of male officers nearby looked at her and raised their eyebrows.

She snarled and gave them a nod.

"I've gotta give you something."

"Oh, he speaks." Her phone vibrated in her pocket. She pulled it out and read the text message from Special Agent Benjamin, one of the few men in the Bureau she considered a friend.

You'd better get in here. Now.

Not bothering to text back, she pressed his phone number and put it to her ear.

"What's going on?" Tedescu asked.

"Better come in here," Benjamin said by way of greeting.

His voice was just above a whisper. "I have to go. We're having a division meeting."

He hung up before she could respond.

"What the hell? They're having a division meeting without us. Benjamin said we'd better get in there."

Tedescu went wide eyed and pulled out his phone. He tapped the screen and started walking to the car, the cell pressed to his ear.

Luke followed close.

"Hey," Tedescu said with clear relief, "are you all right? Where are you? Listen, don't get on the plane. Stay there. Don't ask me why, but do not go to the airport this morning. I don't care. Turn around and go back. I'm going to have an agent come pick you up from your sister's. I love you. I love you so much. Tell the kids I love them ... I have to go."

He tapped the screen and pocketed his phone.

Luke opted to keep silent as they marched toward the car, but she was reeling at the phone call he'd just made.

They reached the vehicle and Tedescu flung the keys at her without looking. She caught them and got in the driver's side.

Luke remained silent for the ride back to the Denver field-office building, letting her partner do some thinking as he stared out the window, while she did her own.

Tedescu had been interested in a dead lawyer named Lethbridge and his family, been spooked by an empty envelope at the crime scene, and then called his wife and told her and the kids to stay in Missouri, where she knew they'd been on vacation, visiting relatives for the past few days. Not only that, he'd essentially told his wife goodbye, as if he was dying, with that final "I love you and the kids" bit. He'd also clearly been worried about their safety. Did he expect they were in the same mortal danger as this family?

He would talk when he was ready.

She looked over at the agent next to her. Tedescu was gnawing on a fingernail and staring out the window, clearly seeing none of the city flashing by.

Or perhaps he wouldn't talk.

She reminded herself that she knew little about her new partner. And then she reminded herself that people were not to be trusted—men in particular. That was one of her deepest beliefs and it had served her well so far in life and career. This guy was caught up in something dangerous and she needed to keep a safe distance.

Lifting her chin at the thought, she pulled into the parking lot, flashed her credentials at the guard, and parked the car.

Two-by-two, agents were exiting the front entrance and climbing into their vehicles.

She got out and waved to Agent Benjamin. "Hey, what's going on?"

Benjamin hurried over. "You'd better go talk to Frye."

"And why's that?"

"Because we're going up to Rocky Points."

Her heart hammered. "What? Why?"

Benjamin shrugged with an apologetic twist of the mouth.

"Thanks."

"Luke." Tedescu grabbed her arm.

She tried to wrench it free but his grip was powerful. She turned to him, and was unnerved by the wild fear in his eyes. "What? Let go of me."

He blinked and let go. "Take this. Go to Trout Creek Moving and Storage in Gunnison Colorado and go to this number." He held out a key with a plastic tag that said #62 on it. "It explains everything. Your friend in Rocky Points is innocent. It's the ghosts. Smith and I were right, and the proof is in that storage unit."

"Innocent of what?"

He thrust the key against her chest and she took it.

"They're executing some sort of plan." He looked at his watch. "I can't explain everything now. I have to go get my son."

"Your son? I thought they were in Missouri?"

"Not my oldest." He gripped Luke by the shoulders and stared with psychotic eyes. "You have to go to that storage unit soon. It proves everything. You have to ..." The sentence died in his throat, and he twisted to look over his shoulder.

Luke followed his searching gaze. "What? Who are you looking for?"

"I have to go." Tedescu ran away, calling out as he went, "Go to Gunnison!"

Tedescu fled across the parking lot. He stopped and got into his SUV and fired it up, backing out in front of Benjamin and his partner, who had to jam the brakes to avoid a collision.

She stared in confusion for a few more seconds and then darted into the building, veered right, and took the stairs three at a time. Dodging another pair of agents as she reached the fourth floor, she went straight for the ASAC's office.

"Agent Luke," Agent Frye greeted her as she poked her head in.

"What's going on?"

Frye loaded some papers into his briefcase. "We're moving on Wolf, and you and Tedescu are staying here."

"What? Why now? What have you got?" Luke asked between breaths.

"A tip." He avoided eye contact.

"A tip? What kind of a tip?"

"On a weapon."

"A tip from whom?"

"Anonymous."

"Sir, this is—"

"Not. Your. Concern!" Agent Frye's gray eyes bore into hers. "Now report to Agent Samson—we've got another matter you'll have to cover while we're gone."

Luke's mouth hung open. Her eyes darted around the room as she thought about what to do. She needed more information, and she needed to speak to Wolf.

A weapon? A murder weapon? There was no way Wolf had killed Sarah. She knew that without Tedescu telling her.

What exactly had he said? *It was the ghosts.* Tedescu was either the crackpot agent everyone feared he might be, or he was telling the truth. She opted for the latter, because there was no way Wolf was a cold-blooded killer.

"Sir, it's the Ghost Cartel. Tedescu just told me that it's they who are framing Wolf, and he's the expert."

He looked at her like she'd just passed gas. "Jesus, *Wolf* is the cartel. Don't you get it?" He opened another drawer.

Her phone chimed and vibrated in her pocket, and she pulled it out. She absently hit the silence button and looked at it.

Every nerve in her body fired as she stared at the name on the screen.

She pressed the green answer button and held the phone to her side.

"Sir," she said, "I can't see how an anonymous tip on a weapon is enough to move on Wolf." She raised her voice. "David Wolf is not a killer."

Agent Frye looked up and exhaled, his face softening. "Look, I know your history with this guy isn't without a little heartache, so I'll cut you some slack with your tone, and I'll explain this once. The first part of the tip was that Gail Olson's body would be found south of Rocky Points. The sheriff's office checked on it last night and they found her, exactly where they were told.

"The second half of the tip told us the location of the murder weapon in Wolf's shed." He held up his hands. "It's enough for me. It's enough for all of us who've been looking for answers for three and a half months. We're moving."

"Sounds fishy. An anonymous tip?"

Frye ignored her.

"Sir, there's no way Wolf did this. This isn't him. He doesn't kill people."

"So you think, because you used to screw him, and that's exactly why you're not going to be involved." Frye closed and latched his briefcase, grabbed it, and ushered her toward the door. He pulled out his phone and made a call.

Luke turned. "Sir, they're going to eat him alive. And if ... if you're wrong about the cartel—"

Frye's briefcase knocked against her back and pushed her closer to the doorway.

"This is Frye. Keep your post."

Luke held the phone with the microphone pointed to her rear.

"Nobody, and I mean nobody but us, goes in or out of that road ... wait until I get there ... as fast as we can."

She went out into the main room and stood still while Frye pocketed his phone and locked his door.

"Report to Samson. There was a quadruple murder in Park Hill last night and it involved a lawyer who does a lot of business with many of us." Frye shook his head. "Damn nightmare. The whole family was executed. I want you two there."

Before Luke could tell her boss that she and Tedescu had already seen the carnage first hand, that her partner had inexplicably brought her to the murders that morning, thrust a key into her hand and then run like the world was about to end, Frye disappeared around the corner.

She considered chasing after him, but her phone seemed to keep her from moving. Like it was planted in space and had some sort of localized gravitational field she could not escape.

Two lone agents sat at desks, pecking away on their keyboards. The rest of the vast room seemed left in disarray.

She twirled full circle to make sure she was alone, then pressed the phone to her ear. "Wolf?"

CHAPTER 7

WOLF WOKE to his alarm at sunrise and muscled down breakfast even though he felt no hunger.

An hour later he'd completed his daily stretches—spending an extra few minutes on his leg—and was dressed to leave.

He checked his old department Glock and shoved it into his paddle holster. After tucking it on his hip, he put on his fleece jacket, pulled open the drawstring on the waist to let it fall over the gun, took one last look in the mirror, and left out the front door.

A warm wind buffeted him from the south. By the looks of the crystal-clear sky, a high-pressure front was pushing up from Arizona. The snow that had dusted the peaks yesterday was a distant memory.

Stopping on the grass, he stretched his back and checked the side of the mountain ahead. To his surprise, the pinpoint reflection was missing.

Perhaps his spies were looking elsewhere, or had finally lost interest in him.

Wolf pulled out his phone, keeping his eyes on the spot.

This was go time. If it took fifty phone calls, he was going to get some answers from the Denver FO. He scrolled through his contacts and pressed the number for Special Agent Kristen Luke.

The phone trilled and then clicked.

"Luke."

He was stunned that after so many months of screening his calls, she was picking up after one ring.

There was no response.

"It's Wolf. Hello?"

Then Luke spoke, but her voice was far from the receiver. She had clearly hit the wrong button.

"Luke?" Wolf paced with the phone against his ear, and then froze at the sound of his name.

His pulse climbed with each word.

"The second half of the tip told us the location of the murder weapon in Wolf's shed."

He twisted and stared at the workshop door on his barn. Listening to the continuing conversation playing out in his ear, he walked silently toward it.

The padlock was missing. There were no scratches on the latch to indicate it had been pried at, but there was a tiny sliver of metal partially buried in the dirt at his feet. He picked it up and rolled it in his fingers. It was jagged and silvery, a piece of debris left after cutting the lock with bolt cutters.

He listened to the remainder of the faint conversation and then there was a loud scratching sound in his ear.

"Wolf?" Luke asked.

"What the hell was that?"

Standing up, he felt a jolt of pain in his spine that had vanished by the time he straightened.

"Did you hear what my boss said?"

"If I heard that the FBI is moving on me for suspicion of murdering Sarah, then yeah, I heard."

He flipped the latch on the shed door and pushed it open.

"Shit." She breathed into the phone.

"An anonymous tip says I killed Carter Willis and Sarah? And what did you say? They found Gail Olson?"

"The tip was called into Sluice—Byron Sheriff's Department last night. Said you killed Gail Olson. The person gave the location of the body, and the location of the weapon, which I'm assuming is at your house. Apparently, SBCSD just found her, and now we're coming up to bring you in."

"This doesn't make any sense. I can see right here that my workshop's been broken into. You guys should have seen everything. This place was crawling with your surveillance yesterday, and now it's gone. And now I'm being framed?"

Studying the wood-plank floor, he regretted cleaning the place a week ago, because now there were no signs of foot-prints. He stepped in and gazed down at the dirt outside the door and saw it looked freshly smoothed over.

He stood motionless, scanning every inch of his work-bench and the surrounding shop area. Nothing seemed out of the ordinary.

"... men."

"What?"

"Are you listening to me?"

"No."

"I said Vincent and Buntham? That's hardly a surveillance operation. They were just keeping tabs on you while you left your house."

Wolf narrowed his eyes. "What are you talking about? You had at least eight men on me yesterday."

"That wasn't us."

He held his breath.

"Wolf, are you there?"

"Yeah, I'm here."

"What men are you talking about?" Luke asked, her voice just above a whisper.

Wolf ignored her and stepped to the first drawer of his workbench. He pulled it open, then moved to the next one, and the next.

He knew exactly what he was looking for: a 9 mm pistol.

"Wolf, talk to me."

"Just a second." He grabbed his hunting binoculars off the workbench and walked outside. He pressed the cold rubber eyepieces against his cheeks and studied the mountainside to the west.

The dark SUV that usually sat parked behind a copse of trees in the saddle was no longer there. There were no more men milling about, with their plumes of cigarette smoke drifting on the breeze.

"Does the Bureau use black SUVs, dark SUVs, for surveillance stake-outs?"

"What?"

"Answer."

"No. They're in a fleet of Crown Vics coming up right now. I'm sure we have some SUVs in the motor pool, but I've never used one down here in Denver." She paused. "Wolf?"

"Yeah."

"I have to tell you something else."

"What?"

"Carter Willis was ours."

The ground seemed to tilt.

"He was FBI," she said. "Undercover."

Wolf switched phone hands. "You've been screening my

calls for months. Ignoring that one question I asked over and over—Who's Carter Willis? I asked you dozens of times if your databases turned up anything, if your contacts had any info. Patterson's been asking you."

"I was under orders to not speak to you about it."

"Fuck your orders!" His chest tightened. "That's a pretty big clue you were keeping from me, Luke."

She exhaled into his ear. "I'm sorry. But whether or not I told you about him is not important right now."

"Not important?"

"No, it's not. From what I've learned this morning, I think you just had a very dangerous element watching you. It wasn't us. I know for certain, because I've been all over this case from the beginning, and the only two men we had up there watching you were Buntham and Vincent. That's it."

Wolf paced in the dirt. "Then who? A dangerous element? Start using simpler words. I'm not in the mood."

"There was a dead family this morning down here, and then my partner said you were being framed and you're innocent. Whatever the connection, this dead family spooked the shit out of him and he just drove away with squealing tires. He was freaked out, and he used to be partnered with Agent Smith."

"Who the hell's Agent Smith?"

"Carter Willis. Smith is his real name. Crap, Wolf, there's a lot you don't know. And you have less than two hours until we get there."

Wolf squeezed his upper thigh and his femur protested beneath his bruised muscle. "I'll get a good lawyer. This is bullshit and everyone knows it."

"I'm not so sure that's a good idea."

"Why?"

"Okay, let's say you're taken into custody and eventually charged. Tonight or tomorrow you'll be put in with general population in Quad County. These guys just killed an entire family down here. They've got my partner spooked. By the looks of it, they're responsible for Sarah's death. Something is clearly going down. Some sort of plan. You think it's a stretch that they might have someone on the inside at Quad County? Think about it. They're framing you. After that, keeping you alive would be a major liability. Like you said, what if you get a good lawyer?"

Wolf stared into nothing.

"Wolf, I'm right. Get out of there, and then call me when you do."

He hung up and took the battery out of his phone, pried out the SIM card with his fingernail, and pocketed all of it.

Special Agent Luke had his attention.

Wolf had a lot of questions, and he would surely fail to get answers from behind bars. Justice for Sarah would be locked up right with him, he was sure of it. And with all the strange action happening lately, he was sure Luke was right in her assessment of the dangers of being locked up.

His watch said 7:45.

The gun that killed Sarah was here. Feet from him, tucked away somewhere inside his barn.

MacLean's laughing face flashed in his mind.

He walked back inside the workshop and stepped along the plank floor to the dirt. His dirt bike, his father's old tractor, some rusted farm equipment, a canoe, and an ill-working snowmobile slept unmoved and untouched, still blanketed in months of dust.

No footprints anywhere.

He stepped to the barn doors, unlatched them, and pulled them open, letting the morning light flood inside.

He stepped out. A black tassel-eared squirrel stood staring at him on the path to his right. A tree trunk creaked as it swayed back and forth in the wind.

He walked to the motorcycle and pushed it upright off its kickstand. The gas tank sloshed, still full.

Swinging his leg over the dusty seat, he winced as his hip protested. Bending over, he swung out the kick-start lever and gave it a try.

Nothing.

He tried once more. The motion of loading his weight, jumping, and slamming down on his right leg was excruciating on his hip and it felt like his femur was about to crack again.

Stepping off, he dug his thumb into cramped leg muscle. Leaving on foot in his condition was a ridiculous thought. The road south dead-ended two miles away in the middle of remote forest. And then what?

That left one option.

Wolf's breath echoed in the canoe as he balanced it upside down on his head and walked down his dirt driveway.

Reaching the bull-horned headgate, he stopped and dumped the fiberglass boat on the ground. It crashed hard and bounced, sounding like timpani in the still morning air.

For the past month, the two FBI goons on Wolf-surveillance had parked a mile down the road. Thankfully, today was no different.

Dropping the paddle inside, he grabbed the rope on the front of the boat, pulled it down the inclined drive to the dirt road, and then crossed, stopping at the steep drop-off on the other side.

The Chautauqua was flowing high on the banks, fed by the recent rain.

Pulling until the boat teetered over the edge, he gave it a shove and then grabbed the side to prevent it from going over too fast.

His footing gave out and he slipped onto his ass and slid down the embankment alongside the boat, scraping his back what felt like to the bone, all the while the booming vessel bouncing against him.

The bow jabbed into the water and started drifting down current fast. The keel slid and connected with his back, pushing him toward the water.

"Shit," he said, realizing he was now leaning out over the water and about to go in.

With the most athletic move he'd accomplished in over three months, he twisted and grabbed the boat and jumped up. It slid underneath him, and he landed inside, belly down.

He landed on his thighs on the bow seat, crashing head and elbow first into the floor of the canoe.

Rocking back and forth, the boat scraped along the rocky edge and was then adrift.

Wolf blocked out the pain of the sledgehammer blow to his femur and rolled onto his back. After a wrestling match with himself, he managed to pull his legs in, roll back over, and balance on his knees in the wobbling boat.

He was flying down the river, bouncing up and down on the rapids.

With a thud, the canoe slammed into a rock and stopped, and Wolf went face first into the stern thwart, the cross beam that kept the hull sturdy in front. With barely an inch to spare, Wolf put his hand up just in time to soften the blow.

He righted himself, grabbed the paddle, sat on the bow seat and started steering.

Thinking two, three, four moves ahead, he picked his lines, moving the boat side to side with the aid of adrenaline-charged muscles.

Looking up to his right, he could see nothing but the steep embankment, and then suddenly the slope dropped away and he was looking all the way to the mountains to his right.

Mountains, and the dirt road.

Thankfully, the FBI vehicle was not parked along the visible stretch.

Again, he slammed into a rock, and he cursed himself for taking his eye off the water for too long.

Crouching low in the canoe, he felt alive for the first time in months. The pain in his hip screamed, but barely registered in his mind. His femur throbbed, but he didn't care.

As he rounded a bend to the right, the unmarked came into view and he saw the two familiar agents Luke had called Vincent and Buntham milling around next to it. A puff of cigarette smoke blew from one of their mouths, and the other was stretching his arms above his head.

Wolf crouched but knew that simply getting lower in the boat would be of no use. In fact, to do so would probably bring more suspicion on him.

The only consolation was that the two men were parked on the crest of a hill, and there was an embankment blocking their view of the river below.

Maybe he could pass completely unnoticed. His only chance was to hug the right-side of the shore as closely as possible.

He paddled and got into position in the right-hand rapids, and just as he'd hoped, the slope grew higher and the vehicle disappeared above.

The last he saw of the two agents, they looked preoccupied in the downriver direction. They were anxiously awaiting their colleagues.

Wolf's stomach dropped as he looked further ahead.

The road descended back down to only a few feet above the river, and Wolf was going to be in plain view until the next bend, which meant roughly a hundred yards of the two agents looking right at him.

Shit.

He searched the shore for a place to land. Maybe he could stop now and try to create a diversion, and then slip by unnoticed.

Before the options had finished running through his mind, he was out in the open.

With slow, deliberate paddles, he pumped twice on the starboard side, then once on the port. He sat straight, high on the seat, a man out for a leisurely morning paddle. No hurry.

"Yeah, this'll work," he said under his breath, dodging another rock with a precise swing of the stern.

He could feel the eyes of the Bureau agents on his back. He could imagine their conversation, deciding what to do about the man in the boat. Should they come after him? Should they keep their posts?

Had they even noticed him?

Of course they had.

Wolf passed around the next bend and exhaled, and then he paddled hard.

CHAPTER 8

Deputy Tom Rachette fired six rounds in quick succession, hitting the grayed area he'd aimed for.

The red cease-fire light flashed and the horn sounded for good measure.

Rachette exhaled and put down his pistol.

"Getting better?"

He turned at the feminine voice. It was her again. He pulled off his ear protectors, pretending like he hadn't heard. "What?"

She gave him that cute, bashful smile act she seemed to think worked on men. "I just wondered how you were progressing. You going to be ready for the test tomorrow?"

Rachette turned his back to her and pushed the button. The motor on the pulley whirred and the target sped towards him from twenty-five yards away.

He had always been a good shot. Growing up on a farm in eastern Nebraska, it was something that happened naturally. That, and he was a Rachette. The Rachettes had always been good shots.

Throughout his childhood he'd picked off birds, squirrels,

and groundhogs with his pellet gun, and then he'd graduated to shotguns and rifles, hunting bigger game with his father and grandfather as he grew up.

It had been one of the only things the Rachettes ever did with their fathers—shooting and killing things out in the wild.

"You'll never be a perfect man, but you can always make the perfect shot."

His father used to tell him that out in the bitter chill of autumn as they followed the dogs up the corn line. It made zero sense to him today, just as it had back then.

Assholes rarely made much sense, otherwise they wouldn't be assholes. But, he had to admit, his old man had taught him how to shoot.

In his first run through the police academy in Lincoln, Nebraska, he'd scored a perfect hundred percent on his proficiency test, and then scored the same when he was hired into the Sluice County Sheriff's Department in Rocky Points.

He'd never felt nerves when shooting until now.

The target zipped all the way in and fluttered to a stop in front of his face.

Three of the shots had missed the grayed target area.

"Oh, no. Well, you'll do better when it counts, outside on the course. I'm sure of it."

Rachette turned. "I didn't ask you. Now are you here to clean up my brass or something? Or what?"

The girl smiled and raised her eyebrows. "No. Did you need help cleaning up your brass?"

"Yeah, please. Thanks, honey." Rachette unloaded his weapon and placed it inside his case.

Still deemed unfit to carry the weapon on his duty belt until he passed the test tomorrow morning at ten a.m., he already felt like an inadequate fool walking around the station with no piece or badge. Now he was missing targets, standing still, at twenty-five yards.

It was his damn shoulder. It just wouldn't hold his arm steady like it had before he'd been shot.

And on top of that he had to deal with this chick pretending to hit on him? He was tired of being the butt of that joke.

She showed up with the hand broom and scoop, and pushed Rachette's brass into a tinkling pile.

"Hey, what are you doing? Give me that." He grabbed the broom and finished cleaning up after himself.

The woman watched quietly.

"Seriously. Don't you have somewhere else to be, Deputy,"—he read her name patch—"oh yeah, Munford?"

He finished gathering up his stuff and froze. With a jolt of realization, he sagged his shoulders. "You?"

"Hello, Deputy Rachette."

"You."

"Yes, me. Besides Sheriff MacLean, I'm currently the only Law Enforcement Standards Board-certified instructor in this department, so I'll be administering your test tomorrow."

"Sorry I called you ..."

"Called me what?"

In slow-motion horror, Rachette felt his gun case slip from his fingers. It tumbled onto his foot, and with a muscle spasm he kicked it into Munford's leg.

"Sorry." He scooped it up and stood.

She stared, clearly enjoying herself.

Her manicured eyebrow lifted, creasing the taut, tanned youthful skin of her forehead. Her lipstick-free lips widened, displaying perfect rows of ivory teeth and a good dose of gum on top. Her blonde hair bobbed side to side as she shook her head.

He looked down at her name patch again, and perused the rest of her body with an undetectable peripheral-vision assessment. Just as stunning as the first time he'd met her a few weeks ago.

She was even more intimidating than Patterson, because this woman was downright irresistible.

She probably had a six-five husband or boyfriend with mountainous muscles. Would probably have a heyday laughing about this with her fellow Byron County cronies.

"Like I said, sorry." He stepped past her to the plastic chair, grabbed his jacket, and began walking.

"Bye, honey. See you tomorrow. Ten a.m. sharp," she said with a chuckle.

Rachette's face went hot as he ducked past a deputy in the next shooting stall watching the whole thing.

Lost in dreadful thoughts about his abysmal aim and luck with women, he stepped out the doorway to the hallway outside, where he heard sounds of excited chatter echoing off the walls.

Curiosity piqued, he walked toward the commotion, which seemed to be coming from the squad room. He stepped down the hallway and entered the cathedral-like space where the bulk of the SBCSD deputies had desks. Unlike the old HQ building, the new county building's squad room was airy and natural light flowed in the floor-to-ceiling windows on the west and east sides. The two dozen desks were empty, because their occupants were lining up and pushing into the situation room.

He searched for Patterson, Baine, Wilson, or Yates. Anyone he recognized.

"Hey, Deputy," he called after the nearest passing uniform, "what's going on?"

The man stopped and pointed at his name patch, and then the chevron on his uniform. "Deputy Sergeant Barker."

"Yes sir, Sergeant. I'm Deputy Rachette. What's happening?"

Barker stepped close, eying Rachette up and down, assessing him like a piece of meat. "Not yet."

"What's that?"

"You're not a deputy yet."

Rachette blinked and stood straight when he saw Barker's lip curl.

"Not yet, correct sir. I have my shooting proficiency test tomorrow. I've been in the Sluice County department for four years now, though."

"And if you pass then you'll be involved with official department business of the Sluice–Byron SD. But until then, you won't be."

Dick. Rachette backed away. "See you around."

Barker raised his eyebrows, as if Rachette had meant it as a challenge. A threat. Maybe he had. *Serious dick.*

"Hey," a feminine voice said behind him.

Rachette twisted around and saw Patterson.

"Hey, what's going on?"

Patterson was ghostly white, and she was rubbing her hands together.

"What is it?"

"They found Gail Olson this morning. Last night."

"They did? 'Bout time that chick showed up."

"Dead."

"Oh."

"Someone called in an anonymous tip. The phone number

was encrypted, the voice garbled, but whoever it was said exactly where to find Gail Olson, and then said Wolf had the weapon stashed in his barn."

"What? Wolf?"

"Tammy took the call. She said the person signed off as *a disgruntled partner of Wolf's*. I guess Lorber's got her body now, and we're waiting for the FBI before we move."

"Move on Wolf?"

She nodded.

"Why are we waiting on the FBI?"

Patterson shrugged. "Above our pay grade."

Sergeant Deputy Barker stood on his toes and then marched over. "Hey, I thought I made myself clear."

Rachette ignored him. "Keep me posted."

"I will."

"Hey!"

"Yeah, asshole, I get it."

Barker stepped close to Rachette again.

Rachette held firm, pressing his pectorals into the man's ribs.

"Easy there, boys."

A different feminine voice materialized next to Rachette and then a firm hand clamped onto Barker's bicep, pulling him away.

It was Deputy Munford again. "Come on, Barker. Deputy Patterson, right? Let's get going."

Barker backed away, using a psychotic glare aimed at him, then he reluctantly turned away and marched toward the dwindling line of deputies.

"Dick."

"Whatever. Forget him," Patterson said. "I'll keep you posted."

He nodded. "All right. Guess I'll go get a cup of coffee or something."

Patterson pulled her lips into a line and turned away.

"Call me."

"I will."

Rachette waved to Patterson and found Deputy Munford in the crowd. She was walking away, and then before she entered the situation room she looked back at him and smiled with one side of her mouth.

He stood, thinking of that gesture until the door clacked shut and he was the only one standing in an empty room.

He shook his head, clearing his thoughts.

A disgruntled partner of Wolf's? What in the hell was going on today?

Deputy Munford's tiny smile flashed in his mind again.

He pressed his thumb on his right shoulder. The starfish-shaped scar was still tender underneath his sweatshirt. His muscle ached, and was less bulky than he was used to feeling.

Not quite healed. But he was here with that test scheduled for tomorrow because he could wait no more. No more daytime television and feeling sorry for himself.

As if that drive to get back into the department hadn't been enough, now he had two more reasons he absolutely needed to pass that test tomorrow, if it was the last thing he ever did in his life: *A disgruntled partner of Wolf's, and that tiny smile.*

CHAPTER 9

WOLF PADDLED to the western shore of the river.

He was tucked in the pines on the southern outskirts of town now, having floated his way undetected along the entire 2.7 mile stretch of sage country.

Undetected? It was probably not an accurate word. Wolf didn't envy the two FBI agents when his escape was discovered.

The canoe bumped ashore and twisted a hundred and eighty degrees. He hopped out and pushed it back into the flowing water.

He stretched his limbs overhead, and as he pulled down on his fleece he realized his paddle holster was missing.

With a sinking stomach, he thought back on his fall down the slope near his house and his dive into the canoe. That was the only feasible spot he could have lost it. Cursing himself, he hiked through the pines toward the rear deck of the Beer Goggles Bar and Grill.

It seemed early to see Jerry Blackman's old pickup in the parking lot on a Wednesday, but Wolf decided it was a good piece of luck.

He walked to the rear door and knocked three times.

The barred trashcans lined up along the outside wall kept the bears out, but failed to keep the smell of stale beer and bar food from spilling into the damp morning air.

He swore he heard a thump inside, but over the trickling river and referee-whistle calls of humming birds behind him, it was tough to say.

Three more knocks.

Still nothing.

Wolf walked around the side of the building to the front, knowing he was clearly visible to Jerry inside as he passed each of the windows in front.

Stopping to peer inside, he saw no movement, but a single light glowed behind the bar counter.

Crunching along the puddle-strewn parking lot, he eyed the entrance road and thankfully heard no vehicles approaching. He stepped to the front door and pulled on it, but it was locked.

He knocked three more times. "Jerry! It's David Wolf! Can I come in, please?"

No answer.

Wolf picked up a rock the size of his head and slammed it down on the doorknob. The knob snapped from the door and fell to the ground. He pushed his finger through and the other side of the knob fell onto the floor inside. He pulled the door open and stepped in.

Jerry Blackman stood behind the bar, his eyes wide and his lips puckered.

Wolf stopped. "Hey, Jerry. Don't shoot. It's me, David Wolf."

Jerry held his pose. His lips glistened with spit, and his eyes seemed like they were going to explode out of his head.

"Sorry about the door. I have an emergency. I knocked on the back door. Did you not—"

A cloud of smoke burst from Jerry's mouth. Drool streamed from his lips as he coughed.

Wolf squinted and waved his hand as he stepped into the pungent cloud of marijuana smoke.

"Hey, Dave. How's it going?"

"Sorry about the doorknob. I'll pay for it."

"Ahhh." Jerry coughed again. "Doorknob?"

"The door ... Can I use your phone?"

"Don't you have a cell phone?"

"No, it died on me. Listen, I've gotta use your phone."

"Sure, bro. Have at it." Jerry stood back and pointed at the cordless on the counter. He leaned forward, grabbed the smoking bong and put it on the shelf next to the liquor bottles.

"Thank you." Wolf pulled out his cell phone and inserted the battery, then powered it on.

"It works." Jerry smiled. "Nice."

He scrolled through the contacts and found Luke's phone number, then dialed the cordless landline.

"Wait. Your phone works now."

Wolf put the phone to one ear and his finger in the other. It rang several times then went to voicemail. Wolf dialed again and waited.

"What?" Luke voice was barely audible over a loud hissing in the background.

"It's Wolf."

"Shit! Where are you?"

"I'm ... is this line secure?"

"I hope. Where are you?"

Wolf looked at Jerry, who was staring at him and blinking. "I'm in town."

Luke exhaled hard into her phone. "You need to get to Margaret's office as soon as possible. I'll take care of everything else."

"I've gotta get to MacLean."

"No, to Margaret. Call me when you get there."

The line went dead.

He pressed the call end button and looked at Jerry. "Can you give me a ride into town?"

Jerry nodded. "Wait, no. I can't drive after doing this stuff. That's against the law."

"I don't care. I'm not sheriff anymore. Please, I need a ride."

"Okay." Jerry shrugged and walked past Wolf.

———

Wolf leaned back away from the filthy windshield as a line of Ford Crown Victorias sped past with lights twisting on their roofs.

"Whoa, must be a fire or something." Jerry leaned toward his filthy side mirror, pulling the truck into oncoming Main Street traffic in the process.

Wolf reached over and straightened the wheel. "Jerry! The road."

"Whoa, yeah." Jerry turned bright red, and then combed back his mop hair.

"Up here." Wolf pointed ahead.

Jerry mashed the brakes and Wolf caught himself before slamming into the dashboard.

"No, up there. Another block."

"Okay, yeah. Man, this stuff is really potent. Sorry."

Wolf wiped his palms on his jeans and scanned outside. All the trouble just blew by them at sixty miles per hour. So he hoped. There was no sign of sheriff's-department SUVs, and as far as he could see through the dirt-caked windows, no sign of anymore FBI vehicles.

"This is perfect."

Jerry slowed at a more reasonable rate this time, his front tire popping up on the curb as he stopped.

"Thanks, Jerry. If they ask you what you did, just tell them you gave me a ride into town. You don't know anything else."

Jerry's eyes glazed over like he was trying to add two ten-digit numbers in his head.

"Never mind." Wolf shut the door.

"Hey, Dave." Rich Chancelor, a local having a cigarette outside the coffee shop, nodded at Wolf.

"Hey, Rich." Wolf felt exposed already after the exchange and buried his face inside his fleece collar. He walked fast to the end of the block and hung a right.

On the opposite corner squatted the abandoned Sluice County Sheriff's Department station building he'd spent so many years of his life in.

The blinds inside the windows were drawn and the dirt parking lot was overrun with hip-high weeds.

He gave a silent greeting to it and marched to the front door of Margaret's office.

The Hitching Post Realty logo was frosted on the glass of the door, and when he pushed it open a string of sleigh bells clanged.

Margaret stood up from her desk and her wheeled chair slammed into a filing cabinet behind her. "David."

"Margaret."

The door swished shut behind him.

His friend pulled her mass of silver curls into a ponytail and fastened it back, all the while locking her eyes with his.

Normally cool and confident, quick to speak with a razor-sharp tongue, Margaret was mute, her face tight, mouth clamped shut.

It was a side of Margaret he was unused to seeing. "Kristen Luke told me to come here." He stepped to the windows and peered outside. When Margaret kept silent he turned to look at her.

She had her desk-phone receiver pressed against her ear and was tapping the keypad.

"Whoa. Who are you calling?"

"Kristen." She stood straight and closed her eyes. "Come on. Come on."

He turned back to the windows.

"Hey. He's here ... okay ..."

"Let me speak to her."

She held up a finger. "Okay ... seventeen ... I'll call her. She'll come. Okay, I have to go ..."

"Wait." He held out his hand. "I need to talk to her."

Margaret reluctantly handed him the receiver.

"What's going on? Where are you?" he asked.

"You have to go with Margaret. I'll meet you guys."

"Where?"

"Margaret knows. You have to move, now. They're going to see you're gone from your house and they're going to throw up containment road blocks."

"Wait. I don't care. I need to stay here. Here's where we'll get answers."

"You have to leave because I have the answers. So get your ass moving and get in Margaret's car. Now."

The line went dead.

He exhaled and gave Margaret the phone.

She put the receiver to her ear. "Hello?"

"She hung up. So I guess I'm going with you."

Margaret grabbed her keychain from the desk and walked.

Wolf eyed the empty room. The computers on the other desks were running, screensavers bouncing across the screen. There was an email on the nearest screen, abandoned in mid-creation.

"I sent them all away." She walked to the door and pulled it open. "Move it."

Her tone and the sleigh bells snapped Wolf into action. He walked fast outside and followed to her SUV.

The engine was already howling when he climbed into the passenger seat, and they were backed out of the parking spot before Wolf had closed the door.

"Shit, duck."

Wolf saw what she meant, but it was too late.

Tom Rachette stood on the corner, staring wide eyed as Margaret rolled through the stop sign and turned north on Main Street.

"Get down."

Wolf ignored her, locking eyes with Rachette.

Dressed in plain clothes, Rachette held a coffee in one hand and stood with his mouth open.

As they drove down Main, he twisted in his seat and kept staring, until Rachette turned and walked the opposite way.

"Cops, cops, get down."

Margaret slowed to the side of the road as a line of screaming and flashing Sluice–Byron SD vehicles flew past.

Wolf never saw them go by, because he was curled up on the passenger-side floorboard.

CHAPTER 10

PATTERSON TOOK another deep breath and steeled herself for the inevitable sight that would confront her as they drove up the inclined driveway to Wolf's ranch property.

Wolf was hands down the best man she'd ever known. Someone was doing this to him and everyone was taking the misdirection hook, line, and sinker.

As they passed through the headgate, the scene rising into view was mayhem: unmarked Fords flashing, men and women pouring out of the SBCSD vehicles, their turrets flashing blue and red through the haze.

Lancaster was unable to drive very far, so he pulled into the grass and parked.

He got out and marched double-time down the driveway. Patterson took her time following, in no hurry to see David Wolf being arrested for murder.

She passed Wilson and nodded.

"You hear?"

"Hear what?" She stopped.

"They found the gun." He nodded toward the barn and smiled. "But not him."

"Are you serious?" A jolt of electricity passed through her body.

"Yep."

"What did you say, Sergeant?" Lancaster walked toward them.

It was always startling for Patterson to hear Lancaster's voice, because the man spoke at an octave lower than everyone else, and he did so very rarely. And at this volume? She could hardly remember him enunciating so clearly in the past few weeks she'd been partnered with him.

For a big man, Lancaster had small, beady eyes. Right now, they narrowed to slits. "He escaped?"

Wilson shrugged. "That's the news."

Lancaster turned and jogged toward the front of the house, and this time Patterson ran to catch up.

A group of suited agents gathered in front of the covered carport, staring at another agent some distance away as he held up a plastic bag with a pistol inside.

The barn doors were wide open, and the Assistant Special Agent in Charge that had interrogated her, and his big-ass sidekick, were conferring with one another. The barn seemed to be off limits to everyone save two white-clad techs with cameras inside, taking pictures.

Upon closer inspection, Patterson saw that Agent Frye was studying the ground intently, and his sidekick—Cumberland, that was his name—was watching his boss.

Frye followed a line on the ground and looked up at Patterson. No, past her.

He walked fast, keeping his eyes down, and the crowd suddenly went quiet, taking notice.

Marching fast past Patterson and Lancaster, Frye snapped his fingers. "Buntham and Vincent!"

"Yes, sir," an FBI agent answered quickly.

Agent Frye continued walking and everyone followed, including Patterson, eager to keep within earshot.

"I'm looking at Mr. Wolf's footprints here, walking off the property. The scrape marks on the ground inside the barn indicate he was carrying something heavy."

"Yes, sir," one of the agents, either Buntham or Vincent, said.

"Ah. Here." Agent Frye paused underneath the headgate wooden arch of Wolf's property and pointed at the ground. A conga-line of agents and sheriff's deputies stopped along with him.

Frye looked up at the agent he'd been speaking to and the agent swallowed. Though a man of slight build and under-average height, ASAC Frye was clearly intimidating to his agents.

"A boat." Frye walked down the hill, across the dirt road, and stopped at the embankment overlooking the river. "Did you happen to see him as he passed you in his boat, Agent Buntham?"

Buntham stared at the water with an open mouth.

"Buntham!"

"Yes, sir. We did. We thought it was a fisherman. Just a ... boatist."

"A boatist?"

Buntham lowered his chin.

"I want roadblocks on north and southbound Highway 734, and a bird in the air checking the river for our boatist." He locked eyes with Patterson.

Patterson stepped back, unprepared for the intensity and focus of the man's gaze searing into her.

"Deputy Patterson."

"Yes, sir?"

"I want to speak with you. Everyone move!"

Another agent raised his voice and started giving orders, and the crowd dispersed fast.

As Frye stepped close, a shadow passed over Patterson's face, and she saw Lancaster stood right next to her.

"What did you and Wolf talk about?"

"What? When?"

"Yesterday. When you were here."

She hesitated.

"Answer the question."

"I ... he ... we went for a walk and he showed me your surveillance teams."

Frye's face soured.

"And, I don't know, he hasn't been back into work for months. He's no longer sheriff, he's healing, he's out of the loop. We meet every week or so to go over the news."

"What kind of news?"

Patterson glanced up at Lancaster's dead-eyed stare.

"News—"

"I want the actual news, Deputy," Frye said. "If you tell me the news by using the word news again I'm going to toss you in this river."

She clenched her jaw and stood straight. *I'd like to see you try.* "He was concerned about the sudden increase in surveillance. He wanted to know what had changed. I told him the FBI had been talking with me and Deputies Rachette and Baine in the last few weeks, but he wanted to know why you had three teams watching him. I think he was getting antsy about his state of being, and was frustrated with the current investigation into the death of his ex-wife, and how he and his deputies were being implicated."

Frye nodded with a humorless smile.

She lifted her chin.

"Sir," Lancaster said, "we'd like to help in any way. And as soon as possible."

Frye looked up at Lancaster. "Yes, Undersheriff. Thank you. Why don't you and Deputy Patterson help with the southern roadblock."

"Yes, sir." Lancaster nodded and twisted on his heels.

Patterson stayed where she was.

Frye watched Lancaster step away and then leaned into Patterson. "Stay available, Deputy." Then he marched away after Lancaster, leaving her alone overlooking the river.

Flowing high on its banks, the gurgling Chautauqua sparkled in the warming sun.

She hoped Wolf had used the river to get far away, and then had gotten off it as soon as possible.

"Patterson!" Lancaster called out.

She jogged to catch up.

CHAPTER 11

"WHAT THE HELL were you doing? He saw you."

Wolf cracked an eyelid. "He won't tell anyone." He could barely hear himself over the growing ringing in his ear.

"This is crazy." Margaret jabbed the power button on the radio.

The country music was silenced and nothing remained but the ringing.

Keeping his eyes closed, he breathed deep to calm his queasy stomach.

"Are you all right?"

He exhaled, inhaled again.

"Wolf?"

"Yeah. I just need a minute."

The minute turned into forty minutes of silence. He wanted to ask about the specifics of their plan, but he didn't have the energy. Through slit eyelids, he observed life happening around him, giving over his trust to Margaret Hitchens and Kristen Luke.

After driving for ten minutes north on Highway 734, they'd

taken a left on County 17, passing a couple of fisherman hanging lines off the bridge into the river, and continued at a steady pace up the dirt road into the forested mountains on the west side of the Chautauqua Valley.

Twenty minutes into the drive, the ringing in his ear had stopped and the nausea had dissipated, leaving only the normality of his throbbing leg and hip.

Now at the fortieth minute into their escape, Margaret finally let off the gas and started taking turns at reasonable speeds.

"What's happening?" Wolf asked, observing Margaret as she leaned into the windshield.

"She's supposed to be around here."

Out the windshield, a woman jumped into the middle of the road, waving her hands. She was dressed in gray sweatpants and a black hooded sweatshirt.

Margaret gripped the wheel with both hands and jammed the brakes.

Wolf recognized the athletic build and movements of Kristen Luke as they ground to a halt in an explosion of dust.

"Crap." Margaret watched as Luke jumped in the back seat and slammed the door.

"Let's go!"

Margaret hesitated for a second, her jaw opening and closing, and then she pressed the gas.

There was no sign of Luke's vehicle outside.

Wolf glanced at her in the back seat and thought of the three-month silent treatment he'd just gotten from her, and opted out of offering greeting.

Luke gave him a sideways glance and then stared past him out the windshield. "Have you talked to her?"

"No," Margaret said.

"Who?" Wolf asked.

Luke leaned forward in between the seats. Her cinnamon eyes were so wide and fierce that Wolf wondered whether they might glow.

The cab filled with her scent, which Wolf knew to be her feminine deodorant and bathing soap, and not perfume, which she despised. He'd forgotten how impossibly smooth her facial skin was, like her face hadn't aged since she was fifteen.

Her brown hair was pulled back tight against her scalp, striped with wheat colored strands that looked to be the recent handy work of a hair stylist.

She flicked him an annoyed glance. "What? It's the workout clothes I keep in my car."

He turned to the windshield. "I'm just wondering when you're going to let me in on the plan."

Luke's finger jabbed past him. "There!"

They rounded a corner and saw an SUV coming at speed. It swerved past them and its brake lights glowed.

Margaret jammed the brakes as they entered a cloud of dust.

"Pull over there."

Margaret did as she was told and Luke was out the door.

"Who's that?"

Margaret put the SUV in park and pressed the emergency brake. "My sister."

"From Aspen? Patterson's mother?"

"Yep." She got out. "Let's go."

———

"Son of a bitch." Margaret's sister climbed out of a new silver

Ford pickup and squinted against the choking dust. "This him?"

Margaret hugged her sister and pointed a hand at Wolf. "Valerie, this is David Wolf."

Valerie Patterson eyed Wolf with a hard gaze that reminded him instantly of her daughter. She stood the same height as Heather, which was to say the woman was short. But with hands on her hips, she presented herself as a much larger woman.

Wolf shook her hand, certain now that Patterson got her tenacity from her mother. "Nice to meet you."

"Wish I could say the same." She shook her head at Margaret and Luke. "I was in the line at the grocery store. You guys freaked me out. You mind telling me what's going on?"

"Sorry," Luke said, "there's no time to chat. We have to move. They're going to be all over these hills in no time."

"Who?" Valerie asked, swiveling her gaze to each of them.

Wolf's ear began to ring again, and when he stepped backward, he staggered and caught himself. "I've gotta go sit down," he said, turning back toward Margaret's vehicle.

"No, we're going in Valerie's truck," Luke said. "Over here."

Wolf stopped and walked toward the passenger side of the silver pickup.

"Christ, he's in bad shape. Should we help him?" one of them asked.

He waved a hand. "I'm all right." His words sounded like a muffled tuba in his head.

The three women stared at him.

"We need your truck," Luke said. "You two go back in Margaret's SUV."

Valerie Patterson gave over her keys. "This dude better be

worth it. Everyone's always talking about how great Wolf is. Wolf did this, Wolf did that. Doesn't look so great to me."

"Val, shut up and let's go. I'll explain on the way to Rocky Points."

"Rocky Points?"

The trees swirled and then Wolf fell to the ground.

CHAPTER 12

"ONE. TWO. THREE!" Luke heaved Wolf's upper body into the passenger seat while the two sisters pushed his legs inside.

"Okay, back up." She pushed on him and slammed the door, hoping all his limbs remained clear.

"What happens if the FBI pulls us over?" Margaret asked.

"FBI?" Valerie's eyes popped. "What do you mean, FBI?"

Luke stepped around the front of the truck. "Just don't worry about it. They won't be looking for you and your sister. They'll be looking for me and Wolf, in my car, not in yours."

"FBI?" Valerie asked again. "What if they ask if we've seen you? I can't lie. I suck at lying."

"She can't." Margaret nodded.

Luke opened the door. "Thanks, girls. I owe you. Just ... go home. We're going to straighten all this out, and we'll be in touch soon, all right?"

The two women stood with raised eyebrows.

Luke got in and fired up the engine, turned around, and drove west. She watched in the rearview mirror as the two sisters jogged to Margaret's SUV, opened the door, and climbed in. And then they were out of sight around the bend.

Settling in, she adjusted the seat and mirrors and cruised on the well-maintained dirt road at forty miles per hour.

Wolf was quiet, bouncing in his seat and leaning against the window. She'd seen him only a few weeks after his fall off the cliff. Back then, he'd looked broken and pale, with a greasy mat of hair and an unkempt beard, an unmoving body that was ripe with the smell of sweat and Scotch. Now, three full months later, he scarcely looked any different, other than that he was fully clothed and not sitting in a hospital bed. His facial hair was short, but his features were sunken, his limbs thinner. He smelled normal. No smell at all, actually. At least that was an improvement.

He slept with his mouth gaping wide open, undisturbed by her violating assessment of him.

Her phone vibrated in her pocket and her heart leapt as she returned to the gravity of the present moment.

Pulling it out, she saw the one number she hoped to God it wouldn't be—Special Agent in Charge Charles Keene.

"Wolf," she said, slapping him in the leg.

He swallowed, and once again his jaw fell open.

She took a sharp breath and cleared her throat, then pushed the answer button.

"Agent Luke."

"Luke, where the hell are you?"

"Sir?"

"Frye's been trying to get hold of you."

"He has? Sorry, I'm not sure what's wrong with my phone."

She pulled the phone away and looked at the screen. She was feigning confusion, but the truth was she hadn't received any calls or messages. Probably because she'd been out in the middle of nowhere burrowing her vehicle in the forest.

"... with Tedescu?" Her boss's voice was breaking up. "... without ... or not."

"I'm sorry, sir, I didn't catch that. Can you repeat?"

She jammed on the brakes and pulled over.

Wolf slid forward, careening headfirst into the dashboard.

She reached over and pushed him back in the seat.

"I asked, where's Tedescu? We can't get hold of him, either."

"He left me this morning, sir. Said he had a family emergency of some sort. I'm not sure where he went. Wouldn't say."

There was a long pause. Luke swallowed and shifted in the seat.

"Frye wants you up in Rocky Points. They've got a situation up there."

"Yeah, I heard about it this morning. He told me to stay in Denver."

"Well, I'm telling you to get up there, now. Your buddy Wolf has gone AWOL."

When it came to the crunch, Keene always reverted to his military jargon.

"Yes, sir. I'll get going now. Can you please let Frye know I'm on my way? There may be shoddy reception on the drive up."

"Yeah. Just get your ass up there ASAP. If you talk to Tedescu, tell him to call me. Yesterday."

"Yes, sir."

The line went dead.

She powered off her phone, then pulled the battery and SIM and put them in the center console.

"Wolf, you're killing me."

Wolf grunted and then began snoring.

She let off the brake and coasted.

Shifting in his seat, Wolf's arms flailed forward.

"Wolf."

He started convulsing.

"Holy shit. Wolf."

A stream of vomit came out his mouth.

She jammed the brakes and pulled over, got out and ran to his side, and opened the door.

He tumbled out and she pushed back, trying to figure out where to grip him without getting covered in puke herself.

A breeze fluttered past, and she thought she heard a thumping sound. She froze, and then she heard it again.

Shit. A helicopter was approaching.

She turned and searched the sky, and Wolf tipped out of the seat and face planted on the ground.

Stepping back, she felt a shock of horror at the unnatural position of his neck. Grabbing him around the torso, she lifted his bulky frame and laid him on the dirt none too gently.

The rotors thumped louder now.

She got to her knees and pushed him as hard as she could, trying to hide him underneath the truck.

He rolled a quarter-turn and she slipped and landed on her chest.

"Damn. Come on."

She shut the door, bent down, and tried again. He moved a little, but it was like he was velcroed to the ground, so she climbed over him, crawled underneath the truck, and tried pulling.

The helicopter was here. *Right here.*

Planting one foot on the inside of the tire, she pulled him fully underneath the truck with an adrenaline-fueled burst of strength.

Then, without hesitating, she rolled over and over and out

into the sunlight next to the driver's side door. As she stood brushing herself off, the helicopter swung into view to the east, banking hard to follow the contours of the terrain.

The black fuselage of an FBI helicopter was immediately recognizable. Rocking back, the craft slowed to a stop in mid-air, twisted, and hovered, pointing its domed cockpit toward her like a huge eye.

She put up a hand as if blocking the sun, hoping she was shielding sight of her face well enough. Then she leaned back and studied the bird, because that's what a normal person would've done.

The helicopter inched toward her and twisted, and she saw binoculars pasted to the passenger window.

She turned and walked away from it to the back of the truck.

Think, damn it. Think.

With unhurried deliberation, she walked past the rear bumper and stopped near a bush at the side of the road, where she then dropped her sweatpants to her ankles.

Squatting low, she relieved herself of a two cups of coffee and forty-five-mile drive pee onto the dirt.

She waited until she was almost done and glanced up at the helicopter again, adding a bashful wave.

The helicopter banked and sped away, disappearing behind the next mountain.

She pulled up her pants with numb, shaky fingers. Her body hummed.

As the rotor sound dissipated to nothing, she walked to the passenger-side door and bent down.

Wolf's eyes were open. "That was interesting."

"Shit, Wolf. Are you all right? I thought you might be dead."

"Yeah. Just a little thirsty, despite what I just watched."

She blushed. "What you just saw was me shaking off the FBI. My FBI. The people who employ me. The people who are going to lock me up in Florence and eat the key."

Wolf rolled onto his stomach and crawled out from under the truck.

She helped him out and swiped the dirt off his back, then put the tailgate down and helped him sit.

"What's that smell?"

"That is your vomit."

He looked down and squirmed out of his fleece jacket, and then tossed it behind him.

"Just a second." She opened a rear door of the truck cab and found four grocery bags. There was a gallon of water in one of them.

She cracked the seal, took a sip herself, and then brought it to Wolf.

His dark hair, normally a swirling wonder of the world, was matted on one side and sticking up and caked with dirt on the other. His skin, normally some degree of tan that defied season, was ghostly. His brown eyes, usually alert and calm, were puffy and distant-looking.

Doubt hit her like a pressure wave.

"What's wrong?" Wolf asked.

"Nothing. Let's get going."

He took a long gulp and looked at her. "I haven't told you yet."

"What?"

"Thanks."

"Yeah. Now get in."

They climbed in and she gripped the wheel with both hands, keeping her speed right at what she considered safe and no more. There was no sense risking an accident or bringing any attention to themselves. They'd already dodged too many bullets as it was.

It was only a matter of an hour or so until they'd be down to the Carbondale area north of Aspen, to where she felt at home, because it had been home for most of her life.

Her brother was there. Her mother was there. But she'd have to avoid them like Wolf's fleece jacket in the truck bed. She had the perfect place in the middle of nowhere for them to stay the night. They just had to get over these mountains first and open some distance between them and the federal government's finest.

"I can't believe we've gotten this far," she said. "And if you hadn't called when you did? You'd be getting cavity searched right now by a big man named Bruno."

Wolf was slumped against his window, eyes closed. He swallowed and his jaw fell open.

"And ... never mind."

She reached over and pulled the open gallon bottle of water from his hand. Pausing to sniff the mouth, she wiped it with her sleeve and took a sip.

"Killing me."

CHAPTER 13

"JUST GIVE ME A QUICK UPDATE," Rachette said into his phone. "They don't have Wolf, do they?"

Another SBCSD vehicle sped past with motor revving high down Main Street. Rachette watched it slam on its brakes at the four-way stop a few blocks up and then accelerate through.

"There's another one. Patty, you gotta tell me what's going on."

"No, they don't." There was a long pause and then Patterson exhaled into the phone. "He escaped down the river in his boat. I'm at a roadblock on Williams Pass and we haven't seen him. Could still be in town."

Rachette smiled to himself, glad Wolfie was giving them the slip.

"I have to go. Lurch is coming. Talk soon." She hung up.

He pocketed his cell phone and walked.

He'd spent the past hour wandering down Main Street's sidewalks, drinking two lattes and replaying the vision of Wolf being whisked away by Margaret.

Her Land Rover had tinted windows, but not the blacked-out drug-dealer kind; just enough tint to make him doubt what he'd seen.

Margaret had ignored him. Not even a second glance. They were usually on a polite-wave basis when they saw each other around town. And he swore he'd seen Wolf in the passenger seat.

And now Patterson had all but confirmed it, and the fifth SBCSD vehicle screaming through town along with the speeding unmarked cruisers made sense.

Rachette's smile evaporated when he saw two men milling around his car.

The unmarked Crown Vic parked on his tail bumper and their suits told him all he needed to know.

Both agents were tall men, late twenties, early thirties at most. One of them pressed his face to the window.

"Can I help you, gentlemen?"

They both sprang upright and drew pistols from their shoulder holsters. "Hands where we can see them."

Rachette froze. "Easy. What the—"

"Now!"

He held up his arms and let the coffee cup drop to the pavement. "Easy, guys. I'm a cop. I'm not carrying."

"Hands on the hood. Turn around. Spread your legs."

He followed their orders and endured a thorough groping. A few seconds later, they cinched his hands behind his back, plastic ties digging into his wrists.

"Am I under arrest?"

One agent gripped him by the forearms and thrust him at their car.

"You two speak English?" he asked, stopping just short of slamming into the side of the vehicle.

Nothing.

"Hey, I just want to point out that this is bullshit. I said I'm a cop."

One agent shoved him against the car, opened the rear door, and pushed him in.

His head hit the back of the seat and he ended up on the floor on his side.

"Okay. Now you've pissed off Tom Rachette. You'd better watch yourself when these zip ties come off, boys."

The agent slammed the door, leaving Rachette panting between the front and back seats, the hump in the middle digging into his hip. He thought he felt a trickle of blood on his wrist.

Neither agent said anything as the car fired up, backed up, and then accelerated forward. It revved hard for a few blocks and then slammed to a stop, which put their stopping point in front of the new county building.

Rachette was relieved, because he was already claustrophobic. Unless they were going to leave him here for some reason. Panic surged through him and he squirmed to take the pressure off his wrists.

The doors in front opened and closed, and then the rear door behind him. Strong arms yanked him up onto the back seat and hauled him out onto his feet on the sidewalk.

Without thinking, he spat straight into the nearest agent's face.

The agent wiped his cheek and pulled back his fist.

"Don't do it," the other agent said.

The rough parade continued as they pushed him inside the automatic doors.

"What's going on here?" Tammy Granger stood up from the reception desk, her face twisted in rage. Just as quickly, she sat as the two agents produced their badges. "Yeah, I know who you are. You'd better not hurt this man. Or you've got a lot of people to answer to, assholes. Including me."

A minute later, they were up the elevator to the third floor and outside the doors of MacLean's glass office, which stood like a human aquarium at the eastern edge of the squad room. Four suited men standing in front of MacLean's desk, along with the sheriff himself, had watched the procession as they passed the windows. Now, as the door swung open smoothly on its hinges, everyone inside seemed to be avoiding eye-contact with their arrived prisoner.

One of the agents let go of Rachette's arm and motioned for him to enter.

There was a snap and Rachette's wrists were suddenly free. He brought his arms in front of him, punched the man holding the door in the nose, and then stepped into MacLean's office.

"Whoa." An older agent inside grabbed Rachette by the arm and pulled him inside. Another, this one much larger and muscular, intercepted Rachette by his neck and held him in a headlock against his ape-like chest.

"Hey! Let him go." MacLean stood up from behind his desk. "Let go of my deputy right now."

My deputy? Rachette had assumed all along that MacLean was rooting for him to fail the proficiency test.

"Let him go," the older agent said. "You two stay outside. Close the door."

The log of an arm punching his Adam's apple into the back of his throat kept its relentless grip for another second and then let go.

He sagged, but the older agent helped him stand up straight.

"They just threw me in the back of their car like we're in Nazi Germany or something."

"Deputy Rachette," the older agent said, "I'm the Assistant Special Agent in Charge of the Denver field office of the FBI. You can call me Agent Frye."

Rachette rubbed his neck and eyed the other occupants of the room. The ape-guy sneered at him with clenched fists. The other two were two clean-cut guys in suits gazing at nothing in particular.

"Sit down." Agent Frye motioned to the chair.

Rachette sat.

"Can I please see your cell phone?" Frye asked.

"Not without a warrant."

Frye looked at MacLean.

MacLean cleared his throat. "Deputy, if you have nothing to hide, let's go ahead and speed this whole thing up, shall we?"

MacLean's tan skin was tinted red. He was not enjoying the infiltration of these agents into his office, and it looked to be Rachette and MacLean against them. Eyes locked on Rachette's, he rubbed his silver goatee and then raised his hands.

Rachette pulled out his phone. "I want this back."

Frye snatched it. "Passcode?"

"1-2-3-4."

Frye raised an eyebrow but kept his eyes on the screen as he unlocked the phone.

Rachette took steady breaths and folded his arms to hide his shaking hands.

Frye navigated the touch screen and after a full minute he tossed it back. "What were you doing at 11:15 p.m. last night, Deputy?"

Rachette pocketed his phone. "Sleeping. I had an early morning planned today at the shooting range."

"Do you have someone who can corroborate that?"

"Nope."

"Do you have a landline phone set up at your residence?"

Rachette frowned. "No. Why? You think I made that anonymous tip call?"

"That's an interesting conclusion to draw from my question. How did you hear about the phone call?"

"I was here earlier this morning. I heard about what was going down."

Frye sat a butt cheek on MacLean's desk and stared at him. "So you've heard that we found Gail Olson's dead body this morning?"

"Yeah. I heard that tip brought you straight there, and then to the murder weapon at Wolf's house. Sounds like bullshit to me."

Frye smiled. "You and Wolf are pretty close, right?"

"Yeah. So?"

"One more time, Deputy. How did you meet Gail Olson?"

Rachette looked up at the ceiling. "This again? I told you guys. She picked me up in a bar. We dated once, and she asked me to take her backpack to her friend. So I did. The end."

Frye glanced behind Rachette.

"You guys can keep asking me that, and I'll keep answering the same way."

"When was the last time you saw Wolf?"

The image of Wolf waving through a tinted Land Rover window flashed in his mind. "I don't know. A week ago?"

Frye leaned forward. "Change of breathing. Tilted head. Shuffling feet. All classic signs of lying."

"Whatever. I saw him a week ago. Drove out to his place and we took a walk."

"What did you two talk about?"

"Not much. Just catching up."

Frye tilted his head. "You're leaving something out."

"I'm just thinking about what you guys are leaving out." Rachette turned and glanced at the other three agents behind him. The big guy loomed close.

"What are you talking about?" Frye asked.

"When I was there last, Wolf and I went on a walk and saw your surveillance teams."

Frye stood and paced in front of Rachette. "You saw them, too?"

"Yeah. I have eyes, don't I?"

Frye looked at him with an unreadable look.

"What?"

"Nothing." Frye splayed a hand. "Continue. You're saying we left something out."

"So, if you had surveillance on his house, why didn't you see whoever planted that gun? Or maybe you did, which tells me you're hiding something. Or it was you guys."

The big guy behind him snorted.

MacLean shifted in his chair. "Deputy, let's please refrain from such"—he glanced at Frye—"accusations."

Frye kept his eyes on Rachette and held up a hand to MacLean. "Please stay available, Deputy."

"That's it?"

"That's it."

Rachette stood up. "He didn't do this. We didn't do this."

They ignored him, so Rachette shook his head and left out the heavy wooden door.

"And, Rachette," MacLean said, "let's go ahead and postpone your shooting proficiency test tomorrow until further notice. We don't exactly have the manpower at the moment."

His stomach dropped.

"You may leave."

"Yeah. Okay."

Outside in the squad room his kidnapper agents straightened at his arrival.

Rachette smiled at the sight of one of them lowering a bloody tissue from his nose.

"Sup?" Rachette slapped his own pectorals. "You want a piece of this?"

The agent looked like he did, but he looked away and shook his head instead.

Walking down the hallway to the stairs, he heard rapid footsteps behind him and turned, ready for a brawl.

"Hey, honey." It was Deputy Munford hurrying to catch up, a smile fading from her lips.

He felt his breath catch, but composed himself. "What?"

She caught up to him and looked back down the hall. "I just kind of saw what happened. Did you say you needed a ride somewhere? To your car?"

He scrunched up his face and looked her up and down. "Nah, no thanks." He turned and walked away, unsure whether he'd seen her face fall in disappointment or not. If he had seen it, it was probably a good act, with reasons why he couldn't yet fathom.

"So, I guess I'll see you at the shooting test tomorrow, then."

"No. You won't. MacLean cancelled it."

"What?" She ran up and stepped next to him.

"Says we don't have the manpower."

"He didn't tell me."

"Yeah, well. He told me."

She swallowed. "What's going on? Why are they bringing you in?"

"You know why. They think I'm involved in all this." He

stopped and looked at her. Everything was suddenly clear. "Is that what you're doing? Are you working with them? Pretending to care, so you can get some inside information?"

"What are you talking about?"

"Come on. A beautiful woman like you? Interested in me?"

She raised her perfect eyebrows, barely creasing her fore-head skin. "You think I'm interested in you?"

He felt his face explode with heat and he turned to leave. "Just—"

"You think I'm beautiful?"

"Just ... step off, all right?"

This time her face really did fall. A damn fine acting job if he'd ever seen one. Or she was serious. And in that case, why the hell did she like him? What was wrong with her?

"Bye, Munford."

"Bye, Tom."

He opened his mouth to speak but thought better of it. Walking away from a woman he'd just hurt was a better option than sticking around and taking whatever she had brewing, so he left.

CHAPTER 14

WOLF OPENED his eyes and stared at the stretched fabric in front of his face, unable to comprehend what he was looking at.

He shifted and the swish of his bare legs rubbing on a sleeping bag pierced the utter silence.

"Wolf."

Flinching, he twisted to his left at the sound of the female voice. "Who's that?"

"It's me, Luke."

She flicked on a flashlight and the interior of a two-person dome tent lit up. She squinted and pointed the beam at her wrist. "It's midnight. You've been sleeping like a dead man, and I mean a dead man, for fourteen hours. Since ten this morning."

Beneath the askew sleeping bag, Wolf saw she was wearing a T-shirt and underwear, and at that moment he realized he was wearing the same thing.

He sat up and ran his tongue across the top of his mouth. "Water."

"Right next to you."

He found the water bottle, sat up straight, and sucked it down in one go.

"Are you hungry? You have to be hungry."

"I'd eat a horse right now."

"Granola bars are next to you, too."

He found the box, unwrapped one and bit into it. As he chewed, his recent memories came flashing back—the canoe ride down the river, breaking into the Beer Goggles Bar and Grill, the ride from Margaret, Kristen Luke with sweat pants around her ankles. It was all a surreal blur.

With each bite, he felt his body gaining strength and his mind awareness, and as he finished the last mouthful and peeled open another bar, he felt wide awake and alert.

"Where are we?"

"Some place safe."

"Where? A campsite?"

"Yep."

"Where?"

"Southwest of Aspen, on the way to Crested Butte. We're going to Gunnison."

"Gunnison? Why?"

"It's a long story."

He ran a hand through his hair and was surprised it felt smooth and clean. "There's no straight shot of highway between Aspen and Gunnison."

"Nope."

"So we're in the middle of nowhere."

"That's the idea."

He tipped the final drops of water out of the bottle into his mouth. "Can I see that flashlight, please?"

She handed it to him and pulled her sleeping bag up against her chin. "What are you doing?"

"I have to go to the bathroom."

"Have fun."

He peeled the zipper back a quarter-circle. "My pants?"

"They're hanging off the back of the truck. They're probably still wet."

"Why's that?"

"Because you puked all over them, so I washed them."

"Oh."

"You're welcome."

"Thanks."

He found his shoes at the foot of his sleeping bag and slipped them on. The inner soles were cold on his bare feet. "I guess the same goes for my fleece jacket?"

"No. I didn't wash that. I'm not touching that."

"Ah."

She rolled over in her sleeping bag and then held up a piece of clothing. "I found this in Valerie's truck, along with all this camping gear. Luckily for us, Patterson's parents seem to be outdoor buffs. This sweater looked like it should fit you, so I didn't bother getting down and dirty with your jacket."

"Thanks."

"You're welcome."

He slipped his arms inside a thick zip-up sweater that was lined with soft fur.

Stepping outside, the skin on his legs tightened with goose bumps as it tried to ward off the damp cold air that smelled like pine and wood smoke.

A lone cricket chirped somewhere nearby, and there was a muffled pop.

He pointed the flashlight beam at a fire pit and saw a few charred logs still smoldering. He swept the beam around in a circle. They were socked in on all sides by dense forest, with no distant view anywhere, at least that he could tell.

He clicked off the light and found he could see plenty fine with the ambient light of the half-moon peeking through the trees. Straight above him, the sky was spray-painted with countless stars.

Feet crunching on dry twigs and pine needles, his eyes stung as he walked through a stream of smoke. A few paces away, he relieved himself and surveyed the area, satisfied they were indeed alone and in the middle of nowhere.

Arriving back, he was surprised to see Luke fully clothed in her sweatpants and sweatshirt and leaning logs together in the fire pit. "Get me that newspaper?"

He did as he was told, and then watched as she expertly kick-started the fire.

With their history involving many hours logged in bed together, he was not in the least self-conscious standing close to the fire in his boxer shorts, letting the flames warm his legs.

"You're looking chipper," she said.

"I am? I feel better."

She stifled a yawn. "Good. You looked like shit earlier. Now you look like you."

"Thanks."

"Really skinny. But like you."

They both sat cross-legged on the cold ground, and he suppressed a wince at the pain deep in his thigh.

Luke's eyes twinkled in the firelight as she gazed into her thoughts. Her hair was pulled back, putting her beautiful, troubled face on full display.

He picked up a stick and poked it in the fire. "So I was out pretty good, huh?"

She nodded. "Yeah. Do you remember anything?"

"I remember a helicopter. You peeing."

She studied him for a beat. "I didn't expect you to be ..."

"What?"

"Nothing."

"Didn't expect me to be such a *wreck*, as people like to put it lately?"

Her face softened. "Why'd you pass out? Is that normal?"

"Some sort of inner-ear thing. A disorder that seems to get worse the more I move around. Then there're all the injuries and stiffness, which won't get any better unless I exercise. It's a nice negative feedback loop I've got going."

They sat in silence for a few minutes, soaking in the heat.

"So, you want to get going on that long story?" he asked. "Preferably starting with why you lied about Carter Willis?"

She kept her attention on the fire. "I have a new partner now. The guy's name is Tedescu. Terrence Tedescu." She wrapped her arms around her knees. "The reason I have Tedescu as a partner is because his partner was killed in the line of duty. Three and a half months ago. Like I said on the phone, the fallen agent's name was Smith. Special Agent Paul Smith, who you knew as Carter Willis."

Wolf pulled the now flaming stick from the fire and stabbed it in the dirt.

She watched him for a beat, seeming to search for her next words. "You know my stellar history with men. I've got a little alarm in my head now that lets me know when there's a real asshole around. Let's just say the recess bell was always going off around Agent Smith.

"Told me I smelled once. One night I was alone in the office, and he just kind of materialized out of the darkness and came over and sat on my desk. Leaned in close, sniffed, and told me I smelled. Normally I would've punched a guy in the nose and watched him bleed for that, make him take back his words, but you've seen Smith. The guy was big. And scary."

He picked up another twig and held it to the fire.

"You know, I never said that I didn't know who Carter Willis was. I said I'd check on him and let you know when I found something."

He snorted.

"I was under direct orders to not talk to you about it."

He stood up, this time wincing at the pain. "So what? You knew how much this meant to me. He was found dead with Sarah, for God's sake."

"Yeah, I know." She rubbed her forehead. "Found dead with the love of your life."

He was startled at her tone, and it stoked the anger inside him. "Yeah, I did love her. Is that what this is about? You were jealous of us and you were holding back this information out of spite or something?"

She lifted her chin. Her eyes shimmered like a rough moonlit sea and then flash-froze. "Get over yourself. I have a career, and I was under direct orders to not speak to you. Damn, that fall did knock you hard on the head. Don't you get it? I was under orders that I'm way beyond defying now, and now my career's as good as toilet paper since I've aided and abetted you. Shit, if it weren't for me dragging your unconscious ass all over Colorado today, you'd be sitting in Denver, sweating and vomiting in an interrogation room with no windows, awaiting a prison shiv in your neck. Holding back? Out of spite? Please. I knew you couldn't, wouldn't have killed Sarah because she was the love of your life. That's what I'm saying."

She stared skyward.

He took a deep breath, letting the tension dissipate from his jaw. "I'm sorry."

She closed her eyes and rolled her neck.

He walked to the back of the truck and felt his jeans were cold and damp.

"Aiding and abetting." He returned and laid the pants down next to the fire. "How did I go from a respectable sheriff of Sluice County to you guys thinking I killed Sarah, a Bureau agent, and now Gail Olson? And what about these guys watching my house? They're the real-deal cartel? With men on the inside waiting to shiv me? Sorry I'm lost, Kristen. How is it that the FBI is unaware of them and going after me?"

"Let me start from the beginning."

He raised his eyebrows. "Good idea."

"Sit. You're freakin' me out."

He exhaled and sat down.

"As long as I've known Smith and Tedescu, since I came to the Denver FO a few years ago, they'd both been on a drug task force. You know, Mexican cartel activity, marijuana grow sites in the national forests, that kind of thing, and now that weed is legal, they were monitoring fraud activity—people trying to circumvent the crop-tracking software, point-of-sale monitoring, stuff like that.

"A few years before legalization, when I was still up in Glenwood Springs, apparently Tedescu and Smith were involved in a big operation that went nuclear down in southern Colorado. I guess they'd encountered a few strains of pot in huge quantities that couldn't be traced to the normal list of suspects south of the border. They took what they had to the SAC. The SAC gave them the go-ahead and a few men to monitor closer, and they concluded that there was a big widespread operation happening right under every official nose in the state.

"Smith and Tedescu were calling these unknowns the 'Ghost Cartel.' The problem was, they had no solid evidence of its existence. But they had plenty of indirect clues. They worked on it for a number of months, six or seven, and eventually one day came out triumphant because they'd recruited an informant. Their new asset wanted immunity and federal protection for himself and his family if he gave them the location of the Ghost Cartel's main distribution center. We agreed, and the guy pointed us to some huge farm property in southern Colorado, southeast of Durango, near the New Mexico border.

"Armed with a SWAT team, a grip load of agents, and the information everyone thought was legit, the SAC led an operation to the farm compound. But the informant went silent on the day of the bust, never showing up at the agreed meeting spot. Just changed his mind or, they thought, more likely he'd been silenced. Whatever happened to the guy, the operation went ahead, and they sent everyone in.

"Long story short, the place blew up, turning the sand to glass for a square mile. Huge freaking explosion. Eleven SWAT-team members killed instantly, six agents, and a lot of casualties."

"I heard about this," Wolf said. "We were told it was a Mexican cartel responsible for the explosion."

Luke nodded. "After the smoke settled, literally and figuratively, they looked closer into the informant and found that he was a well-known commander in one of the cartels in Mexico, and not a low-level lackey they'd all thought. He'd been up in the States on business under a different name. Big screw-up. None of the brass could figure out how they'd messed up so big. In the end, the Special Agent in Charge took the blame and got canned, and Agents Tedescu and Smith were suspended and kicked down a GS level. And that was basically that. Until the whole Gail Olson thing."

Wolf narrowed his eyes. "Our famous drug runner from Byron County."

She nodded. "Yep."

"Our famous dead drug runner."

"Yeah. So she is." Luke massaged her neck. "Anyway, when she was pulled over nine months ago, the Bureau's ears perked up at the details of her case. She had over twenty pounds of weed, no license of any kind to be carrying or distributing it, and it looked to be a hybrid of the same strain of pot Tedescu and Smith had been tracking years ago. And then this third-year college student brought in a team of high-priced lawyers who managed to get all charges dropped completely."

Wolf frowned. "I thought she'd been charged and somehow had her record expunged with MacLean's help."

"Nope. Never even had a record. Not with the team of lawyers she had. They ended up proving she had no knowledge of what was in the car. They slapped a counter-suit on the Ashland PD for unlawful search and seizure, and everything ended up getting washed."

Wolf shook his head. "That's not what Baine found out."

"Well, that's what happened. The point is, after Gail Olson, Tedescu and Smith got a second chance and were somewhat vindicated, because it was clear that something big was going on, just like they'd said a few years ago. So Tedescu and Smith were partnered up again, and the first thing they did was start following Gail Olson's activities, which eventually led them to Deputy Rachette, and the Sluice County Sheriff's Department."

Wolf straightened. "Are you saying they thought we were the Ghost Cartel?"

"They've been looking into you and the department. Let's just put it that way."

He stood and laughed out loud. "So what? That's what this is? They think I'm some sort of drug lord?"

"I'm not sure what the brass really think about you. But I know that the consensus with the agents is that you definitely had something to do with Agent Smith's death."

Wolf glared at the flames.

"And this anonymous tip didn't help."

He shook his head. "They got a warrant to go in with this anonymous tip?"

"To find a weapon that killed one of ours? We pretty much have a warrant print button on our computer keyboards for situations like that."

"What did they find?"

"I don't know. I'm incommunicado. But I'm betting my career that they found a pistol that shoots 9 mm Parabellums. Matching the gun that shot Sarah and Agent Smith, and probably Gail Olson. Like you heard Frye say on that phone call, the first half of the tip was right. They found Gail Olson's body right where the caller said they would."

"But this guy, Tedescu, Smith's old partner, he told you I was innocent."

She nodded.

"So what? These guys, Tedescu and Smith, were caught up with the cartel?"

She fished in her pocket and pulled out a key. "We have to go to a storage unit in Gunnison that supposedly explains everything."

He stared at the glimmering key. "Where'd you get that?"

"Tedescu."

"Where's he? With the rest of them, coming after us?"

"I don't think so. He gave me this, told me, 'Smith and I were right, and the proof is in that storage unit,' and then he took off, clearly freaked out for the safety of his family after seeing that quad murder."

"What quad murder?"

She exhaled and looked up, as though shuffling thoughts in her head. "Agent Tedescu came to my apartment and got me out of bed at four a.m. yesterday morning, and then he drove me to Park Hill, where DPD was working a family of four found shot in their home. A lawyer and his wife and kids. Real messed-up stuff. The DPD didn't call us in. I have no clue why we were there, other than Tedescu just wanted to see the scene. Had some sort of personal interest. I could see it in his eyes.

"We went in, checked the bodies, and then he stormed out like he was spooked. Then that's when we got the call for the emergency meeting. Everyone was mobilizing to come up after you. Tedescu handed me this key, and told me you were innocent. He said whatever they found, it didn't matter, that you were innocent, and it was all a set-up, and it would all be explained if we went to this storage unit." She pulled a crumpled piece of paper out of her pocket. "Gunnison. Trout Creek Moving and Storage. Number 62."

Wolf looked at the piece of paper in her hand. "Tedescu was spooked, and then knew that I was about to be framed. Why didn't he go to the Agent in Charge with this?"

She shrugged. "Like I said, he was spooked. He called his wife, told her to stay put where she was, and then he hung up and told me he had to get his oldest son, and drove away in a cloud of smoke."

"Why didn't you tell your SAC about this?"

"About a key and information in a storage unit that may or may not exist in the middle of the mountains? Not likely to sway the momentum this morning." She lowered her voice. "You met Agent Frye, right?"

He nodded.

"He's partnered with an agent named Cumberland most of the time."

"Yeah, I've met him, too. Hell of a guy."

"I watched him staple a picture of you on a target and empty a clip into it once. That's the general attitude about you in the Bureau. I'm not sure you would've survived the raid."

He exhaled. "Thanks."

She stretched her arms overhead and yawned. "Whatever. Listen, if I'm going to be lugging you across Colorado tomorrow then I need to sleep." She held up the key and dangled it. "So we'll go here at sunrise, and we'll get some answers. Until then, goodnight."

He was wired and still had questions. Lots of them. But he held back at the sight of her drooping eyelids. "Goodnight."

She crawled into the tent, zipped it shut, rustled around for a second, and then was still.

The fire crackled and a shower of embers swirled. Like the questions in his mind, they burned bright, full of glowing energy, and then they were gone as more arose underneath.

Carter Willis had been FBI, and had been following Gail Olson. That meant MacLean was somehow involved with the FBI, because it had been MacLean who'd taken those pictures of the fake Gail and Rachette drug-drop.

Agent Tedescu had known that Wolf was being framed. A frame job that made Wolf look like he was some sort of drug lord running a cartel. How exactly was Tedescu involved? How had Smith been involved, and why was he with Sarah?

Then there was the dead family in Denver. They clearly had something to do with all of this.

It was futile trying to come up with answers when he knew he lacked pieces of the puzzle.

Luke was right. They had a destination, one that would hopefully explain everything. They needed more answers to a lot more questions, and that key might help.

He shifted his thoughts to Jack, as he did at least ten times every waking hour. He thought of his son's youthful flop of hair, his lanky build due to his huge growth spurt that Wolf and Sarah had marveled at behind his back. And he thought about the pain on his face yesterday.

Wolf pulled another granola bar out of his pocket and forced it down. He found a bottle of water standing near the tent and guzzled it all. Then he unzipped the tent, took off his shoes, and crawled inside. He lay on the hard ground, stared at the tent ceiling for a couple of hours listening to Luke's soft snoring, and then finally drifted off to sleep.

CHAPTER 15

POPE STOOD STILL inside the house, looking through the tiny sliver between the wood slat blinds.

The SUV pulled into the driveway outside and screeched to a halt. The driver stayed inside the vehicle, rummaging around for something.

His prey had finally arrived.

The top-of-the-line Audi SUV was decked out with all the bells and whistles, a car that could theoretically match up with an eighteen-year veteran of the FBI who was savvy with his money. But Pope knew better.

Pope was unaware of the agent's GS level or the salary associated with it, but he was certain it could not pay for this house, with its one-acre plot, three stories, four bedrooms, six baths, and more granite in it than on the slopes of Pike's Peak —which was now a pink monolith in the light of the sunrise out the southern windows.

Tack on the Lexus SUV in the three-car garage, which his jobless wife drove, all while paying for two children in private schools in Douglas County, and it was downright ridiculous other people had failed to wonder about the agent's extracurricular activities.

The man outside finally climbed out of the vehicle and stepped quickly to the front of the house.

The front door lock twisted and the door silently glided open.

The agent stepped in and shut the door fast, twisting the lock. He stepped to the illuminated alarm keypad.

Dropping his briefcase on the ground, the agent stared at the keypad in disbelief for an instant and then pulled his pistol and twirled around.

Pope was already there. With a precise and powerful movement, he blocked the agent's gun. The pair of muffled cracks beneath the skin told him the radius and ulna had broken even before the agent howled in pain.

As the gun clattered onto the hardwood floor, Pope kicked it away and stepped back.

The man sank to his knees, cradling his arm, and looked up with equal parts disbelief and agony.

"Special Agent Terrence Tedescu. Nice to finally meet you."

"Ah, my arm. Who are you?" Tedescu's voice was a whimper.

"I'm the man who's going to kill you and your entire family."

The agent's eyes narrowed and widened with fear. "Pope?"

Pope said nothing, letting his previous statement burrow into the man.

"My family's not—"

"Not safe in Missouri, I'm afraid. We have quite a presence in the Midwest. I'm sure you're aware of that."

Agent Tedescu shook his head. "Please. Please don't hurt them."

Pope paced and glared down.

"I'm not sure what's going on," Tedescu said. "I thought everything was going fine. I thought we had a deal. It was win–win. We did everything you wanted."

"Win–win?" Pope knelt down and clamped the agent's face between thumb and fingers. His leather gloves were tacky on the man's sweaty face. "No. Ever since you assholes poked your heads into our business, it's definitely been a win–lose situation, with us on the losing end. You had to have seen this coming. This is the inevitable end to what you started."

He hurled the man back and his head thudded against the wall.

"You have a choice, however." Pope pulled his phone out of his pocket. "You can choose the finale. I'm going to call my men." He pushed the number and listened to the ringing. "And one of two things is going to happen."

"What are you doing?"

"You are either going to tell me who else you've told about all this, or I'm going to ... hold on ... Hey. It's me. Are you in position? Okay. Hold on ... This is my Midwest team leader on the line. You want to say hi?" Pope shoved the phone in Tedescu's face.

Tedescu closed his eyes and shook his head. Sweat slid down his cheeks onto his neck.

"He says your two daughters are cute. Says he'd rather not go through with this."

Tedescu kept his eyes closed tight, as if still refusing to believe the situation.

Pope narrowed his eyes. "Hey, you listening to me?"

"Just shoot me, you asshole. There's no way you're getting

my family. They're with the FBI—I made sure of that today. You're not getting to them. I don't care how powerful you assholes think you are, you're not getting them. Just shoot me. It's me you want."

"Joplin."

Tedescu's eyes sprang open.

Pope shook his head. "They're in Joplin, Terrence. Once again, your disrespect is mind-boggling. We've been on them for days, watching them visit your sister-in-law, at that nice countryside manor of theirs. We followed them to the airport, and then back to the house. And then we followed the FBI team as they took them to the safe house. And now," he held up the phone, "we're there. In Joplin. We might have lost you all day but, believe me, we never lost your family for a moment."

Tedescu's eyes clamped shut again and he sagged into the wall.

"You're in the middle of a well-executed plan, here, Terrence. Not some short-sighted shit show you and your partner would've concocted."

"Hold your position," Pope said into the phone.

Tedescu opened his eyes and glared at him.

"You have a choice. Tell me who else you told about all this, or else I give the word. Did you hear about your lawyer and his family yesterday?"

"I saw them." Tedescu clenched his teeth. "I saw them, you sick bastard."

"You made me do that." Pope pulled out his pistol and pressed it against his head. "You made me. You made me do that." Pope's hand shook. His whole body trembled and his breath came in short gasps as he remembered what he'd done. "Now tell me who else you told."

"About what?"

Pope stepped away and his face went slack.

"Nobody." Tedescu gritted his teeth. Defiant. "I didn't tell anyone."

The agent's eyes glimmered, and then he convulsed, a small shot of saliva shooting from his lips.

Pope wondered whether the man was having some sort of seizure.

Then the agent smiled. "You idiot. My family's not in Joplin. You'll never get my family." Then Tedescu laughed like a maniac.

Pope shot him in the eye and then twice more in the side of the head as he dropped.

He stood breathing hard, his ears ringing, the acrid smoke choking his nostrils.

"Sir? Hey, you there?"

He pressed the phone to his ear. "Yeah?"

"What was that all about? I thought I told you they lost the family in Joplin. Not that they were holding them in Joplin. You knew that, right, sir?"

Pope stepped back from the encroaching pool of blood. "I know. I was bluffing this asshole."

"Oh."

He turned and stared out the window at the majestic fourteen-thousand-foot Pike's Peak. It was really quite a view in the first light of day. Only the top half of the mountain glowed.

"Sir? You there?"

"Yeah. Which house are you at?"

"Four. I'm the only one here. I can't leave. Unless you can get someone."

"And everyone else?"

A clearing of the throat. "Chairman's at camp two, if that's what you mean. At least as far as I know."

"Who's manning three?"

"I think it's Pepper."

Pepper. The biggest screw-up in their entire organization. House two was the closest to Gunnison, but next to the bleeding corpse a few feet away, inept men like Pepper were the biggest detriment to their entire organization.

"What do you want me to do, boss?"

"I want you to stay put. And I want you to continue to keep your mouth shut until this is all over."

"Hey, you know that."

"What's the news on our Rocky Points guy?"

An exhale in his ear. "I hear they're still looking."

His palms broke into a sweat. "Still looking? They still haven't found him?"

"Yeah. I guess he got away or something."

The image of Pike's Peak blurred in his vision. "Okay. They'll find him. Change is underway, my friend."

Pope thought he heard a swallow on the other end.

He pressed the end-call button.

Like a master chess player, he'd already had his next move planned well in advance, but the maniacal laugh this agent had just let out had got to him.

The agent had called his bluff, clearly unconcerned for his family. How could he have had such certainty up against a man like Pope? What was Pope unaware of?

He pressed his map application, and then typed in Gunnison, Colorado.

The blue line materialized, showing him a drive time of three hours and forty-three minutes. It was 6:20 a.m. With the half-mile walk back to his car, he could be there by 9:45, give or take a quarter-hour, depending on how fast he drove.

Pocketing the phone, he steeled his thoughts and looked at the FBI agent, now lying in a lake of red.

He was going to have to be careful. He was walking a fine line between cut and run and stay the course and become nothing short of God in his world.

He gritted his teeth, just about punching himself in the face for even thinking cut and run.

Today was no different from any other day in his life, looking over his shoulder for feds. As always, he would use caution.

And this Wolf guy escaping the FBI? They would find him. They had plenty of motivation to stay the course there. Despite the setbacks, Pope was progressing.

Feeling better, he walked to the front door.

With one last glance at his watch, he unlocked the latch and stepped out into the brisk fall air.

CHAPTER 16

WOLF WOKE to the sound of a wailing woman, which when he jumped awake morphed into the true sound of a long zipper being pulled back on the tent.

"Morning, sunshine. Get enough sleep yesterday? By my count, you're pushing twenty hours."

Lying back down, he smacked the back of his head on a rock underneath the tent floor.

He winced and cracked an eye, and then watched Luke's shapely, mostly bare, rear end exit the tent. Aroused for an instant, his thoughts went to Sarah, and then he was hit with a lightning bolt of guilt.

What was Sarah doing right now? Watching down on him? Sitting here in the tent with him? He suddenly had an image of her, hands on her hips, tapping her foot, wondering what the hell was taking him so long. Why hadn't he brought her justice yet?

Rubbing a hand through his hair, he pulled off the sleeping bag and poked his head out into the cold morning air. He brushed his bare feet free of debris, pulled on his socks, and put on his shoes.

It was bright on the tops of the trees, but shaded and brisk at ground level.

He stretched his arms overhead, taking in the view of lumber for three-hundred sixty degrees. "Wow, this is a good spot you found here."

A jet of fog shot out of Luke's mouth. "It's as secluded as I could find. I wasn't looking for picturesque views."

"No, I'm serious. You can't see fifty yards in any direction." He twisted and looked at the truck. "It's perfect. There's not even a road in."

"There's a two-track over there." She pointed east into the trees. "It leads to a pay campground. Then there's a county road that goes south and ends up near Crested Butte. I've been on it a few times before."

Wolf looked at his watch—8:05 a.m. "How far to Gunnison?"

"Shouldn't take more than an hour, hour and a half."

"We're going to have to figure out how to change vehicles."

Luke ignored him and concentrated on lacing up her shoes. They were a black athletic style, something that went well with a pantsuit and chasing criminals in a full sprint.

"Hey, Luke."

"What?"

"Did I say thank you yesterday?"

"Yeah, you did." She gave a final pull on her laces and looked up with a nod. "Let's tear down camp and haul ass."

They took down the tent, packed up the sleeping bags, and stowed everything in the spacious back of the interior cab of the truck.

Luke drove them out of the woods, along a loop that passed a group of deserted campsites to a dirt county road, and turned south.

The drive started out bumpy and progressed to smooth: starting in the deep woods on a rarely improved road in mountainous terrain, then dropping down into the East River Valley just south of the Crested Butte Ski Resort mountain and connecting with Colorado State Highway 135 made of dark, newly paved asphalt.

The land was flat as a board on the bottom of the valley, with low sage-covered hills on either side.

Behind them, Crested Butte Ski Resort jutted up, reminding Wolf of a breaching submarine launching up from beneath a calm sea. Every year they held a free skiing competition at the resort, filled with contestants who had somehow slipped through the Darwinian cracks.

The last time he'd been there to ski had been with Sarah, all the way back in their senior year of high school.

It had been arctic cold that weekend, and he remembered little of the skiing, but memories of shacking up next to Sarah on the floor of her cousin's dorm room at Western State College in Gunnison, zipping their cloth sleeping bags together and using each other to keep warm, were as fresh as if they'd happened yesterday.

"We need substantial food."

He blinked, arriving in the present. "What do you have in mind? These groceries are pretty useless." He turned and looked at the paper bags on the rear floor that Valerie Patterson had left in haste yesterday. "Flour, yeast, sugar. A bag of tortillas. Some cheese. Waffles. You want another granola bar?"

"No, I don't." Luke's tone was razor sharp. "I need a meal. When you were asleep yesterday I had a candy bar, a granola bar, and some beef jerky I got at the gas station."

Wolf eyed her. "I hope you paid cash."

"Yeah, yeah. I'm hungry."

"I think it's a bad idea to stop at a restaurant. Every law-enforcement agency in the state is probably on the lookout for us now. It's dumb."

"You should see the color of your face," she said. "You need food, too."

Wolf kept quiet, watching barbed-wire fence posts fly by next to the Gunnison River. "Let's get into Gunnison and see what we can find. I have twenty bucks. I hope you have more cash."

They rode in silence for another ten minutes, and Wolf zoned out watching the meandering route of the water. The Gunnison was a destination river for die-hard anglers. This morning they were thick, casting their fly rods amid the rising steam and bugs. If he could come out of this whole thing alive and free, he thought it would be a good idea to go camping and fishing with Jack. That is, if he could come out of this whole thing with a relationship with his son.

They arrived at the outskirts of Gunnison and Luke slowed as they cruised down Main Street.

"There it is, Trout Creek Moving and Storage. Kind of a little shithole."

Laid out in rows perpendicular to the street, the aluminum roll doors of the storage facility were visible for only a second and then obscured by a concrete wall, but Wolf saw that the units were low and skinny, made of sagging metal and coated with flaking paint. Mini storage units rather than full sized, and it looked like a strong kick would peel one open.

"There's a restaurant." Luke let off the brake. "Up there. We'll park here, halfway between. Walk both places. What do you think?"

He nodded. The truth was, he was ravenous. He would kill

for a chicken fried steak with eggs and hash browns, and he failed to see any law enforcement in every direction.

They parked and walked a block and a half along old western-looking storefronts, to a floor-to-ceiling-windowed restaurant.

Walking inside, the sight and smell of breakfast dishes atop the tables made his mouth gush in anticipation.

The hostess sat them at a booth in the rear underneath a mounted elk head, and they ordered their meals.

As they waited for their food they sucked down water and coffee and surveyed the room.

"No cops," Wolf said. "No one staring at us."

"Speak for yourself. Those hung-over college boys over there keep looking at me."

He sipped his coffee and eyed the group of five college kids. All male. All nodding and whispering behind sly grins. "That's just because they like the view."

"Psh."

A group of tourists came in and sat down.

"I was serious," Wolf said. "I have twenty bucks, and that's it."

"Don't worry. I have money."

He leaned back and relaxed. "Tell me about your Assistant Special Agent in Charge, Frye. He a good agent?"

"He's definitely smart."

"What do you think he's doing now?"

"Let's see." Luke took a sip of coffee. "I'd say he's figured out by now I'm involved, so he'd be checking my cell-phone records. He'd see that the last phone call I made was with Margaret Hitchens. So he'd track her down and see that her sister, Valerie, was in town, and then talk to both of them. According to Valerie, she's a terrible liar, so she'd give the whole thing away immediately. Then they'd have an APB out on our car."

She froze with her coffee against her lips. "And then the Gunnison police would spot Valerie Patterson's truck parked along Main Street, and two units with flashing lights would speed by the restaurant that we were sitting in."

Wolf caught the tail end of a third flashing cop car as it flew past the windows. The blur and revving engines drew gasps from the diners inside the restaurant.

"Geez, something's going on out there. Hi, my name's Toby. I'll be taking care of you two today. Where you guys from?"

Luke peered around the waiter. "Listen, Toby, we need a few minutes."

"Sure. Let me know if you have any questions. Our special this morning is—"

"Thanks, Toby. We'll let you know if we have any questions."

Toby closed his mouth and nodded. "Sure." He moved to the next booth.

"Let's go out the back," Wolf said.

"If there is a back."

"There is. Behind you, down the hallway to the right, past the kitchen window."

She shook her head. "Damn it. I'm hungry."

They got up and both walked toward the back hallway.

Toby intercepted them halfway. "Hey, you guys taking off?"

Wolf smiled. "Gotta go to the bathroom. We've been in the car for a while."

"Me too." Luke smiled.

"Ah, I see. Straight back down the hall."

Wolf followed Luke around the corner and almost slammed into her.

She'd stopped, poking her head through the window to the kitchen where three plates of food steamed under the heat lamps.

"Hello? Hello!"

"What are you doing?" He swallowed at the sight of the glistening breakfast burrito with cheese oozing over its sides.

"Hi, there. Can I please get a to-go container?" Luke said through the window.

There was a muffled response in accented English.

"A to-go container?"

An arm handed her a Styrofoam clamshell box.

"Thank you so much," she said with a winning smile.

Without an instant of hesitation, she set the to-go box down on the aluminum shelf, grabbed the plate and tilted it.

"Ah, shit." She clenched her teeth and clanked the plate back down. "Hot."

Two arms came from the other side to the rescue, grabbing the plate with two rags.

She caught the green chili dollops first, then the heavy tortilla wrap slapped into the box and she flashed her smile again, this time bashful and flirty. "Thank you so much."

"De nada."

"You have any silverware?"

The arms handed her a silver fork and knife.

Toby spotted them from the dining room and approached.

"Are you sure? Thank you." She winked, took the box and walked after Wolf. "All right, let's go."

"I can't take you anywhere," he said, stepping fast to the rear door.

"You'll be thanking me in ten minutes when we're loosening our belts."

Wolf pushed on the bar of the rear door and they were into the bright parking lot.

"Hey!" Toby said as Luke slammed the door shut.

CHAPTER 17

PATTERSON ROLLED her eyes and gripped the phone tighter. "Just tell me, Doc. Come on. It's me."

Dr. Lorber exhaled long into Patterson's earpiece. "I'm sorry, Heather. I've been sworn to secrecy by the ... hold on one moment ... federal agents"—a door squeaked and closed in the background—"and I've assured them that ... I ... will ... not ... okay, they're not here but I don't have much time. They'll come back any second. The time of death on Gail Olson's body is no longer than seventy-two hours."

Patterson stood frozen to her spot on the shoulder of the highway, watching as two deputies peeked inside the windows of an old woman's Buick sedan down the road. "Seventy-two hours?"

"Yes. And I've heard a bigger, juicier piece of information."

"Spit it out, Doc."

"Gail Olson's mother is missing from her home in Las Vegas as well. Has been for, wait for it, seventy-two hours."

Patterson instinctively turned to the forested slopes of Williams Pass to hide her exasperation. "Could she just be on vacation?"

"I heard it looks like abduction. Forced entry, broken furniture. If I was placing bets there, I'd bet on her being dead, too."

Patterson never knew how to respond to the macabre statements that flew from Lorber's mouth so freely. She turned and looked over at the roadblock. Lancaster was on his own phone call, studying her intently. "What do they think? Wolf got on a plane and flew to Vegas and offed her?"

"And I'm thinking that ... if you could get me a sandwich, you know the one. No mayonnaise, and no pickles. And for God's sake, don't be late this time."

The line went dead.

Patterson looked at her phone screen, pocketed it, and walked to Lancaster.

The big man kept his dead eyes glued to her and then ended his own call as she drew close.

"What's up?" she asked.

"They want you at the station," he said, turning away and walking toward the SUV.

She followed in silence.

Taking in the new-car smell, she took a deep breath and relaxed in the passenger seat.

"Who were you talking to?" he asked, climbing behind the wheel.

"It was my mom. Always needing the latest 4-1-1 with my life."

Lancaster stared out the windshield with no response and fired up the engine.

As they cruised down the valley into town, things were as silent as ever. Spending time with this guy was like wearing sound-isolating headphones.

As she often did, she looked over at Lancaster and wondered why the hell she had been paired with the man. It was as if she were being observed, which was probably the truth.

"You know, Wolf didn't do this."

Lancaster moved a few centimeters up and down as the car bounced.

"And I had nothing to do with this. And neither did Rachette. Or Baine, or Wilson, or Yates. Or anyone else from our department."

Still no response.

"Is that why MacLean has us paired up together? So you can all report back to him or something?"

Lancaster swallowed and glanced in the rearview mirror.

"Thanks. Nice talk."

When they pulled into the county-building parking lot, she got out and walked fast, not caring whether she left Lancaster in the dust. Stepping through the rear entrance, she let the glass doors shut behind her without looking back.

Only when she'd turned around to climb up the second flight of stairs did she see that Lancaster was following silently, only a few steps behind.

Freak!

She reached the third floor and walked down the hall. Reaching MacLean's glass cube of an office, she stopped dead in her tracks.

Lancaster walked past her and she lashed up and caught his tricep in a vise-like grip.

"What's my mother doing in MacLean's office?"

Lancaster looked down at her hand and shrugged.

She kept her hand clamped. "Thanks for the heads-up, partner."

He blinked. "I thought you said you were talking to her on the phone."

She let go and walked to MacLean's office door, which was propped open.

To her surprise, Lancaster veered away from her and walked toward the squad room.

"Deputy Patterson, please come inside." Agent Frye said from inside.

She walked straight to the cloth-upholstered chair in which her mother slumped.

"What are you doing here, Mom? Are you all right? What's going on?"

Her mother looked up with red eyes.

"What did you do to her?"

"We've done nothing, Deputy. Please take a seat and we'll explain," Frye said.

Patterson stood motionless for another second.

"Deputy, please."

She sat.

MacLean nodded at her, looking none too happy that his office was being used as an FBI command post for the second day in a row. His silver goatee seemed to have less luster, his impeccably groomed hair a dollop of grease too heavy.

His eyes were creased with a hint of worry, devoid of the cock-sure glow they normally possessed.

"Deputy Patterson, do you know where David Wolf is?" Frye asked.

"No. Now explain to me why my mother is sitting in this office. Did you bring her here from Aspen? Don't you know that her husband and two sons are extremely accomplished lawyers?"

"And she's going to need them," Frye answered without hesitation.

Patterson looked at her mother.

"I'm sorry, honey." A tear fell down her mother's cheek. "I didn't want to get you in trouble."

"Your mother had a busy day yesterday, colluding with your Aunt Margaret to help Wolf escape from Rocky Points. Your aunt drove him out on County 17 and met your mother, where Wolf swapped keys and got into your mother's truck, with her consent of course, and escaped over the mountains to the west. We have your mother's confession all on video."

Patterson looked her mother in the eye and squeezed her hand. "Good job, Mom."

Frye smiled and sat on the edge of MacLean's desk in front of her. "Not a good job, Mom. Jail time, Mom."

Patterson lifted her chin and glared at Frye.

"Have you spoken with David Wolf, Deputy?"

"No."

"May I please look at your cell phone?"

"Not without a warrant."

Frye flicked a finger. "Cumberland, can you bring Deputy Patterson down to a holding cell until we line up that warrant, please?"

Patterson pulled out her phone and flung it at Frye.

He caught it and poked the button with his index finger. "Thank you." Keeping completely silent with his head down, he perused her phone.

Patterson reached over and squeezed her mother's arm.

Her mother nodded and tried to smile.

"As you can see, I have not spoken with David Wolf."

He turned the screen and thrust it toward her. "What did you two speak about on Tuesday morning?"

"You've already asked me that and I told you."

Frye smiled. "I don't believe you."

She shrugged. "Like I said, we spoke about how you guys were suddenly so interested in him. And now that all this is happening, I've gotta say, I'm finding the whole thing very interesting."

Frye raised an eyebrow. "Oh, really? Do tell."

"Gail Olson's time of death was seventy-two hours ago."

"And how do you know that?"

"So why is it that she was killed seventy-two hours ago, supposedly by Wolf, and yet you guys didn't see him leave his house to do it?"

Frye blinked rapidly and turned down the corners of his mouth. "Care to elaborate?"

"Yes. You were watching his house with three surveillance teams, and the two guys in the unmarked on his road, and yet he escaped and went to go kill Gail Olson?"

Frye raised his hands. "You said it yourself, he escaped. He's a very slippery man."

Patterson shook her head. "No. Your teams would've seen him leave. He's not in any condition to be walking out of there across the wilderness. Hell, Gail Olson was found twenty-five miles away over the other side of Williams Pass. Wolf couldn't walk up the low hill we climbed and back without passing out after we were done, much less hike a mountain range. No, you guys are hiding something."

MacLean closed his eyes and rubbed his temples. "He could have used the motorcycle in his barn and taken some trails to go kill Gail Olson."

"He hasn't used that motorcycle in ages. The gas is probably bad in the tank. Otherwise he would've used it to slip away yesterday morning, and not risk floating by your two agents in a canoe."

She leaned forward. "And what about Gail Olson's mother going missing in Las Vegas? Are you thinking he had something to do with that? Are you thinking I, or Deputy Rachette, or any of the other Sluice County deputies had anything to do with that? No, of course you're not."

She looked over at her mother.

Her mother was glaring at Frye with the hint of a satisfied smile.

"You've been working your own investigation, Deputy," Frye said slowly.

"I'm a cop. It's what I do. And my investigation is telling me that someone is setting up my old boss. Who happens to be the best man I've ever met."

Frye pointed at her and smiled. "ME Lorber. That's your source."

She ignored him. "This investigation is BS."

"We found the murder weapon in Wolf's shed yesterday."

"Brought to you by the anonymous, garbled, untraceable voice on the telephone."

"That voice was right about Gail Olson, and right about the weapon's location."

"It would've been a crappy frame job if it had been wrong."

"Wolf was jealous of Carter Willis and Sarah Muller's relationship and killed them both."

"Wolf loved Sarah Muller with every fiber of his being and would never have hurt her."

Frye stood up abruptly and paced in front of her, his hands clasped behind his back. Then he stopped.

The door to the office flew open and an agent leaned inside. "Sir."

Frye looked up, annoyed.

"The Gunnison County Sheriff's Department has found Wolf and Special Agent Luke."

Patterson sat straight. "Luke is with him?"

Frye ignored her and stepped out of the office, Cumberland on his heels.

MacLean, Patterson, and her mother watched silently as Frye's head bounced up and down outside and the agents scattered at a full run.

Frye walked back into the office, his eyes locked on Patterson, and stalked to the edge of MacLean's desk. Resuming his seated position, he breathed deeply through his nose, contemplating something.

"You're free to go, Deputy. Please stay available."

"What are you going to do with my mother?"

"Put her back in the holding cells downstairs with your aunt."

"Sir," she looked at MacLean, "surely you gentlemen know my mother and aunt were just trying to do the right thing. They had no intention of breaking federal laws."

MacLean held up his hands and flicked a glance at Frye.

Frye stood up and walked from the room. "Agent Cumberland," he said, and Cumberland followed him out.

Patterson sat with her mouth open and then glared at MacLean. "Mom, just stay strong. We're going to prove that Wolf is innocent of any wrong-doing, and then they're going to let you go."

"Okay, honey." Her voice was barely audible.

Patterson looked at her and gripped her arm. "I promise."

MacLean stood with an apologetic look. "Deputy, please."

Patterson left the office, and her mother to cower in a jail cell.

Lancaster materialized next to her. "Let's go."

"Where?"

"To work."

Patterson followed silently behind the undersheriff, giving a final glance back to her mother, who was being escorted out of MacLean's office without handcuffs. At least that was something.

CHAPTER 18

WOLF JOGGED FAST through the rear parking lot of the restaurant and veered to the right, down a dirt two-track alley backing the Gunnison Main Street storefront buildings.

Luke strode next to him and cracked the lid of the to-go container.

"I hope that's the best breakfast burrito you've ever had in your life," Wolf said. "When Toby figures out you stole food, there's no telling what he'll do. Maybe he'll call the cops."

She ignored him and jabbed the fork inside the box.

"I hate to tell you this, but holding that burrito is now a liability."

She looked down at the container she'd worked so hard for, closed it, and slam-dunked it into the next dumpster. "Damn it."

As they approached the first cross street, Luke held out the storage unit key to him. "You go to the storage yard across the street. I'll be behind you."

"Good idea. They're looking for two of us." He glanced backwards. Still no pursuit from Toby or anyone else. "I'll cross the street here and walk up the other side."

"I'll wait a bit and cross at the next block." She leaned against a brick wall.

Wolf fingered a small plastic puck dangling from the keychain. "What's this?"

"I don't know. Just go."

Wolf ducked back into the alley next to her and then took the plastic puck off the key ring. "It's a magnetic key fob. It must be to get into the exterior gate. They had a concrete wall around the whole place. I'll leave this on the ground outside next to the gate so you can get inside."

"All right. Go."

He walked around the corner and immediately saw two police officers milling around on the corner a half-block straight ahead. He stepped off the curb and crossed the street, keeping his hands in his jeans pockets and his head down.

In his peripheral vision, he saw the two officers walk to his right down the sidewalk, toward the restaurant.

He needed to move.

Reaching the intersection of the side street and Main, he stopped, pushed the crosswalk button, and then stood patiently.

A couple of officers were jogging down the sidewalk toward him, and he held his breath as they drew nearer.

The light turned, and the little white man told him to walk, so he did.

He stepped fast, resisting the urge to break into a run.

Crossing onto the other side of the road, he saw that every single patron on the sidewalk was either slowing or already at a complete stop, gawking at the action on the other side.

As Wolf swerved between people, he decided to openly gawk himself. Because to not do so would bring attention.

Directly across the street, a growing group of law-enforcement personnel from the Gunnison County Sheriff's Department and Gunnison Police Department swarmed around their abandoned truck.

He locked eyes with a cop, who assessed him for a second and then slid his gaze further down the sidewalk.

Wolf zipped up the sweater and caught a glimpse of Luke crossing the street to his left.

He smiled at a nearby patron and walked on. After crossing another intersection, he reached the entrance of the Trout Creek Moving and Storage, which was a bent wrought iron gate with a magnetic key panel mounted on a concrete wall next to it.

He placed the key fob on the reader and the door clicked and squealed open with a gentle push. He walked in, and then bent down and slid the fob up under the gate as it latched closed.

He stood up and walked inside, feeling a small sense of relief being obscured by the concrete wall of the grounds and hidden from the eyes of his gaggle of pursuers.

The numbers of the near units were in the single digits and he needed to get to #62, so he got his bearings and walked to his left.

Stopping at the next row, he counted the units along one side and calculated it ending at #50, so he moved on to the alleyway of doors.

As he reached the next row he heard the metal gate in the distance close. Luke had made it inside, but he didn't bother looking back, because his eyes were locked on a huge diesel pickup truck parked down the row of units he was about to enter. Up on the left side of the alley, a man leaned inside the passenger door of his huge, lifted, vehicle, while his piece-of-crap storage unit door yawned open behind him, revealing a darkened space.

Hopefully it wouldn't come to stealing this man's truck, compounding the severity of their criminal spree, he thought. But, at the moment, there was no other way out of here, other than on their own two feet.

Hopefully inside their destination storage unit was so much evidence, such a glaring nullification of Wolf's guilt, that he and Luke could simply walk across the street and hand it over to the nearest cop.

Passing #54, he counted two digits at a time so he could lock eyes with the unit and will it to contain what he needed as he approached.

His heart skipped when he reached the number 62 and landed on the man with the truck, who was now walking back into the open storage unit.

Wolf counted again and came up with the same destination.

Walking back out into the sun, the man eyed Wolf for a second and then disappeared again inside.

Wolf shoved his hands in his pockets and walked at an even pace, veering slightly to his right to give the truck a wide berth. When he passed the unit, he glanced over at the darkened interior and was surprised to see wide eyeballs staring back at him. Like a ghost in a dark room, a white-skinned, muscular, man stood inside, looking out like a rabid, albino, animal.

Wolf suppressed any facial expression and gave a curt nod. "Morning."

Then his view was blocked out by the huge pickup, which upon second glance looked more ominous than before. It was lifted with knobbed tires, with an extended cab lined with jet-black tinted windows. The truck bed was covered, it too lined with obsidian-colored glass too dark to see inside.

Head down, Wolf continued past the truck and felt the man's eyes on his back.

Wolf was unarmed, and with each footstep he felt more vulnerable as he thought of the laser glare of the man in the unit.

"Sheriff Wolf!"

A jolt of adrenaline shot through him at the mention of his name, but he kept walking.

"How about this. Stop right there, Sheriff Wolf, or I'm going to shoot you in the back of the head."

He stopped and turned around, holding his hands out from his sides.

The guy was outside of the storage unit now, thrusting what looked to be a Beretta M9 handgun in his direction. His skin glared like snow in the sun. His blonde hair was cropped to the skull, almost as white. With eyes now squinted, he used his free hand to block the sun, displaying an elaborate tattoo on his skin.

Wolf saw the ink running up the man's arm was a rendition of the Pope, dressed in his papal tiara and costume, pointing his staff as if firing a machine gun. The holy man's teeth were bared, lips curling, eyes dark red. Fire shot from his staff into a crowd of people, which had been expertly drawn as exploding into chunks of flesh down his forearm.

He noted the barrel of this pigment-challenged man's gun shook in his meaty fist.

"I think you're mistaken." Wolf cowered down submissively, keeping his hands high. "My name's not Wolf. I'm not a sheriff."

The guy stepped all the way to Wolf and put the barrel

inches from his forehead. Four months ago, Wolf would've had the pistol and the guy on the ground. Today, he hesitated, doubting the speed and strength of his vastly injured body against this man who was clearly a fan of lifting weights.

Stepping back quickly, the man smiled, revealing crooked teeth. "Not a sheriff, huh?"

"My name's John. I'm just going to my storage unit, there."

"I know exactly who you are, Sheriff Wolf. And I'm damn glad I caught up with you. I heard you'd escaped."

A siren whooped in the distance and the man's eyes bulged. "Wait a minute, you brought them here?" He looked over his shoulder toward the concrete wall at the end of the row and did a double take at the sight of a woman walking toward them.

Lowering his pistol, the white-skinned man bared his teeth. "You say a word or make a move, I shoot you in front of this bitch, and then I shoot this bitch. Got that? Now lower your hands, damn it."

Wolf lowered his hands.

Glancing between Wolf and the approaching woman, the man turned to the side and lowered his pistol to his thigh.

For a few moments, Wolf watched as thoughts went through the guy's brain. One second the man was looking at the ground, and then he creased his forehead and looked up, locking eyes with Wolf.

When the man's eyes widened and he turned to study Special Agent Luke walking closer, Wolf stepped straight into him, blocking the rising gun with his left arm while he punched as hard as he could in the man's throat. In his peripheral vision, he saw Luke spring forward, bounding toward them like an Olympic sprinter.

Momentarily stunned, the white-skinned man croaked and his eyes bulged; then he erupted into frenzied action.

Wolf gripped the man's gun arm with both of his hands and backed into him, and it felt like grabbing the hoof of a rhinoceros after kicking its balls.

A vicious blow slammed into the back of his head while his body was thrust forward. Tasting blood as he bit into his own tongue, his vision blurred for an instant as another flurry of blows hit him from behind on the neck and skull.

But Wolf held his relentless grip, knowing that if he gave back control of the arm he and Luke were both dead.

Then he was lifted from his feet and everything swirled, and then he was on his back and staring at the gun from a new, worse, angle.

But still, he had a hold with both hands, and the pistol was aimed at the ground a few inches to the side of his head.

Behind the gun, the man's face was shaking but otherwise completely calm. With sheer force, the barrel of the gun twisted ten degrees, then twenty, then pointed at Wolf's left eye, the cold steel almost touching his eyeball.

"Don't shoot. They'll hear you," Wolf said. "Then they'll come for you."

The man's eyes narrowed.

Then the black blur of a shoe came into view, accompanied by a slap as it connected hard with the man's white face.

His eyes rolled to the back of his head as he toppled sideways. His grip on the pistol let up and Wolf wrenched it away.

As the man teetered, Luke reared back and kicked his face again, and when she connected, it was even more of a vicious blow, whiplashing the man's head back.

Chin to the sky, he rocked back on his knees, stopped, and started falling forward.

Luke timed it right and stomp kicked the back of his head, and the man's face bounced on the concrete.

With a grunt that sounded like it came from a demon possessing Luke's body, she landed on his back and gripped his shaven head with both hands.

"I think he's out," Wolf said.

Panting through gritted teeth, she released her grip and stared at his motionless form as if daring him to move again.

"Luke."

She looked at Wolf. Her pupils were pinpoints, her lips pulled back, her chest heaving.

Wolf rolled to his hands and knees and climbed to his feet, feeling a lance of pain in his spine and renewed ache in his thigh. Before standing, he shook his head, expecting a ringing in his ears any moment, but none came.

"You all right?" she asked.

"Yeah." He sniffed. "I smell smoke."

Luke walked to the storage unit and looked on the ground inside. "Fire."

There was a loud clank somewhere around the corner and then a continuous squeal. "What the hell is that?"

"I think it's the rolling gate of the entrance. A car must be coming in." She grabbed the unconscious man's feet and pulled, managing only to twist him. "A little help here?"

They turned the guy over and each took a foot, pulling him into the unit.

The inside was hazy with smoke rising from a scorched pile of papers on the smooth concrete floor. In the corner stood a plastic file box with the lid propped open. Other than the two anomalies, the small space was starkly empty.

Wolf kicked the pile of blackened paper and it crumbled and fluttered airborne. In the ash and debris there was a portion of a glossy photograph the size of a dollar bill that had remained unburned.

"It's a picture," Luke said, bending down next to him.

He blew gently on it and held it up. "Looks like grass. Weeds and wildflowers." He dropped it and sifted through the ashes some more.

Luke stood and went to the door. "Shit. Cops are inside. They just drove by. There's nothing in here. We're too late. We've gotta move."

She cupped her hands and put her face to the truck window. "Keys are in the ignition."

He pushed the pile with a finger. "There were five or ten photos here. Manila folders." He stood up and looked down at the unconscious man.

"Great, whatever. Get in the truck."

"We have to bring this guy with us so we can question him when he wakes up."

"Yeah, and tie him up and load him in the truck. All before the freaking cops drive up on us. Forget it. Get in the truck and get down. They're looking for us, damn it."

"Wait." He patted the man's pockets.

"I have the keys. Let's go."

He pulled out the man's cell phone and then flew out the door to the truck. He heard the police radio echoing through the rows of storage units as he got in the passenger side and closed the door.

The combined tints of the rear and topper windows dimmed the scene outside like it was midnight, but he saw a Sheriff's Department vehicle swing into view and roll toward them just as he sank to the ample floor of the passenger seat and curled into a ball.

He dared not rise from his position, but he heard a scratching police radio edge closer with each passing second.

Just when Wolf was wondering whether Luke had up and run, he heard the roll door of the storage unit close outside.

The radio lowered in volume and Wolf heard a squeak of brakes and then two thumps of car doors closing.

"Hello, ma'am." The voice was right outside the truck.

Wolf froze, his eyes fixed on a pair of leather gloves on the floor, and the specks of dried blood on the knuckles of the right glove. Next to the gloves was a crumpled fast-food bag, stained with grease.

"Howdy, Officers. I swear I've paid my bill here! What? Ya'll bustin' me? Haha. Jus kiddin'. What can I do for ya'll?"

Wolf pulled his eyebrows together.

"Are you okay, ma'am?" the officer asked in a more playful than official tone.

A pause. "Don't I look okay?"

"Were you just burning something?"

"No, just putting the charcoal barbecue in. Upgraded to one of those fancy propane models."

There was a slight movement of the truck, a jostling back and forth, and then a slap on the sidewall of the truck bed. "Have you seen a man and a woman walking through here?"

"Nope."

There was a pause that escalated Wolf's blood pressure, and then the voice said, "Okay, thank you. Have a good day, ma'am."

"You got it. You too, now."

Luke opened the door and climbed in.

When the door slammed closed, Wolf gave her appearance a double-take.

Her hair was a frizzed mess, hanging down to her shoulders. Her sweatshirt was tied around her waist, and he could not help but notice her dark nipples clearly visible underneath the thin white fabric of her T-shirt, which was smeared with dark soot.

She twisted the key in the ignition and the truck's big diesel engine roared to life.

She smiled, revealing teeth also smeared with soot. Then she finger-waved in the rearview mirror. Add the dark streaks on her lips and cheeks, and she'd knocked herself down to the lowest tax bracket in a hurry.

"That's a nice look on you."

"Shut up," she said without moving her lips. "They're right behind us still." She shifted into gear and moved forward.

Wolf remained silent and watched her drive. She slowed to a stop and he heard the familiar squeal of the gate outside.

Her quick glance in the rearview told him the cops were following them out.

"Back to Rocky Points," Wolf said.

"Are you sure?" she said like an out of work ventriloquist.

"Back to Rocky Points."

She exhaled, twisted the wheel, and hit the accelerator. After a few seconds, she deflated in her seat. "Shit. All that for a pile of ashes?"

"We got a vehicle, and we bought us some more time."

"If we don't get stopped in the next two minutes at the roadblock they're undoubtedly setting up ahead." She slapped the wheel. "Damn it! Who was that guy?"

He climbed up into the passenger seat and massaged the pain out of his hip flexor. "No match for you. Thanks, by the way. If you'd been a second later, I'd be dead."

She scoffed. "All that and we got nothing."

Leaning forward to stare at the receding turret lights in the side-view mirror, he fished inside his jeans pocket and pulled out the cell phone he'd lifted from the man. "We got a cell phone."

She leaned toward him and eyed it, then sat back hard. "Ah, this guy practically drove lying down. What the hell?"

He pushed the wake button on the phone and an image of the Pope smiting a crowd of horrified people filled the screen.

CHAPTER 19

"No, no, no, no." Rachette punched the wheel and the horn emitted a dog-toy like honk.

With a practiced move, he downshifted, popped the clutch and hit the gas, and the car lurched and sputtered to life.

Crisis averted.

Something was seriously wrong with the engine of this tin can he drove, and it was time to get rid of it once and for all. He had his eye on a Ford truck parked with a for-sale sign on the north end of town.

The blue pickup looked pretty worn down, but the price was right at two grand. And having four-wheel drive in the winter and no more breakdowns? That had to be worth it.

As he pulled to the curb in front of the coffee shop, he sat idling for a few seconds, then reluctantly shut off the engine, knowing that could have been the last time it ran for a while.

He got out and stepped to the curb. A flashing SBCSD vehicle sped by so fast he failed to catch a glimpse of who was driving.

"Damn," he whispered. He was stuck on the outside with no date set for getting back in.

His life was spent wandering through town, with coffee in the morning at the Chairlift Coffee House, lunch from a drive-thru on his kitchen table in his tiny apartment, cheap reconstituted dinners, and beers at night to forget the monotony of it all.

And when he finally did get back in, if that day ever came, what was it going to be like? If it was without Wolf, and with dicks like Deputy Sergeant Barker, it was going to be abysmal.

Then he thought of Deputy Munford's tiny smile and knew it wouldn't be all that bad.

"Same as always?" the stoned-looking barista asked behind the counter.

Rachette nodded. "Same as always."

Another department SUV sped past. There must have been a development.

He decided he would go to the department and poke around, that is, if he could get by Tammy with a little sweet-talking.

With a quickened stride he walked to his car and got in.

The key turned and there was a click. The dashboard gauge needles spasmed and then went still.

"Ah!" He punched the wheel again. This time when he pressed the horn no sound came out.

After trying the key again with no result, he got out and kicked the door, leaving a tiny dent.

"Shit."

Putting his head down, he walked away from his pile of scrap metal on wheels, vowing it would be the last time he touched it.

CHAPTER 20

LUKE SLAPPED the wheel again as they passed a strip of fast-food restaurants. Her stomach churned nothing but air and her general mood was murderous-angry, the former exacerbating the latter. "I really need that breakfast burrito right about now. I'm gonna come back here and beat Toby's ass one day."

She flexed her foot, feeling a wicked bruise welling up from her soccer kick to the guy's face. As she watched another restaurant slide by, she wished she could kick it again.

Forcing herself out of her dark mood, she looked at Wolf. He was zoned out next to her, still pecking away at the screen of the cell phone. His face was white and shiny.

"Hey, how you feeling?"

He pointed at the screen. "Listen to these text messages, from a phone number, not a name. First one says: *Wolf escaped.* That was yesterday morning. Then this one that came thirty-five minutes ago: *He's on the run with an FBI agent named Kristen Luke. They found them in Gunnison just now. Where are you?*"

She raised her eyebrows. "That sounds like someone in Rocky Points relaying information to this guy."

He put the phone to his ear.

"What are you doing?" she asked.

"Calling the number."

The digital trill of a ringing phone suddenly filled the cab of the truck, blaring from every speaker.

"Hello?" a deep male voice answered.

Wolf grabbed her arm and put a finger to his lips.

She nodded.

"Hello?" the voice said again.

The phone call ended with a loud click.

She reached up and turned down the volume. "Who was that?"

Wolf shook his head. "I don't know. Did it sound like anyone you know from the FBI?"

"No." She checked the rearview mirror for the thousandth time. Still no cops. "What about—"

Once again, the speakers erupted in sound, this time a call coming in.

Wolf raised the phone, pressed the button, and said nothing.

The speakers hissed. The person on the other end breathed into the receiver at a steady rate, but otherwise kept silent.

Wolf pressed the call-end button and the speakers went silent again.

"We're almost at Crested Butte. I'm going to say this one more time. I'm hungry, currently braless in a scuffed-up T-shirt, have charcoal on my face and a knotted bird's nest for hair, and haven't showered in days. But you, my friend, look like shit. You need to eat."

Wolf twirled the phone in his hand, then rummaged

around at his feet. He produced a pair of leather gloves and handed them to her.

"Thanks?" She dropped them in the center console.

Then he fished out a fast-food bag and held it up in the light. He opened it and dove his face inside.

Teeth-clenching frustration rushed through her. Jamming on the brakes, she pulled into a supermarket lot and parked. "Screw it. I'm going in to get food. Fried chicken? Great. Fried chicken." She opened the door.

Wolf put his hand inside the greasy bag.

"Hey, are you deaf? I'm going to go get food."

"Look at the blood on those gloves. The right hand."

She climbed back in the seat and picked up the right glove with her index finger and thumb. There was blood spatter on the knuckles. She dropped it back in the cup holder. "Ugh."

"Looks pretty fresh, right?"

"Yeah, sure, I don't know."

Wolf pulled a piece of paper from the fast-food bag and held it out. "Look at the date, time, and location on this receipt."

"Two days ago ... Tuesday afternoon ... Colorado Boulevard, Denver. 2:24 p.m."

Wolf held up the bag. "And this."

There was a smudge of blood on the outside of the fast-food bag. "Shit," she said, putting the puzzle together.

"When did you say that family was killed?"

"We went to the scene Wednesday morning. It was dark still. 4:30 a.m."

"He got this food bag Tuesday afternoon in Denver, then smudged it sometime between then and today."

She flinched as the vision of the two dead children sandwiched between their dead parents flashed across her mind.

She eyed the gloves again, suddenly wanting them out of this truck. She wanted to get out of the seat where the man had sat.

"It was that guy who murdered the family." She leaned back and exhaled. "Damn it. I should have kicked him again."

"I have to make some phone calls," Wolf said. "Go get us some food."

She watched as he dialed a phone number from memory and pressed it to his ear.

"I hope you're not calling Patterson or Rachette, or anyone else that the Bureau's going to be monitoring. Remember, they had to have gotten to us through Margaret and her sister."

Wolf ignored her, completely oblivious to her presence. His free hand clenched into a fist and his eyes were wildly darting around.

She swallowed, remembering the last time she'd seen him like this, which had been in a bar room back office, the moment he'd realized his son was in mortal danger.

"Is Harold Burton there? Put him on ... now!"

She got out and closed the door.

CHAPTER 21

PATTERSON SAT inside the quiet cab of the SUV and watched Lancaster's profile in the side-view mirror as he stood outside with a cell phone pressed to his ear.

The silence was absolute, but she still heard nothing.

The guy was officially giving her the creeps.

He'd just received a phone call and said hello twice into the receiver. Apparently, nobody had answered him because he'd hung up. After ignoring her questions about it, he'd simply stopped the car, gotten out, and put his phone to his ear.

Now Patterson watched the reflection of him stand on the sidewalk and make calls.

Lancaster's lips hadn't moved yet. Not only that, it was like he'd never intended to say anything with the person on the other end of the call he was making.

He pocketed his phone and walked back to the SUV.

Before he climbed back inside she flipped the radio volume back up and brought her hand to her lap.

The big man eyed her as he got in and she stared back.

"Who was that?"

Lancaster answered with pushing the ignition button and shifting to drive.

"Because I watched your call, and it looked like you just dialed a number and stared into another dimension. What? You calling the weather hotline?"

He pulled out onto Main Street.

A few tourists with backpacks and ski poles stood outside the coffee shop, and some clearly high-on-marijuana twenty-somethings played hacky sack in the grass field near Town Square.

"Hey, pull over here. I want to talk to these kids." Three teenaged boys wrestled at the next intersection.

Lancaster ignored her.

She flicked the lock and pushed open the door. "It wasn't a request."

He slowed to a stop and she got out.

"Excuse me."

The three teenaged boys stopped and faced her.

"Oh, yes, Officer," one of them said with a fading laugh.

"Do you three know Jack Wolf?"

They looked at one another.

"It's a simple question. You know him?"

"Yeah," the short one said. "We know him. He's in the grade above us."

"Why are you three out of school right now?"

The tallest took a defensive posture. "We all have fourth period off, and then it's lunch. So we're on lunch."

She held her hands up. "Okay, okay. I was just wondering if there was some sort of short day at school or something. So, what is it now? Like, fourth period?" She looked at her watch.

They relaxed. "Yeah, like middle of fourth. It ends at twelve, and then it's lunch."

She nodded. "Thanks, boys. Have a good day. Stay out of trouble."

"Bye," they said in unison.

She walked back to the SUV, ignoring the catcall and whistle from one of them, and got inside.

Lancaster stared at her with half-closed eyelids. "You mind filling me in?"

She strapped her seatbelt on. "I want to go to the school and find Jack Wolf."

"And why's that?"

"Wolf's son has a right to know what's going on, and I want him to hear the news from me, not an FBI agent, or you, or anyone like you."

Lancaster raised a corner of his mouth. "Anyone like me?"

She glared at him. "Yeah, people like you, who think he's guilty until proven innocent, when you have no clue what a good man Wolf really is. His son needs to know that not everyone is like you and the people chasing after his dad. That the rest of us still believe Wolf's innocent and we're getting to the bottom of everything. However slow that might be." She pointed out the windshield. "Go up to 4th and take a right."

To Patterson's surprise, Lancaster put the SUV in gear, let off the gas, and drove without protest.

CHAPTER 22

POPE LAID his cheek on the cold concrete and pushed his eye up to the small crack of light at the bottom of the door.

The vehicle engine shut off outside and a car door squeaked open.

A civilian car. A cop car would've been better oiled than that.

"Pepper?"

There was no answer.

"Pepper?" he said again. He knocked on the inside of the door. The sound was like a kick to the head. Not nearly as painful as when he'd actually been kicked. Making that bitch pay was going to be one of the first orders of business.

"Who's that?" came a quiet voice from the other side of the door.

"Who's that?" he countered.

A pause. He pictured an idiotic look in Pepper's bloodshot eyes.

"Pepper? Is that you? It's Pope." Doesn't get clearer than that.

"It's Pepper. Who's that?"

Pope closed his eyes and took a deep, relaxing breath. "It is Pope. I'm stuck in the storage unit. Help me out of here."

A shadow passed in front of the sliver of light and dreadlocks fell to the ground. Then one of Pepper's eyeballs was inches from his.

"You're stuck?"

"Yes. Do you have a crow bar in the vehicle? Any bolt cutters?"

"I think so."

Pope suppressed his optimism. There was a good chance this moron had no clue what either of those objects were. "Check."

The shadow disappeared. A minute later it returned and he heard a metallic clank on the door.

Pope stood up in the darkened storage unit. His balance was off, like he was on a ship at sea, so he leaned a hand on the door. Feeling the scrape of metal on metal on the door through his palm, he closed his eyes and hoped.

There was a clank, and suddenly the door was rolling up and light was flooding in.

When it rose all the way, Pope shielded his eyes against the hammering sun and saw the silhouette of Pepper and his Medusa head of dreadlocks.

"Hey there, boss. You get yourself in a little trouble?" Pepper stepped inside. His thin, greasy facial hair framed a stupid smile.

"You're an hour late, Pepper."

"Sorry 'bout that," he said. "Got a late start, and then there's some serious stuff going on out there. Cops galore. Had to wait until the action died down a little before I drove in here."

Pope held out his hand.

Pepper reached out to clasp it in a handshake and Pope pulled it away.

"No, give me your phone."

Pepper patted his pockets and pulled out his cell. Handing it over, he smiled again. "Lucky I had this truck, 'cause the bolt cutter from the other day was still in it. What a coincidence, huh? What if I hadn't driven this truck? We'd be screwed right now."

Pope nodded. "Or what if you had shown up on time?"

Pepper squirmed under Pope's glare.

"Give me the bolt cutters."

The stoner looked down at the snipping tool in his hand and swallowed. "Yeah, sure."

Pope reached out and took one of the long red handles.

Pepper held firm for an instant, and then let go.

Pope took the other handle and jabbed upward into the smelly, dreadlocked moron's neck while he clamped the jaws shut.

A spurt of warm blood shot onto Pope's arms and he jumped back.

The hippy gurgled and clamped both hands on his neck, trying to staunch the life pouring from his body.

Pope raised the cutters above his head and brought them down onto Pepper's nest of hair, and then again, until he'd slumped all the way to the ground. One more blow for good measure, and the man who'd caused this whole storage-unit mess was motionless, certain never to move again. Not many people lived with brain showing through a hole in their skull.

Looking down at his red streaked arms, panic surged through him. His palms were slick on the handles of the cutters, his left foot standing in the blood.

He peeked outside and saw no one, then ducked back in.

The corrugated steel walls were covered with oozing blood spatter. His shirt was like a Jackson Pollock painting. So were his jeans. His face must have been a mess.

Quickly, he took off his shirt, turned it inside out, and began wiping his face and arms.

He found a half-full bottle of water and dumped it on his T-shirt, and finished cleaning himself. But no matter how hard he scrubbed, his arms were coated with a permanent pink hue. He checked the side view mirror on Pepper's truck and saw his face was the same color. Surprisingly, a light coat of blood spatter made him look more normal.

His fingerprints would be on the plastic box and the bolt cutters, so he put them both in the truck cab, rolled the storage-unit door shut, and got in the truck.

Shirtless, with bloody jeans, red arms, an angry red face, and one red shoe, he drove away.

Outside the Trout Creek gate, he took a right and followed the hand signals of a pig waving traffic around a cluster of other pigs that were focused on a silver truck.

With an affable grin, he nodded at the gutless clones and sped north out of town.

After dialing a number from memory, he held the phone to his ear.

It rang once and went to voicemail.

He dialed again.

Again his call was screened.

"Come on." He dialed again, and this time the deep voice answered.

"Hello?"

"It's me, Pope. Listen to me very carefully."

CHAPTER 23

FOR A SMALL TOWN in the middle of the mountains, Rocky Points Middle and High School was quite a large building. Built of red bricks and brown-painted steel, it was a sprawling one-story, surrounded by flat fields and, beyond that, forest.

Boys and girls kicked soccer balls in the field to the south, and they looked to be about Jack's age, but Patterson failed to see his tall, lanky form amid the other kids.

A trip to the administrative offices would tell Patterson quickly enough where Jack was.

She and Lancaster walked up the long sidewalk toward the school.

She took the lead, once again not caring whether Lancaster decided to join her. This was her gig.

Lancaster's phone rang again, and again he screened it.

When it rang a third time she stopped and turned. "For Chrissakes, are you going to get that?"

He pushed the button. "Hello?"

True to form, he turned away from her and walked in the opposite direction.

Her curiosity piqued, she listened closely.

He slowed and looked at her, listening intently to his phone call. "Yes, sir ... We're actually in the process of doing that right now," he said.

A few seconds later he pocketed the phone.

"Who was that?"

"MacLean. Apparently he's on the same page as you. He wants us to find Jack Wolf and for you to inform him of everything that's going on."

She tilted her head. "And you didn't know MacLean's phone number when he called the first two times?"

"He was calling from a number at the new building. I didn't recognize it."

Nodding, she turned around and walked into the school.

Inside was an entryway with a trophy case housing brass statues, pictures, and ribbons.

Perusing the plaques and pictures on the way by, she stopped at the sight of a familiar face beaming a smile in a line of fully uniformed football players.

It was a much younger Wolf with wavy black hair. Handsome as ever. Downright hot, really. He stood in shoulder pads with his helmet under his arm. The plaque said *State Champions, Division 4A, 1993.*

She continued down the hall to the administrative offices and entered.

"Hello, Officers," the woman nearest them said from behind a wooden desk.

"Deputies, ma'am. With the Sluice–Byron Sheriff's Department. We are here to locate and speak with a student named Jack Wolf."

"Okay." She punched her keyboard and then did some navigating with her mouse.

Patterson turned to Lancaster. "So MacLean had the same idea as I did? To locate Jack and tell him about his father?"

Lancaster shrugged. "That's what he said. He thought you were the best for the job. You know Jack well, right?"

Perhaps MacLean had a brain after all. It was tough getting a read on the man. He'd been treating any and all Sluice County deputies like spoiled fruit so far, never including them in anything. And now he was saying she was *best for the job*?

"Miss ... uh ... Deputy, I found him. He's in room 183. Earth Science class. We can call him over the speaker and have him come down, or you can go to him. Which one would you like?"

Patterson always liked moving better than waiting. "We'll go to him. Thank you."

The woman exhaled. "Excuse me, but what's this about? Do we need to contact family?"

Patterson shook her head. "No. His father is with the department, too. Sheriff Wolf?"

"Oh, really? I thought he wasn't sheriff anymore."

"He's not. My point is, we're just relaying some important news from his father."

"Ah." She nodded and winked. "All righty. Have a good day. I can get someone to show you the way. Maybe pull him out of class for you, so it's not a couple of cops doing it?"

"No, thanks," she said with no more patience. "If you could just point us in the right direction."

"To the left. Straight down. It's on the right a ways up. Can't miss it."

Patterson led at a brisk pace and a minute later they were at the classroom.

Patterson knocked and stuck her face against the rectangular window.

A man with a beard and wire-rimmed glasses stopped in

mid-lecture and walked to the door. He hesitated at seeing the uniforms and stepped outside.

"Hello, Officers. May I help you?"

Patterson noted the way the man started sweating. "We're here to see Jack Wolf. Could you please send him out?"

The man leaned and looked over Patterson's shoulder, and then at his watch. "He went to the bathroom a few minutes ago. I'm usually not one to let students get out of class to go mess around in the bathroom when they could have relieved themselves between classes. But it seemed like an emergency." He whispered the final word.

Patterson pointed down the hall. "Here?"

"Yeah, just down the hall. On the left side."

"Thank you."

They walked to the men's bathroom and stopped.

Patterson held out her hand and Lancaster pushed his way in. The door swung shut and she was left standing alone in front of a line of lockers. With an exhale, she leaned against one of them and a memory of being pinned against her locker and kissing Brad Quinley flashed in her mind. Before Scott, there had only been Brad.

She wondered what Scott was doing today. Probably wondering why she was avoiding his calls. Probably wondering why she had yet to give him an answer to his proposal. And probably wondering why she'd paused after the question as he'd popped it—sprung it, thrown it in her face—when they'd been out to dinner a week ago.

Why had she frozen up and told him she'd think about it? Her hesitation had clearly devastated him.

The memory of Scott's jaw falling to the floor made her push from the locker and pace the hallway.

She certainly loved the man. Their physical chemistry was

great. They made each other laugh. They made each other think. So what the hell was her problem?

And what the hell was taking so long with Lancaster?

She barged across the hall and pushed on the bathroom door, which swung open a few feet and stopped with a bang.

"Ah!"

Backing up, she let the door swing shut.

A second later, Lancaster came out, holding the side of his face.

"I'm sorry, I'm sorry. I was just ..." She paused at the sight of Lancaster's eyes.

For a split second, she saw hatred within his glare, and for an instant he leaned toward her, like he was about to do something about it. And then, just as quickly, the look was gone.

"It's all right," he said with a forced calm.

She turned away and let him get out of the doorway. Like she'd just stared at the sun and the after-image was floating in her vision, she still saw the hatred burning in Lancaster's eyes. Christ, she'd had no idea the guy was so disgusted by her presence.

Jack. She remembered why they were there.

"Where is he?"

Lancaster shrugged. "Not in there. Checked every stall."

She pushed her way into the bathroom. "Jack?"

No answer.

She bent down and saw that the stalls were all empty, then walked back outside.

Lancaster stood with his arms to his sides, his cheek bright red.

"There's gotta be another bathroom he went to." She marched back toward the classroom and then past it, then around a corner, and finally to a set of double doors that led outside.

Pulse now racing, she jogged past Lancaster and back down the hall, past the classroom, all the way to the administration office.

"I need you to page Jack Wolf on the intercom and tell him to come here."

The woman read her expression and tone and jumped into action. "Jack Wolf, please come to the principal's office. Jack Wolf."

A door opened and a tall woman in a pantsuit stepped out. "Everything all right, Claire?" She looked expectantly at Patterson.

"I'm looking for Jack Wolf, ma'am."

She stepped forward with her hand extended. "I'm Principal Ulfers. What's going on?"

"Jack Wolf is missing from his class. I'm looking for him."

The principal smiled. "Well, that's not exactly out of the ordinary for Jack Wolf as of late."

"Is that right?"

"Yes. I'm ... sure you heard about his mother. He's been absent quite a lot lately."

Patterson frowned. "He just leaves class? He says he's going to go to the bathroom and leaves? Doesn't come back?"

Principal Ulfers shrugged her bony shoulders. "Well ... no ... but I wouldn't put that past him."

Patterson shook her head and left out of the admin area, back into the hallway.

Lancaster was leaning against the wall, watching her as she flew by.

Reaching the classroom again, she opened the door.

Everyone's heads turned her way, teacher and student alike. "I need to know where Jack Wolf sits."

A girl pointed at a vacant desk in front of her.

She walked over and plucked the backpack out from underneath the plastic chair. "Is this his?"

The girl nodded. "Yes."

"Did he tell any of you where he was going?" She turned full circle, imploring the young faces in the classroom.

"He was on his phone for a little bit," said a boy sitting next to where Jack would've been. "I saw him, like, texting, and then he left."

"Are you sure?"

"Yeah."

"Officer," Principal Ulfers was breathless in the doorway, "can I please speak to you a second?"

Clutching the backpack, Patterson walked to the doorway and pushed past the principal into the hallway. She stopped and turned, feeling a familiar heat in her cheeks like that of when she'd been caught skipping class in tenth grade. "Yeah?"

Principal Ulfers closed the classroom door and turned to Patterson and Lancaster. "What is going on?"

"Jack Wolf is not in his class. We're looking for him. If he shows up, please give us a call." Patterson pulled out a contact card and handed it over.

Ulfers blinked her long eyelashes and took the card reluctantly. "Like I said, he skips a lot of class."

Patterson turned her back, walked down the hall, and back outside.

Halfway down the pathway to the parking lot, she looked over her shoulder just as a bell rang on the side of the building. Lancaster was leaving the doors with a crowd of students. Eyeing her, he had his phone pressed to his ear again.

She put her hands on her hips and waited, ignoring the flow of kids as they scattered to cars to have off-campus lunch.

Lancaster slowed to a stop and spoke into his phone.

"Screw this." Patterson took out her own phone and dialed.

"Sluice—Byron Sheriff's Department. How may I direct your call?"

"Hi, Tammy. It's Patterson. Can you please connect me to MacLean's office?"

Patterson waited patiently as the phone trilled.

"MacLean."

"Sir. This is Deputy Patterson. I have news."

"What news?"

"We, Lancaster and I, just learned that Jack Wolf is missing from school."

"Okay. How do you know that?"

"We just stopped by his school and found that he's missing."

"You stopped by his school? The high school?"

She paused. "Yes. To find him. To tell him about his father, you know, let him know everything that's been going on. Didn't you talk to Lancaster about this earlier?"

"And so what? He's gone?"

"Yes, sir. His backpack was still here. In class. But he disappeared."

"Are you sure he isn't just, I don't know, taking a leak?"

"That's what the teacher thought he was doing. We checked the bathrooms. He doesn't appear to be on campus."

"Doesn't appear to be? Appear to be?"

Patterson's face went hot. "Yes, sir."

MacLean chuckled into her ear. "Did you learn who his girlfriend is? See if she's missing too? Check out the make-out spots up in the trees? How about where the kids sneak away to have a smoke? Hell, was he given a wedgie and shoved in a locker? Maybe he likes a particular shitter on the other side of the school and is having a rough go of it."

Her breathing escalated. She turned around and looked toward Lancaster, who was mouthing something and ending his own phone call.

"Yes, sir," she said.

"Bother me when you have a reason." The phone clicked.

Pocketing her phone, she took some deep breaths and walked to meet Lancaster halfway. MacLean had a point. She had been hasty, thinking Jack was missing after a few minutes of passionate pursuit. They needed to be one hundred percent sure before they left these grounds.

Lancaster approached with his phone held up. "I just told MacLean about this. He wants us to check around town to find him. I told him you know better than I do where he could be." Lancaster motioned to the SUV. "Let's go. You navigate."

Patterson stopped, almost stumbling. She opened her mouth and closed it. She might have made a noise but it was unintelligible beneath the pounding pulse in her ears.

"You all right?" Lancaster asked.

She swallowed. "Yeah."

Lancaster narrowed his eyes. "Were you going back inside?"

She froze, her thoughts unable to keep up with the momentum of the situation.

"What's going on?"

She shook her head. "Nothing. I was just thinking that maybe we missed him somewhere. I'm just freaking out. We have to find him."

"You think he's still in there?" he asked, looking back at the outpouring of students.

"No," she said.

"Then let's go." Lancaster marched to the parking lot.

Heart hammering in her chest, the pores on her body leaking sweat, she steeled herself like she was about to karate chop through a stack of pine boards. Then she followed the man.

CHAPTER 24

WOLF SAT PERFECTLY STILL, concentrating on deep inhalations and exhalations to counter his anxiety.

"The guy's still locked in the storage unit. No phone. Out cold," Luke said.

He ignored her. She was trying to make him feel better, but until he got a return call, there was no taming the dread.

"Wolf, we have to move. Every second we waste in this parking lot means the FBI and cops are closer on our tails."

He picked up the phone and pushed the button again. Nothing had changed: the phone was still on. The battery was still charged. There was still cell coverage. Still no call.

"Okay. Never mind. We'll wait." Luke sat frozen in the driver's seat, her eyes wide and gentle. Impatient and yet with all the patience in the world.

When Luke and Wolf had dated for that brief period, Jack would stutter and trip on his words in her presence. She was that kind of beautiful to his son. And when she'd spoken, Jack would give her all his attention, as if terrified he might miss a word coming out of her lips. He used to over-laugh at her jokes, unconsciously follow her from room to room.

Wolf smiled briefly at the memory, then thought of Jack's smile. His forest-green eyes. The pain on his face the last time they'd spoken by the river.

He lifted the phone again.

At the same instant, it vibrated and rang. He pressed the button and brought the phone to his ear. "Yeah?"

"Got him. I'll take care of everything. Just get here safe and keep me posted."

Wolf hung up and leaned back. The tension flowed down his legs and out his feet, leaving his body weak.

"Are we good?" Luke asked.

He nodded. "He's safe. Let's go."

The truck fired up and she reversed with squealing tires.

She pulled forward and immediately slammed the brakes. "Crap."

He saw why she'd stopped. Outside the parking lot there was a line of traffic dribbling forward on the northbound lanes of the highway. Four police cruisers with flashing lights were checking vehicles as they passed at a snail's crawl.

As if on cue, a black helicopter sped by overhead, going south.

She let off the brake and crept forward. "We're screwed."

He pointed. "Go out the north exit of the parking lot to the other strip mall across the street."

"Yes." Luke accelerated, narrowly missing an old man stepping out of the grocery store.

"Without killing anyone."

"No promises." Her face was pressed against the windshield. "Idiots, they left a bypass route wide open. We're going to make it."

And they did. In a matter of minutes, they'd passed the roadblock and were on their way north on the highway.

A half-mile later they took a right on the county road they'd come in on earlier that morning, and ten minutes after that, the truck hummed over gravel.

Luke shoved another chicken drumstick in his face and he waved it away. "I'm all right."

"You have to have more food. I'm not going to carry you around for the rest of the day."

He grabbed the cold piece of chicken and forced down the meat.

He didn't say that exhaustion had almost overtaken him after the wait for Burton's phone call. Almost. The ringing in his ear had started, but it had stopped before gaining any traction. Perhaps it was because he'd been sitting, or maybe some form of resistance to his condition was building, spurred by the danger to Jack.

"That was the best chicken I've ever had in my entire life, bar none, hands down. The best."

He eyed Luke. "That bad, huh?"

"What's the plan here?"

Wolf threw the bone out the window and wiped his hands on a napkin. "We go talk to MacLean."

Luke spat Coke out her mouth and coughed. "MacLean?"

"Yep."

"You want to, what? Saunter back into Rocky Points and walk into the station?"

"No, I want to go to his house."

She set down the plastic bottle in the center console. "And that's safe? That drop off the cliff really did knock you on the head."

Wolf grabbed his Coke and took a sip. "I've made sure Jack's safe. The next thing we need is for you to be safe. The only way that can happen is by proving I was framed for this whole thing. And as far as I see it, everything points to MacLean. He brought those photos of Gail Olson to me and tried to blackmail me to drop out of the race. Gail Olson admitted that the whole thing was a set-up and that MacLean was behind it.

"You said Carter Willis, or Agent Smith, brought those photos to your boss to get the go-ahead to watch me and my department. So that means MacLean brought those photos to Agent Smith. They were somehow partners in all this. And since it's looking like Smith and Tedescu were involved with some really bad guys and we can't talk to them, we need to talk to MacLean." Wolf squeezed the plastic bottle. "I'll beat the truth out of him if I need to."

"Yeeaah. Beat it out of him? We need to be a little less heavy-handed and a little more careful about things when we get into town. The Bureau's going to be everywhere. They're probably going to have surveillance on MacLean's house. Are you sure there's not another angle of attack when we get there?"

"Yeah, but if you're right about how they found us, our angle of attack is probably sitting in jail, or in FBI custody."

"Who? Margaret?"

He nodded. "Margaret was Sarah's employing broker at Hitching Post. She has access to all of Sarah's records—every transaction she's ever made since she hung her license there three years ago."

"You think this has to do with Sarah?"

"She was shot dead in the same car with Agent Smith, wasn't she? In the last few weeks I've looked at her history, but found nothing. I'd like to take a second look."

They rode in silence for a beat.

"I don't think she was involved with this Carter Willis-

Agent Smith guy. You know, sexually. I saw it in her eyes the first time I met the guy. She was scared of him for some reason. I think he was using her for something, and she got caught up in all of this without meaning to, and then paid the price for it."

Luke kept silent.

In his mind, Wolf repeated the words he'd just said, feeling less sure about them the second time around.

He activated the white-skinned, tattooed man's cell phone and scrolled through the contacts again.

"Still don't recognize any numbers in there?"

He shook his head. "They're mostly Colorado numbers. A few 303s and 720s, but mostly 970 area codes."

"So, either the mountains or the northern third of the state," Luke said.

"But there're no names in here. He uses numbers to signify each phone number. And there are fifty-one of them. He must have some sort of cipher, a list of the corresponding names to the signifying numbers to know who's calling him. Looks like he was prepared for this scenario—a cop getting hold of his cell phone."

"And WCB Holdings," Luke said, referring to the commercial insurance and registration cards they'd found in the glove compartment.

"We need to look into that, too."

Luke shook her head. "If only we had the resources of the Bureau. Wouldn't that be nice?"

Wolf leaned back and sighed.

Luke eyed him, her demeanor much improved after the solid meal.

"I noticed you said you were going to, quote, *beat it out of him* when you saw MacLean. From what I've seen so far, you couldn't best a second-grade schoolboy at arm wrestling."

He smiled. "With the hormones they're feeding these kids nowadays? Probably not."

She smiled and he laughed, and he felt more grateful than ever for her being there.

Folding his arms, he leaned back and closed his eyes.

"Oh no, here we go."

"Wake me up in an hour."

"Yeah. I'll try."

CHAPTER 25

RACHETTE SNUCK to the hallway that led to the squad room and peeked around the corner.

At the end of the corridor, MacLean paced inside his glass aquarium office with a cell phone pasted to his ear. His gruff tone echoed all the way to Rachette, but he couldn't make out the words.

"Can I help you?"

Rachette turned around. A deputy whose name eluded him waddled forward, his pear-shaped body swaying side to side. His eyebrows were propped up in a superior expression.

"Hey, I'm Deputy Rachette," he said, holding out his hand.

The other deputy shook with a cold palm. "Rachette?"

"Yeah, I was in the Sluice Department. I got shot a few months ago. Been recovering, so I haven't been around much. But I'm just about back in action."

The deputy eyed Rachette up and down as if looking for the wound.

"Right here." He patted his shoulder. "Took a nine-mil hollow point. Blew my shoulder pretty much to shreds. Luckily, though, wasn't a direct hit on the joint. Could've been worse."

The deputy stood frozen with those eyebrows.

Rachette eyed his name patch. "Well, Deputy Prough, it was nice to meet—"

"Prough," he corrected, pronouncing it *Prow*, rather than rhyming it with the bodily function as Rachette had done.

"Prough. Cool. Nice to meet you. Later." Rachette double-timed it the opposite way toward the stairwell.

He'd gotten nowhere with the visit to the department. The FBI had all gone, and none of the deputies were there except a few low ranks that were holding down the fort for admin duty —deputies Rachette had met once at most and whose names he'd forgotten instantly, so he'd decided against engaging them in his plain clothing.

Trotting down the stairway and stepping outside, he pulled out his cell phone and considered who to call.

His derelict car was parked six blocks away, hidden behind a line of vehicles. It could rot there for all he cared.

He had a long walk home to his apartment, with nothing waiting for him when he arrived. Eyeing the Sunnyside Café, he decided on a meal first.

His phone vibrated.

Jack is missing. The text message was from Patterson.

Rachette's chest tightened. What the hell?

He pushed her phone number.

"Hey." She sounded breathless.

"Jack's missing?" His armpits broke into a sweat. His phone vibrated again and there was a beep in his ear— another call coming in from a number he didn't recognize. "Tell me everything. What do you mean he's missing?"

The connection crackled. "Just a ... school ... there, so we're going to his grandparents' house."

"He's missing from school so you're going to his grandparents' house?"

"Yeah."

He paced in front of the county building. "I think his grandparents are out of town. I remember Wolf telling me that they go up to Vail a lot now for a development project Sarah's father's involved in."

The connection crackled again.

"Hello?"

There was no answer.

His phone chimed and vibrated again, and it was the same random phone number.

Again he ignored it. "Patterson? Are you there?"

"Just a second."

"Okay."

A full twenty seconds passed and then Patterson's voice was a whisper. "... might be bad. I don't know ..."

"What?" Rachette asked. "Might be bad? The connection?"

"No." Patterson's voice was a plea.

Rachette stood listening to dead silence. "I can't hear you. Call me back when you get into good cell range."

"... breaking up. I'll keep you ..."

Damn it. "Keep me posted!"

No answer, and then the connection went dead.

He stood breathing heavily and then forced himself to relax. Jack was at an age where it was normal to skip school. And hadn't Wolf recently been concerned that his grandparents were spending time away this month for a project in Vail?

And who knew how Jack was holding up after his mother's death? Maybe he was skipping a lot of school now. Maybe he was even thinking about running away. Maybe he'd heard about his father being on the run and had done the same.

His phone vibrated and rang again.

It was the same number he'd screened before.

"What?"

"Tom?"

"What? Who's this?"

"It's Harold Burton."

"Sir." His face went instantly hot. "Thank God you called. Patterson says Jack Wolf is missing."

"I know. I have him."

He blinked. "You do?"

"Yes. And I need your help, right now."

"How?"

"I'll explain everything when you get here. Where are you?"

He turned and looked at the glass façade above him. "I'm in front of the county building."

"I don't want you to repeat any of this conversation to anyone, above all to MacLean or anyone from his department. Not to any Byron County deputies. In fact, better to tell no one at all. Am I clear?"

"Okay, yeah, sure. What is it?"

"We have reason to believe MacLean is behind Wolf's framing."

"Really?"

Burton paused. "We're not sure who else could be involved. But it's probably best not to trust anyone from Byron County."

Rachette thought of Patterson and how she was with Undersheriff Lancaster. Then he thought of Deputy Munford's beautiful face and his heart dropped. The odds of her playing him for a fool had just gone up.

Then he turned around and flinched, because Deputy Munford stood only a few feet away.

"... of the firehouse?"

"Uh ... sorry ... what was that?"

Deputy Munford was staring, listening. And for how long? He turned away and walked down the sidewalk.

"I asked if you know where my wife's family's place is, a few miles south of the abandoned firehouse on 328?"

"Yes, I do."

"Good. Bring every gun you have and plenty of ammo. See you there as soon as possible. Don't tell anyone about this, do you hear me? Anyone."

"Sir, my car just broke down."

"What?"

Rachette felt like a kid who'd just told his father he'd crapped his pants. "It just died. Minutes ago."

Burton exhaled hard into the phone. "Can you fix it?"

Rachette calculated the odds of that. "No."

"Can you get another car? From a friend?"

He looked back and saw that Munford was still standing on the sidewalk, still intently listening to his every word.

"I'll work on it."

Burton said nothing for a few seconds and then hung up.

Rachette pocketed his phone and walked to her.

"Jack Wolf is missing?" Munford asked. "Dave Wolf's son?"

He ignored her, scrolling in his mind through the images of his friends outside the force and the vehicles they drove. He crossed off the first three guys he could think of. Two of them rode their bicycles everywhere and used the bus to get to work in the winter, and the third one would never let him use his BMW SUV. Not in a million years, unless maybe he told him about Jack being in danger, which Burton had instructed him not to.

"And you were talking about your car being dead, right? Do you need a ride somewhere?"

For an instant, he was sucked into her eyes, then snapped out of it. "I don't know what you're talking about."

"You said, *Sir, thank God you called. Patterson says Jack Wolf is missing.* That's what I heard you say into the phone. I was right here. Then you said, *My car just broke down.*" She tapped her ear. "I have pretty good hearing."

Idiot. How had he not seen her?

"Tom, tell me, do you need help? Do you need a ride somewhere?"

"No." He thought of another friend he drank beers with at Beer Goggles, but he didn't have the guy's number and had no clue where he lived. "Shit. Maybe."

Munford's voice softened. "Listen, if you need help, we're here. Jack Wolf is missing? Let's get everyone mobilized, damn it."

"No. No. It's not like that. I was mistaken."

She straightened. "So he's not missing?"

Rachette thought of Gail Olson's seductive smile, and of the humiliation that had followed. It had been the start of this entire mess.

He held out his hand. "Just give me your keys."

"Yeah, right."

His hand-held air for another few seconds and he lowered it. "Shit."

For a second he entertained the idea of forcibly taking the keys from her pocket. But she'd heard his phone conversation. Even if he managed to wrestle her keys away from her, she would go inside and tell MacLean what he'd said. Burton had specifically told him to keep the information on the down low.

Hell, he didn't even know which cruiser she drove. He'd probably still be outside in the lot searching for her vehicle when the bulk of the department came out to chase after him.

He looked to the sky, hoping a solution would present itself.

Why was Jack with Burton? And why did Patterson think he was missing? He must be in danger. Burton had said to bring every gun and all the ammo he had.

"Hey, you look like you're about to have a seizure. You want my help or not? Either way, I have to tell you, Rachette, as a cop I'm not comfortable keeping silent with this. You say Jack Wolf is missing? And you want me to walk away and pretend I didn't hear that? No can do."

He wiped the sweat beading on his forehead.

She stepped forward and hypnotized him. "Hey, I'm paired with Deputy Wilson. He just went inside to use the restroom. When he gets back out, we'll take you wherever you need to go. You can tell us all about it. Okay? Great."

Rachette stared at her. It was impossible to say no to her, but more importantly, it was the best choice he had. The only choice. Rachette's read on this woman was a moot point. And besides Patterson and Wolf, Wilson was as trustworthy as they came.

"Okay, Munford, you win. I'll take that ride."

"Yeah?" She nodded. "Okay, good. I just want to help."

"But if you try to screw me over, I'll kill you."

She chuckled. "Oh really?"

Rachette stared at her.

She hardened her gaze and nodded, then cracked a smile. "I'd like to see you try."

"I'm sorry, Munford, but I'm serious. About this, I'm dead serious. Dave Wolf has killed people to protect me. I wouldn't hesitate one second to do the same to protect his only son."

She narrowed her eyes. "Okay, I think you've officially turned me on, Tom Rachette."

His face caught fire.

Burton was going to be pissed.

CHAPTER 26

As Pope drove Pepper's truck over another batch of rocks sticking out of the unmaintained road, he grasped the wheel with both hands to counter the terrible pull to the left, hoping the neglected, piece of crap, whining engine would make it to camp.

His left forearm skin stung when he flexed his hand. No longer pink from the smeared blood, it now glowed bright red, having been slow roasted through the untinted window on the drive.

His sunscreen was in his truck. His truck that had been stolen by David Wolf and that field goal kicker fed bitch.

He'd be able to borrow a shirt from someone, but he'd never show such weakness as to ask whether any of the men at the compound had sunscreen. Damn his pigment-free skin in the Colorado altitude.

Clenching the wheel, he slowed at the barbed-wire fence and was glad to see that there was no one in sight.

He stopped and cranked down the window.

A few seconds later, a man dressed in full camouflage and carrying an M4 Carbine assault rifle stepped from the trees.

It was Andre. The overweight man squinted and paused at the sight of Pope.

Shirtless and redder than usual, he didn't blame Andre for giving a long second look.

Pope held his breath and watched the M4's barrel closely. It pointed at the ground, never wavering. Andre's finger remained outside the trigger guard.

The compound sentinel gave him a knowing nod and Pope returned the gesture. Keeping a confident air about himself, Pope let off the brake and drove up the double track.

In a matter of minutes, his ambitions would be realized. Or not. He would live, or he would die.

And what if he lived, and all went to plan here? Despite the incredibly important moment facing him now, he forced himself to think even further ahead.

Because his truck had been stolen along with his phone. Those two things alone spelled trouble.

But it was not the feds who had shown up at the storage unit. It had been David Wolf and that woman, who he now knew was Special Agent Kristen Luke, who had been Agent Tedescu's partner until Pope had emptied his brains onto his entryway floor.

Special Agent Luke was being pursued by the feds, just like Wolf. She was helping the former sheriff because she probably knew the truth. Tedescu had probably told her. Luckily, he'd gotten to the storage unit first and burned all the waiting evidence.

The solution to the remaining problem was clear: Two people had to die.

As he trundled up the bumpy road through the thick lodge pole pines, his inner strength swelled, thinking about the people he'd killed in the past couple of days—all the tiny explosions of red flesh, the streaming blood from gaping wounds.

It was a shame what all these incompetent bastards in the organization made him do. It was no different than the marines had been—they were dropping the ball and he had to take over.

If he'd wanted to, he could have ripped the steering wheel right off with the surge of adrenaline-fed rage that coursed through him.

As he pulled out into the clearing and drove to the doublewide trailers, a swarm of men appeared at the sight of the truck. Some were armed. Most were not.

The sight of Pope inside the vehicle, rather than Pepper, had apparently caused a stir, and those who were armed fondled their rifles—a subconscious preparation of what was to come.

Pope parked and opened the door. Stepping out into the sun, he felt his bare shoulders sizzle under the ultraviolet radiation.

The metal door to the nearest doublewide squeaked open and the Chairman loomed in the doorway. "Pope," his deep voice boomed.

Pope nodded.

The steps squealed under the Chairman's ample weight and then the ground crunched under each footfall. His chin raised and his head tilted to the side, his waxed pate reflecting a tiny version of the sun.

Under the Chairman's gray army T-shirt, ham-like pectoral muscles flexed in turn, pushing the talisman that hung around his neck back and forth.

Pope stood still, fixing a perfect poker face, ignoring the searing glare off his own bare skin.

"Where's Pepper?" the Chairman asked.

"I killed him with a pair of bolt cutters."

The Chairman chuckled as if he was kidding, then nodded at Pope's unflinching gaze. "You look like shit. You know, they told me what some of the men have been calling you lately. *The Pope*."

The Chairman's voice was like a trained actor's. He projected himself well when he needed to.

The men shuffled near one another, keeping a safe distance from the confrontation. Just watching the Chairman in action could get you killed. Stray bullets were certainly about to fly.

"The Pope? You know what I see? I see Poop. I think I'll call you Poop." The man's silverback-gorilla torso bounced up and down as he chuckled.

Three other men in the crowd laughed. Pope knew exactly which three without looking.

"I didn't think you'd be showing your face here ever again."

"Why's that?" Pope asked, matching the Chairman's theatrical volume.

The Chairman stopped ten paces away. "You've put the entire operation in danger. Killing our insurance with the FBI? Killing that real-estate agent in Rocky Points? Killing the runner bitch from Ashland? And I hear your plans are going to shit."

My plans? There was a traitor.

Pope pointed at the Chairman and raised his voice higher. "You put the entire operation in danger long ago. Two FBI agents were running our organization, because you let them."

"Running our organization? They were—"

"They were not insurance, they were a liability, and you sat back and let it happen." Pope shook his head in disgust. "Hell, you didn't care. You've still been getting your cut. But what about us?" Pope extended his arms and twirled in a circle. "What about these men and their families? You're bringing in more partners, and we're getting pushed out on profits. But we're the ones putting ourselves in danger out there!"

None of the men in the crowd made a sound or moved a muscle.

The Chairman took a step forward. His lip curled and his fists clenched into bowling balls. The man had a volcanic temper, and this was a look they all knew well. Mutinous talk like this was not tolerated in the least, and death was coming soon. Doled out by the Chairman himself.

Once, Pope had watched the Chairman strangle a man to death with one hand while punching him with the other. The men that day had all stood in silence, listening to the connections of fist on face mixed with gurgling, each man unable or afraid to look away until the Chairman was done with his tirade of violence, which had been minutes after the man had actually died.

Pope had also seen the Chairman kill twice by gunfire. Each man had been made to suffer long with shots to the arms and kneecaps, the gut, and only after were they put out of their misery with a headshot.

But Pope did not intend to die by the Chairman's hand today.

By God, he hoped not.

Raising his chin high, he puffed out his shirtless chest and pointed at the Chairman again. "Your time is up, Chairman. I've removed the FBI infiltration, which was something you should have done at the beginning. I've fixed your mess and ensured the future of this organization. Once again, we're going to be free to do business the way it was done before you took over, when we thrived under our own organization rules.

Not under the thumbs of a couple of crooked FBI agents that you didn't have the balls to stand up to."

Two men stepped out of the crowd. Both holding M4 carbines, they flanked the Chairman and faced Pope. Their eyes were relaxed and malicious.

Pope's palms began to sweat.

The Chairman smiled and stepped up between the gun-wielding men. "Your time is up, Poop. This conversation is over." He turned to one of the men and held out his hand. "Give me your M4."

The man turned, raised the barrel, and fired three shots into the Chairman's muscled thigh.

"Ahh!"

Pope stepped forward, watching the Chairman writhe on the ground. Blood soaked the man's desert camos. Arterial spurts flowed between his fingers.

The man who'd shot him, Luther, gave Pope the M4 and stepped away.

Three pistol shots rang out somewhere behind them, and the men shuffled and murmured in surprise, but Pope kept his attention on the Chairman's squirming form.

Raising the M4, he aimed at the Chairman's face.

The Chairman opened his mouth to speak.

He pulled the trigger, silencing him for good with a three-round burst to his face.

Handing back the gun to Luther, he reached down and unclasped the talisman from Fred Fontaine's dead neck.

Fingers drenched in blood, Pope stood up and placed it around his own neck.

The medallion known as "the talisman," which hung from a silver chain, was a symbol of the Chairman's power within the organization, and now its warm metal rested on Pope's chest.

It was heavier than he'd imagined it would be. Perhaps it was a harbinger of the responsibility to come.

Raising his hands, he turned full circle once again, giving the men a good look at the historic moment. He made sure that there was no mistaking what had just happened.

Half the men, those who called Pope "The Pope" with genuine reverence, had known this moment was coming. The other half looked down at the three lifeless bodies among them, and the dead Chairman in front of them, and understood—those who were against the changing tide would be dealt with accordingly.

Every man raised his right hand in a fist and hailed him.

"Chairman!" they chanted.

Pope reveled in the glory of the moment for a good sixty seconds and then whisked himself up the steps and into the command building.

Luther and Trey, the two men with the M4s, followed closely.

The door shut behind them, and the noise of the men was drowned out and replaced by a tiny radio playing classic rock. Pope flicked it off and the three men stood in silence.

Pope paced on the low-pile carpet for a few moments, listening to the squeak of the decaying wood underneath. It smelled like coffee and old food. He would need to change that, but there was work to do first.

"We have trouble," he said.

The two men looked at each other.

"The sheriff. Wolf. He's escaped the FBI's clutches, and he's with a rogue agent who's helping him. A woman. I destroyed the information in the storage unit."

Luther nodded. "And?"

"After I burned it, Wolf and this FBI bitch showed up.

They took my truck and phone." He paced some more. "They need to die, fast. We need to move. Get ten men ready. We move in ten minutes. We'll convene at GH 3. It's nearest Rocky Points."

"Wait a minute," Trey said.

Pope felt a flash of rage, but let it dissipate. Trey was much taller and bigger, and he was holding an M4. "What?"

"You killed the lawyer and his family, correct?" Trey asked.

Pope considered not responding—as of two minutes ago, he answered to no man in this organization—but Luther looked interested. It was good leadership to get other men involved. "Yes."

"And you got the second agent this morning."

"Yes."

"That's the original FBI threat taken care of, but what is this female FBI agent doing with Wolf? Who is she?"

Pope stared at Trey. "Agent Tedescu's new partner."

Trey rolled his eyes. "Shit. So she might know everything, right along with this guy Wolf. Tedescu could have easily told her. And now they have your phone and truck?"

Pope walked to the paper-strewn desk and started opening and closing drawers. In the third drawer there was a Glock sitting on a notebook.

"So we've got to move on this Wolf guy," Trey said as if it were his own original thought. "And this other agent. Or else we're really screwed. Where are they now?"

Pope picked up the gun and checked the chamber for a round. Then, with his trophy-winning speed, he aimed and pulled the trigger, shooting Trey between the eyes.

As Trey's eyes rolled into the back of his head, the M4 exploded in fire, three rounds spraying into the wood-paneled wall. Then his body collapsed to the floor.

Pope aimed through the smoke at Luther. "You want to tell me some more things I already know?"

Luther shook his head. "We move in ten minutes."

Pope slid the Glock in his pants and nodded. "Get eight men now that Trey's decided to quit. Then we move. Trey was right about everything. We have to kill these two, the ex-sheriff and FBI agent, or we're screwed." He looked at the wall clock. "Is that right? The time?"

Luther pulled out his phone and checked it. "Yeah."

"We still have five men worth a shit near Rocky Points, so I called and mobilized them. They know what to look for—my pickup truck—and they know where to look for it—on County 17 between Carbondale and Rocky Points. There's no way they're going to risk coming in on highways with all the attention they're getting from law enforcement."

"Who's in Rocky Points? Fellman and Larson? That crew?"

Pope nodded with a confident smile.

Luther smiled back. Besides Pope, Fellman and Larson were the two most ruthless and clever men in the organization.

"They're setting up an ambush."

"Time till engagement?"

Pope glanced at the clock again. "Thirty minutes."

Luther nodded, looking like he had another question but was afraid to ask.

"What?"

Luther shook his head. "Nothing."

"Just ask. I'm not going to shoot you."

He stood straight. "And if they get through the ambush?"

Pope hid the welling anger. "Then we'll hold a knife to the kid's throat to smoke them out. Then we'll cut off his head in front of them. Then we'll give the bitch to Reichlund, and if she's not dead after that we'll give her to the rest of the men until she is. And only then, after that guy Wolf watches the entire thing, will we start on him."

Averting his eyes, Luther looked down at the lifeless man at his feet and swallowed. He was probably thinking how much the dead man had sacrificed to get Pope into power, only minutes ago shooting the deadliest man Luther had ever known in the leg, and how quickly Pope had disposed of him for insubordination.

That's the kind of leader Pope was going to be. "Move. And get someone to clean this shit up."

Luther nodded and was out the door.

Pope's body was electrified. He felt a pang of regret looking down at Trey, but knew he needed to be quick and decisive, using measured doses of violence to rule this dangerous mob of men.

So help him, if these two weren't taken out, the violence was going to be biblical.

CHAPTER 27

WOLF'S HEAD bumped against something and he opened his eyes.

After a couple of blinks, he realized he'd hit his head on a window inside a truck cab, and then he remembered just where he was and who he was with.

"He lives!"

He stretched his arms and straightened up in the ample passenger seat. "How long was I sleeping?"

"An hour and a half."

"Where are we?"

Luke jabbed a thumb backwards. "About fifteen miles past Aspen."

They were rumbling on a two-lane dirt road through God's country. The hills on either side of them glowed yellow from the changing aspen leaves, with an occasional blood-red burst of color near the sparkling river to Wolf's right. Steep hills and mountains sculpted from brown and maroon earth flanked either side.

"What time is it?"

"Three p.m. We'll get into Rocky Points in an hour, hour and a half."

Wolf found an unopened water bottle in their sack of groceries and took a swig. The cool liquid filled his belly and gave him energy.

"You're looking decent."

Wolf noticed that Luke had pulled her hair back again. Her face was cleaned of any soot and when she smiled there was no more discoloration on her teeth.

"Ditto. Except for the slouch outfit, of course."

She looked down and rubbed the soot marks on her T-shirt, brushing up against one of her breasts in the process. "Did the job, didn't it?"

Wolf nodded absently, watching her hand slide across her chest.

"You men are always looking a foot and a half lower than you should be."

He raised his gaze and felt his face redden.

"See?" She shook her head. "Bunch of simpletons. Every last one of you."

He thought about the pile of charred papers and pictures again. "We should have taken all that burned stuff. We could have sifted through it more carefully to get an idea of what we were looking at."

"We need to give ourselves a break. We narrowly missed getting killed by that guy, and then we had him unconscious and bleeding on the floor with cops driving up on us."

Wolf looked at her. "What happened to the doom-and-gloom woman I was riding with earlier?"

"She was hungry."

Another grove of aspens flicked by the window. "It was a

pile of papers that guy was willing to kill for. Willing to kill an entire family for."

Luke's eyes glazed over, as if the images of the dead family were haunting her.

"You said there was an envelope at the family's house? Just an empty envelope?"

Luke blinked. "Yep."

"Was there any writing on it?"

"None. I remember thinking it wasn't mail. No stamps or postmarks. It was torn on the top and empty."

"Did you know the lawyer?"

"No. Never seen him before. But my SAC said he worked with some of the agents in the Bureau."

"Worked with Tedescu?"

She nodded. "Sure seemed like it. I'm not sure why else we would've been there. I guess he could have been a family friend."

They came around a bend and started down a long straight-away. The road cut through a grove of trees with gold leaves shimmering in the afternoon light.

"What do you think that guy's going to do when he gets out of that storage unit?" Wolf asked.

"Gets out? We have his phone and his gun. There were no tools in there to help him out."

"Yeah, but someone could drive up, maybe go into another storage unit down the row, and he could yell for help."

"What are the odds of that? Nil. That guy is screwed. He's gonna starve in there. I hope it's a cold one tonight."

Wolf shook his head. "No, he'll get out today. There's secu-rity at those places. People who work there. If it were me, I'd just bang on the door until someone let me out. Someone would hear the racket. He'll get out."

They rode in silence for a beat. "So what? What are you saying?"

"I'm saying I wish I'd killed that guy. I'm really regretting that I didn't."

She turned down the radio and they both rode in silence.

Wolf opened the glove compartment and took out the Beretta pistol he'd taken from the tattooed man. Racking the slide back, he made sure it was loaded and then put it back in and shut the compartment.

"You thinking we're in danger from him?"

A sudden, uncomfortable feeling came over him and he scooted forward in his seat, seeing the upcoming straight stretch of heavily forested road in a new light.

"What?"

"Slow down."

"What? Why?"

She let off the gas and pressed the brake, slowing to twenty miles per hour.

Twice, Wolf and his squad had been caught in ambushes in his six-tour service as an army ranger. Both times he'd had the same feeling after the carnage had been over—that he'd sensed it before it had happened. Many of the other men swore the same thing. Before both ambushes, their staff sergeant had been vocal about anyone speaking up if they felt anything was off. Both times, the ambushes had happened anyway.

After that, they'd been one of the most skittish and reactive squads the army had ever known. It was a trait that was now ingrained in Wolf's DNA.

A discoloration in the trees caught Wolf's eye. It was silver and shiny, the chrome bumper of a vehicle.

Quickly, he dropped the glove compartment door and pulled out the Beretta, spilling papers out onto his feet.

"Shit, what?"

Pressing his face against the window as they passed the vehicle, he saw it was a big Dodge truck backed into the trees.

Two men sat inside with their elbows out the windows, and both locked eyes with Wolf.

The last fleeting image Wolf saw before it disappeared behind the foliage was the passenger bringing a radio to his mouth.

"Stop!"

Luke mashed the brakes and the rear end swung to the side as they skidded to a halt.

A cloud of dust enveloped them, but not before Wolf caught a glimpse of a patch of red in the trees up ahead on the right.

"We're being ambushed."

Luke squinted and peered over her shoulder. "What? That truck back there?"

"Yes. Get in the back—I'm driving." Wolf took off his seatbelt and started climbing toward her.

She froze for an instant and then sprang into action, flying out of the seat and diving into the back of the cab.

Wolf crammed himself into the seat, which was way too close to the wheel for him, shifted into reverse, and pushed the accelerator.

The diesel engine roared and rocks spat forward as they reversed. He looked over his shoulder, and though it was almost impossible to see through the dark tints and multiple panes of glass, he kept his foot pushed to the floor anyway.

"Open that back window. When we hit them, take out the passenger. Shoot through the window."

"Hit them?" Luke reached up, one hand holding her pistol and the other unlatching the slide window and pulling it open.

Wolf was completely blind now, but sensed they'd reached their target. "Get down!"

She ducked out of the way and he saw he was nearly too late.

Wrenching the wheel to the right, the rear wheels careened off the road and bounced through a dip. He sagged and then shot up in his seat, and his head connected with the roof.

Next, he slammed back into the seat as the truck stopped with a metallic thud.

Feeling the pistol still firm in his hand, he opened the door and got out as fast as he could. Immediately he stumbled, the ground lower than he'd expected.

Landing on one knee, he felt plastic and metal shards needle into his back as a barrage of bullets smacked into the open door.

He dropped all the way down and started pulling the trigger. Only after the second shot did he have a bead on the blaze of fire coming out of the muzzle of an automatic rifle near the trunk of a tree ahead. The third shot was properly aimed, and so were the fourth and fifth. The incoming fire stopped.

Springing to his feet, his ears rang and his eyes stung from the gunpowder smoke as he aimed at the windshield of the truck behind them. The interior cab behind the cracked glass was empty.

Ducking just in time, he stumbled forward as the cab of their truck again exploded in a mayhem of glass and plastic, and then just as quickly it stopped after two muffled shots came from inside their truck bed.

With raised pistol, Wolf stepped to the tree trunk where he'd downed the man and fired two more rounds into a still, bleeding figure lying on the ground, sealing the deal.

He bent over and wrenched the M4 out of the man's

hands, searing his own fingers on the muzzle. The strap caught under the man's arm and he stepped on the corpse's bearded face for leverage to pull it free.

"I got him!" Luke yelled from the back of the truck.

Wolf's hearing was still muted from the gunfire, but he could hear the gurgle of the still-running diesel engine. He sprinted back to the truck, got into the seat, shifted into drive, and stepped on the gas again.

He took a right, toward the second waiting ambush vehicle, which was now pulling out onto the road.

Wolf glanced in the rearview and saw Luke tumbling back in the bed of the truck, light streaming in on the side where she'd shot out the glass.

"Get down and hang on!"

Another big, four-door, diesel pickup wobbled onto the road, then jammed to a stop halfway out, the driver clearly shocked at the sight of them speeding toward him at fifty miles per hour.

Wolf kept his foot on the gas and the speedometer needle climbed higher.

When they were a mere fifty yards away, he swung the truck to the left side of the road to pass and saw three men tumbling out of the doors with guns in hand.

A smattering of bullets connected with the passenger side of the truck as they sped by, leaving the men in a cloud of roiling dust.

They were now up to seventy miles per hour. A bend to the right approached fast and Wolf jammed the brakes. Sliding on all four wheels, he was lucky the turn was gentle, but there was a sharp curve to the left ahead.

Foot still pressing hard on the brake, the beast of a vehicle underneath them fishtailed back and forth. By the time he hit the sharp turn, he'd dropped to a safe twenty miles per hour and they took the curve easily enough. Once around the other side, he pulled to the left shoulder, stopped, and got out onto the road.

"Careful." Luke poked her head out the broken window of the truck-bed topper.

With the M4 in his clutches, he sprinted back to the sharp curve.

Over his straining breath, the pulse pounding in his head, and a tinnitus onslaught in his left eardrum, he heard the approach of a diesel engine coming around the bend.

He slid to a stop, raised the M4 to his shoulder, and fired the instant the red hood of the truck came into view.

With the first three shots, his aim climbed too high, so with the second three round burst he compensated for the muzzle kick, and red spray and flailing limbs told him he'd hit the mark. The truck revved as it rolled out of sight over the edge of the road. Then there was crunching metal, and then there was nothing.

Turning back to the truck, he raised the M4 again, briefly aiming at Luke, who stood in the road, and then beyond her.

He walked forward and kept the rifle aimed up the road, toward danger that never showed itself.

"Holy crap." A stream of blood flowed from a cut below Luke's eye.

"Are you okay?" he asked.

She nodded.

"You're bleeding."

She touched it absently. "Whatever. You think that's all of them?"

He turned around. There was no sound, save the burbling

river below. No sign of movement or men crawling up onto the road.

"It looks like you got them."

He remembered the spray of blood and lowered the rifle. "Yeah. You drive. I'll cover us just in case there's more ahead."

The truck ticked loudly as they climbed in, and Wolf wondered if the sound was normal or if a bullet had caught something vital under the hood. But it fired up fine, and drove well enough as they sped away.

"We can't drive this thing much longer," Luke said.

Wolf nodded, leaning forward and checking the side-view mirror, which was cracked up the middle and had a hole through it. The passenger side of the truck was punched with dozens of holes, mostly concentrated in the door, and the rear topper window was smashed out, clearly by gunfire. "Yeah. Kind of draws attention, doesn't it?"

Luke drove fast, sliding around the next corner.

CHAPTER 28

RACHETTE, Wilson, and Munford drove the final leg of a circuitous route to Burton's wife's cabin.

It was a route that Rachette had insisted on, and in Wilson's family vehicle rather than a department cruiser, which he'd also insisted on. It was one thing that Rachette was bringing two deputies to the meeting place Burton had specified he come alone. It was another that one of the deputies he brought was from Byron County. There was no way in hell he was going to compound Burton's anger by leading anyone to their destination via GPS receiver or any other method.

He gave the side-view mirror of Wilson's Chevy Suburban the hawk eye again and leaned back.

"Relax," Wilson said. "We're not being followed."

Wilson's calming voice did little to loosen Rachette's clenched jaw.

The truth was, he was scared of Burton and always had been. The man was a bear. Sure, a fat, old, out-of-shape bear, but the guy still had fangs and claws and growled pretty loud.

"Here." Rachette pointed up at the next turn off. "Up there."

Wilson slowed and took the turn, and they headed up a hill through the woods.

"It's just up here."

"I know, I've been here before. You know, I'm sure Burton was about to call me, too. No way I'm staying out of this anyway. I'll stick up for my presence. This isn't all on you."

Rachette ignored him, though the words made perfect sense.

He glanced back at Munford, who sat with her hands folded on her lap and staring out the window. Her presence was another matter altogether.

"Just stay in here for a second until we talk to Burton, okay?" he said to her.

Munford's eyelids slid down and she gave him a death stare.

She was pissed. Clearly ditching the Sheriff's Department SUV at Wilson's, stopping by Rachette's to grab supplies, then driving aimlessly through the woods for an hour to get to this point without having a say in the matter had crossed a line in her mind.

"Thanks," he said.

As they reached the cabin, they pulled up next to four trucks parked along the trees. The smell of wood smoke permeated the vents into the SUV's cab, and a haze outside came from a flickering campfire where a group of men sat staring at their approach.

Burton stood in front of the others with squinted eyes. With a shake of his head he walked over.

"Here we go." Rachette slid out of the Suburban.

"Who the hell?" Burton demanded, and then he slowed. "Wilson? I just called you. Why didn't you answer?"

Wilson eyed his phone and nodded at Rachette. "Must've been shoddy reception. We've been driving through the middle of nowhere for a while, making sure we weren't followed."

Burton tilted up his camouflage hat and nodded at Rachette.

Rachette shook his big warm hand, noticing the revolver holstered on the old man's hip beneath his flannel shirt.

Standing straight, Burton lowered his silver caterpillar eyebrows as he studied the back seat. "Who the hell is that?"

"Sir, I know you said to not tell any Byron people ..." Rachette glanced at Wilson.

"But she's my partner, and I can vouch for her," Wilson said. "Her name's Deputy Munford."

Munford took her cue and climbed out of the back seat. She stood tall with her nose in the air and slammed the door behind her.

Rachette cringed, waiting for the confrontation.

Burton petted his mustache and eyed her up and down. It was impossible to tell the draw of his lips underneath the walrus-like growth of hair, which was another reason Rachette could never get a good read on the old man.

With a flip of his hand, Burton turned and walked to the campfire. "Get your asses over here."

"I think he likes me," Munford murmured on the way by.

They walked to the fire and everyone stood from their camping chairs and log seats to greet them.

Burton turned abruptly and shook Munford's hand, staring her in the eye. "I'm Burton. Hal Burton. I used to be—"

"Sheriff of Sluice County, before David Wolf. I know, sir."

Burton tilted his head and nodded. "This is Martin Running Warrior."

The cocoa-skinned Navajo took off a turquoise beaded cowboy hat, revealing long silver hair pulled into a pony tail.

His expressionless eyes were like pools of coffee, the muscles in his extended arm like steel cable.

Though his skin was like worn leather his age was impossible to tell, thought Rachette, as he took the man's iron grip.

As Martin put his hat back on, he winced in pain. The last time Rachette had seen him, he'd been lying in a pool of blood on the side of a mountain, shot through the shoulder. Wolf had pulled Martin out of danger that day, staunched the bleeding of his wound, and had called for help.

Burton motioned to another man. "Phillip Chesmith."

The man was younger, Wolf's age, and was vaguely familiar to Rachette. He had a full head of shaggy brown hair and wild blue eyes. "Hi."

"Fabian Michaels."

Rachette paused. This man was well known by all as the owner of the crystal and spiritual healing shop in town. Normally dressed head to toe in hemp clothing, with long blond hair hanging loose on his shoulders, now he was dressed in all black, his hair pulled up inside a black winter cap. On his hip was a scoped pistol, and on his shoulder hung an assault rifle.

"Hi Tom. Nice to see you." Fabian grasped Rachette's hand in both of his and gazed into his eyes as if reading his aura.

"Hi Fabian." Rachette nodded to his assault rifle. "Didn't know you were a gun enthusiast."

He smiled and pulled it from his shoulder in a lightning move. "This? I'll give you a good price."

"Uh ... no thanks."

"I'm just kidding, Tom. No way I'd sell. Who's this?" Fabian grabbed Munford's hand and kissed it.

She frowned and pulled it back.

Burton cleared his throat and continued the introductions. "Nate Watson."

Rachette knew Nate well. He stood at Rachette's height and filled out his clothes with roughly the same build. Nate had been Wolf's best friend since high school, and Rachette had always had a special kinship with him.

"Hey, buddy." Nate wrapped his muscular arms around Rachette and then turned to Munford with an extended hand.

Munford nodded. "Hello. Charlotte. You can call me Munford, I guess."

"Nate. Nice to meet you."

"And this is Jack."

They all turned to Wolf's son.

Jack stood taller than all of them except for Wilson, but his presence was almost unnoticeable. He stood with stooped shoulders, and his normally vibrant kelp eyes looked sunken, and were focused on the ground.

Rachette had not spoken to Jack for months. Not since his mother's death. There had been a single time when he'd seen Jack on the street and greeted him, and Jack had turned away without a response.

"Hey, Jack." Rachette held out his hand.

Jack grabbed it with a limp wrist and gave it a single pump, never getting anywhere close to eye contact.

Rachette turned away as if their awkward greeting was nothing out of the ordinary, reminding himself that this kid had lost his mother, and now these men were whisking him away and hiding him in the woods, while his father was being chased by the FBI and law enforcement. It was hard enough being fourteen without all that.

"Take out your phones, please," Burton said.

Wilson and Munford looked at one another while Rachette dug his out of his pocket.

"It's not optional." Burton held out his hand. One by one, he relayed the devices to Nate, who removed the batteries and SIM cards.

Burton stepped in front of Munford and glared at her.

Munford looked vaguely uncomfortable, but held his gaze.

"So, what exactly is going on?" Rachette asked. "Have you told Patterson the truth about Jack not being missing yet?"

Burton kept his eyes on Munford. "No. Like I said, we can't trust anyone from Byron, and Patterson's paired with that Lancaster guy. Along with MacLean, he's Byron's poster boy."

"Sir, I was on the phone and she overheard me. I had no choice."

Munford glared at Rachette with something resembling disappointment on her face.

He shrugged. "What?"

"I was in front of the station and overheard Deputy Rachette say that Jack Wolf was missing," Munford said. "He was clearly distraught, and then he told you, or whoever he was talking to, that his car had broken down. I offered him a ride."

Burton looked at Rachette. The disappointment there was clear enough.

"He had no choice," Munford said. "I told him that I'd go to MacLean with the information I'd heard. I'm a cop. You don't go hearing that a kid's missing and then just shrug it off when someone says, *Just kidding*. I told him I would take him where he needed to go, or I would leave him and continue investigating myself."

Burton's mustache curled and his eyes creased. A smile? Rachette couldn't tell.

"Well, you're about to hear some things that you'll just

have to shrug off, as you put it. I know you've never met David Wolf. Never worked with him like these two have. Never had your life saved by him like Martin, Fabian and Phillip have. And never known him like Nate and I or Jack have, or the rest of Rocky Points knows him for that matter.

"I know you're more inclined to believe the bullshit that's going on right now. You're more inclined to believe that just because the evidence says so, that David Wolf has shot and killed all those people." Burton walked up behind Jack, who was now seated in a camping chair next to the fire, and squeezed his shoulders. "One of whom was the love of his life and this boy's mother. But he sure as hell didn't kill anyone."

Munford looked down at Jack and then up at Burton. Her chin was still raised in defiance, her eyes staring hard.

"Wolf's been in touch," Burton said.

Rachette perked up. "Really? Where?"

"He didn't say, and it doesn't matter. He just wanted to make sure Jack is safe, and we're here to do that."

Rachette eyed Jack for a response, but he was still a zombie, eyes transfixed on the fire.

Munford eyed the men in turn around her. Her breathing quickened and she stutter-stepped forward an inch.

"Deputy Munford," Burton said, "you want to talk about it?"

"I just ... didn't know I was getting into this."

"You don't know the half of it. Deputy Rachette, did you bring your guns?"

Rachette nodded. "In the car, sir."

Munford glared at him, realizing the significance of why Rachette had insisted on stopping at his house for a long black duffel bag, and that it had not only been camping gear he needed for tonight. "Okay, now you guys are scaring me."

Burton nodded. "Good. This is definitely a situation where it's appropriate to be nervous."

Then she made a mistake. Her hand lifted and rested on her holstered Glock, and in an instant five pistols were pointed at her head.

"You don't want to do that," Burton said as he cocked back the hammer of his revolver.

Wilson and Rachette stared at one another.

Munford slowly lifted her hand from her pistol and then held out the other.

Jack shifted in his seat. His teeth were bared and his eyes reflected the flames. "What are you guys doing? You guys gonna start killing people for my dad? It's not enough that he killed my mom? You're gonna start killing cops for him?"

Rachette walked over and smacked Jack across the face before he'd even known what he was doing.

Jack cried out and looked up with shimmering eyes.

"You don't really think your dad did this, do you?" Rachette's chest heaved. He felt like someone was holding his heart in a fist. "Do you?"

Jack swallowed and looked back down at the fire.

"No! Look at me!"

Jack did.

"Shit. I can't believe ..." Burton put a hand on Rachette's shoulder but Rachette swiped it away. "Listen, Jack. We got a garbled phone call from someone the other day. It was an untraceable call with a voice-changing device." He looked at Burton. "Didn't you guys tell him any of this?"

Burton shook his head.

Of course they hadn't. They were coddling the kid, or probably hadn't heard all the up-to-date information. These men were acting on an unshakeable faith in David Wolf. What

216 / JEFF CARSON

they'd forgotten was that Jack's faith in his father had been shaken to the core.

"Jack. They're going after your dad for three murders: your mother, the guy in the car with her that night, and a girl they found a few days ago. All three people were killed with one gun. The anonymous phone call said that the gun in question would be found in your father's shed, and they found it there.

"There's a problem with this theory that your dad did it, though. First of all, the girl's body was twenty-five miles south of Rocky Points. You know there's only one way in and out of your dad's ranch. That means your dad would've had to drive past two FBI agents who were parked on that road to get there. Twice. But they didn't see him drive by, because he never did.

"Everyone in town knows he didn't do this, and even the FBI knows. You know Kristen Luke, right? She's the one who helped your dad escape. She's thrown away her entire career because she knows he's innocent."

"And the girl's mother's missing," Munford said.

Rachette looked at her. "What?"

"Gail Olson's mother went missing in Las Vegas," Munford said, "and they think that Gail Olson was killed then moved, not killed where they found her. They're saying now that she was killed up to twenty-four hours before they found her, and the post-mortem hypostasis and the position of the body didn't match up. She was bruised all down her side but was found on her back. I heard this a couple of hours ago."

Munford kept her hands out, staring down the barrel of Martin's Smith & Wesson. "I haven't even told Deputy Wilson about it yet. I heard it from a friend, a deputy who used to work in Byron County with me ... anyway, I hadn't gotten a chance to talk about it. I really hadn't even gotten time to think about it until now, because I ran into you, Rachette, and then this whole thing happened. But," she looked at Jack, "if you think about it, Gail Olson was missing for months. Maybe whoever was looking for her got to her through her mother in Vegas, and that's where they were both killed, and then Gail Olson was moved here to Colorado. Or something like that. But we know for a fact that your father has not traveled for months. The FBI can swear to that. He's been too laid up with his healing wounds to leave."

Jack stared at Munford with streaming eyes.

"Your dad didn't do any of this," Rachette said. "You know that, right?"

Jack's mouth spread wide and his eyes clenched shut, sending a fresh deluge of tears down his cheeks. He nodded and then his head dropped and his shoulders bounced as he sobbed.

Rachette knelt down and hugged him. "I'm so sorry I hit you, man. Shit, I'm so sorry. I'm sorry about everything."

A few minutes later, they all stood in the fading light, elated and energized by the tears that had flowed out of each of their eyes.

Nate handed Rachette, Munford, and Wilson their phones back, now with the SIM cards and batteries separate and loose.

Burton held out his hand to Munford. "Sorry. I'd still like to keep that. Just in case."

She looked at him. "Why do you think the Byron Department had something to do with this?"

"Just a precaution. Now hand it over, please."

She held the phone away from him. "I want to know. You said earlier that you haven't told Patterson about all this because of Lancaster. Why? You think our deputies are involved?"

"That's our initial suspicion. Wolf's initial suspicion. And Wolf is usually pretty tuned into things."

"I think it's smart not to tell Lancaster," she said. "I've always had a bad feeling about that guy. But I think Sheriff MacLean's a good man."

Burton stared at her, his hand extended.

She dropped her phone, her SIM, and the battery in the fire and swiped her hands together. "There. Now you know what side I'm on."

Burton dropped his arm.

They all gathered close to watch the electronic device sizzle and warp in the flames.

"That was completely unnecessary," Nate said.

"I disagree," Martin Running Warrior said. "Completely necessary. You all should follow her lead and toss your electronic collars into the fire."

After a moment of sober reflection, Burton roared with laughter. "Okay, you've won me over."

"That's not everyone she's won over," Wilson said.

"What?" Rachette's face fell. "Shut up."

"Move over, Patterson," Wilson continued. "Jack has a new crush."

Rachette broke into strained laughter and looked at Jack.

Jack shook his head and picked at a smudge on his jeans. His face bloomed crimson, almost as red as Rachette's felt.

"Let's get your hardware out of the car, Rachette. And now we have a lot more to talk about."

Nate led the way and Rachette followed.

On the way by, he snuck a glance at Munford and saw the tiny smile.

CHAPTER 29

PATTERSON PRESSED the call-end button on her phone and shrugged.

Lancaster kept his eyes locked on the road. "Still no answer?"

"Still no answer," she said. "They must be together."

The radio squawked to life. "Delta 329, please respond. Delta 329, please respond."

Tammy was calling for Deputy Wilson, who'd gone unaccounted for an hour ago, reported in by Deputy Yates, who had been trying to call Wilson earlier with no luck. Further investigation by Yates and his Byron County partner had shown that Wilson's squad SUV was parked at his house, and his family vehicle was missing.

This was the fourth try via dispatch that had gone unanswered, and Patterson was having no luck getting Wilson via phone.

She needed to look like Wilson's disappearance had totally bamboozled her.

Then there was Rachette. Clearly he had missed what she'd said about Lancaster, and her suspicions of him "being bad," as she'd put it. She'd barely gotten the sentence out of her mouth in time, but she was certain it had been undetected by Lancaster. And now every time she called Rachette, his phone went straight to voicemail.

Of course, she acted confused about that, too.

Nate Watson's absence at home tonight after work? That was odd.

She was out here on dark forest roads, pretending it was a mystery that Rachette, Wilson, Nate, and Jack Wolf were missing. She failed to mention that it would be a good idea to call Burton. Because it was too good an idea, and she already knew they were all together.

And she was here with this freaky-ass mute who reminded her of Lurch from *The Addams Family*. She could feel his beady eyes on her skin as he glanced between her and the road.

Then he pulled over without warning.

As the vehicle shuddered to a stop, she rehearsed counter-attacks in her mind: eye gouges, throat punches, pressure-point applications.

"What's up?" Her voice was tense, just like her muscles.

Lancaster lifted his phone and pecked the screen, ignoring her question.

Outside, the northern slopes of the ski resort were a silhouette dotted with lights in the post-sunset hour. The headlights illuminated a deer trotting out of the woods. It paused on the dirt road, showed its shining eyes, and then darted away.

"I'm not sure what to think about all this." Patterson swallowed.

Lancaster was a dark statue.

"You know, it's a little freaky when you just sit there all silent. Has anyone ever told you that?"

Lancaster looked up from his phone at her.

"Yeah. That's the freaky-ass look."

"Available units, we have a report of a stolen car and a vandalized truck at the Tackle Box Bar and Grill at Cold Lake Marina. Available units, please check in."

Patterson snatched the radio and pressed the button. "Bravo 39 responding."

Lancaster let off the brake and accelerated.

She half expected a showdown then and there with the big man, but apparently Lurch wanted to see what the commotion was.

"Copy. Bravo 39 responding to stolen car and vandalized truck at the Tackle Box Bar and Grill at Cold Lake Marina."

Cold Lake. Patterson thought about the bullet that had whizzed past her head that rainy day three and a half months ago, and then the sight of Wolf jumping headfirst off that cliff.

Her heart skipped a beat. That day was over. But something told her the danger wasn't.

Patterson and Lancaster pulled into the Cold Lake Marina parking lot in between two Sheriff's Department vehicles.

Outside, the humid, fishy air next to the lake carried a mix of music from the Tackle Box and the static voices of police radios. Turret lights flickered off the other parked cars, and as they ducked underneath the police tape they were hit with three flashlight beams.

Lancaster walked up to Deputy Baine. "What do you have?"

Baine started at the sudden presence of Lancaster next to him. "Oh, hey. Hey, Patterson." He composed

222 / JEFF CARSON

himself and waved them to the other side of the pickup truck, which was the focus of all the activity. "You can see here on this side—shot to hell with a bunch of 5.56 calibers."

"Any blood inside?" Patterson asked.

"None that looks like it's from gunshot wounds."

"What does that mean?" Patterson asked.

"There's a pair of leather gloves in the back of the cab with a couple of drops of blood on them, and a fast-food bag with some blood, too. Doesn't look fresh or like it's from the shots, though."

A light behind Baine drew Patterson's eye. It was a deputy with an LCD-screen device that lit up his face as he stared down at it. Their new portable fingerprint identifiers were a luxury that came with the new combined budgets of Sluice and Byron Counties.

"What do you have there, Deputy?"

Deputy Yates pulled his mask down, revealing his signature blond mustache, worn in a style that had been all the rage two hundred years ago.

"Oh, Yates," Patterson said. "What d'ya got?"

Yates beckoned them with a finger. "You guys should see this."

Lancaster led the way.

The cell-phone-sized digital screen showed a headshot picture of Special Agent Kristen Luke in a dark-blue suit. Yates pressed a button and it changed to a headshot of Wolf dressed in a brown sheriff's uniform.

"I found a lot of their prints," Yates said, "but most are from this guy."

He held up the device again and it showed a man with snow-white skin, almost albino. His eyes were baby blue rimmed red, unsmiling, just like the rest of his face. He was dressed in desert BDUs.

"Ex-military. A guy named Clayton Pope."

Two unmarked Ford sedans came squealing into the lot.

Agents Frye and Cumberland jumped out of one of the vehicles, and two other agents took up the rear.

"I want every law-enforcement officer over here now!" Agent Frye said as he ducked under the tape.

Yates, Baine, and Lancaster stood still as Frye came to them. The other three deputies on scene materialized from the other side of the lot and joined them.

"This is officially a federal crime scene from now on, and the deputies of Sluice–Byron County Sheriff's Department will proceed under my command." Frye held out his hand to Yates. "What did you find?"

Yates handed over the electronic device.

Frye handled the buttons like he'd invented the machine and then handed it to Cumberland. Frye mumbled something unintelligible to his fellow agent and Cumberland walked away.

Patterson watched Frye's mind work. First the agent checked the bullet holes.

"Caliber?" he asked no one in particular.

Yates cleared his throat. "5.56. There's a good one lodged in the center console."

Frye pointed at the license-plate shields on the truck. "Plates are missing. Is there registration inside?"

"No, sir," Yates said. "No insurance either."

Frye's lips drew in a tight line.

"The stolen car was a blue Ford Taurus," Yates said, "Those plates were found over there in the rocks, sir."

Frye nodded. "Call it in right now. BOLO for a blue Ford Taurus with male and female inside."

"Already done."

Patterson looked at Frye's expression—contemplation mixed with a dose of disappointment—and silently cheered for Wolf and Luke's tactics. They'd switched the plates from the truck to the car they'd stolen, and then removed the registration from the truck. It would buy them time.

Lancaster was staring at her again.

"What?"

He blinked and looked elsewhere.

"You have something to say, Patterson?" Frye walked over.

She shrugged and glanced back at the huge pickup in front of them, smashed in the rear and looking like a pasta strainer on the passenger side. "Looks like a bad-boy's truck. That Pope guy in the picture looked pretty bad to me. Muscular, a chip on his shoulder. Must be his truck. Lift kit, dark-tinted windows. I think he drove with road rage, and a sense of entitlement. The whole truck says, I'll drive over you if you get in my way, and I'll get away with it because you won't see me inside."

Frye smiled and shook his head. "I'd go along with that profile."

Baine snorted, and then swallowed when Patterson fired him a bullet look.

Cumberland returned with a sheet of paper in his hand and handed it to his boss. Frye read it and gave Cumberland a knowing look. Without a word, Cumberland walked away.

Frye nodded at Patterson. "Come with me, please." Then he ducked under the crime tape.

Patterson exchanged glances with Lancaster and Baine and followed after him.

The agent walked fast and far, through the cars of the parking lot, onto a strip of grass, and then down to the sand of the lakeshore. Only when the tiny waves splashed to within an inch of his shoes did he stop and turn around.

"Sir?" Patterson stopped a few yards away.

"Wolf and Luke steal a truck and come back in town. On the same day, Wolf's son goes missing. So do Tom Rachette and Deputies Wilson and Munford. Your aunt and mother helped get Wolf out, and all your buddies are helping him now that he's back in. And you're telling me you don't know anything about this?"

"No, sir."

Frye's face flickered blue and red. "Cumberland and I checked. There's a road across the valley from Wolf's ranch. It climbs up the mountainside, switching back and forth. We found the spot where you and Rachette said the FBI were watching Wolf's house."

"Whatever. We saw you up there."

"We weren't up there. But we found evidence that someone was. There was a pile of cigarette butts, all with the same fingerprints on them. Ran the prints and came up with a match."

She frowned. "Yeah?"

"Turns out the man has quite a sheet. Done time in state. Works at a place called Ashland Moving and Storage."

"So you're serious. You guys weren't watching him. It was someone else?"

"If you know where Wolf is, you need to tell me right now."

"I don't." She looked back toward the parking lot. "Sir, why are you talking to me way out here?"

"We need to talk."

CHAPTER 30

Wolf stumbled on a branch and almost went headfirst into a pine.

"You okay?" Luke whispered.

"Yeah, yeah."

The branches slapped and scraped along their faces while brittle pine needles poked into their hands as they groped their way through. The darkness was absolute in the thick trees, but it was too risky to use flashlights at such close range to the house.

Ignoring the ache in his thigh, Wolf pressed on and led them at a steady pace, swerving through foliage that reminded him of Thai and Sri Lankan jungles.

Luke swatted her skin. "Frickin' mosquitos."

She had no idea.

"Shhh, we're close."

A few steps later, the trees ended and they were at the edge of a wide meadow. The whole expanse of flatland was splashed in moonlight, treeless and dotted with lights where houses were built on lots with thirty acres or more between them.

The nearest blob of light was their mark—a single porch

light illuminating the front door of Sheriff MacLean's brand-new two-story home.

"Let's go." Wolf wasted no time hiking across the open space to the road. Veering wide right, he kept out of the light from the front porch and swung around to the rear of the house.

"He's gonna have a light sensor back here," Luke said. "Gotta figure a sheriff has some serious security features on his brand-new house. Including an alarm."

"I hope so."

"You going to tell me what you're thinking?"

"There's no way we're going to get in there without getting shot. So we're going to have to bring him out."

"Okay. And how do you plan on doing that?"

When they'd reached the field off the rear corner of the house, Wolf stopped and studied the building. "That sliding glass door on the second floor and the big windows next to it, southwest corner. We'll stay out of sight of those."

"Why?"

"Because that's where MacLean and his wife are sleeping."

Luke shook her head. "How do you know?"

"I don't for sure, but that's where I'd put a master bedroom if I wanted to take advantage of the sunsets."

"Such a romantic."

He stood up and jogged directly to the north side of the house, Luke following close.

Halfway across the plush lawn there was a click and light blazed from three floodlights mounted on the house, turning night into day.

Luke dove against the house underneath a first-story window and Wolf followed.

Right on cue, a faint ringing in Wolf's ear started, filling the empty space between the sound of pumping blood.

He breathed in through his nose and hard out his mouth. And then again.

"You all right?"

He shook his head to try to launch the noise out of his ear.

"No, you're not all right? What's wrong?"

"Nothing, I'm okay."

"What's the plan?"

A dog barked inside.

They snuck to the corner and looked down the west side of the house, which was the rear and had a large deck with patio furniture. "Go knock that umbrella over as hard as you can."

"What?"

"Quick." Wolf leaned back against the house and blinked, trying to keep his vision from tilting.

"That's your plan?"

"We need to lure them down here. A noise isn't going to do it. We need MacLean to come out with his gun."

"Shhhh, Jeepers!" MacLean's wife was around the corner on the upstairs deck.

Luke looked down at Wolf and then moved out into the open.

"Where are you—"

"Mrs. MacLean?" Luke's voice was a trumpet in the silence.

"Oh, my," Mrs. MacLean said.

"Mrs. MacLean, it's Deputy Patterson. I work with your husband."

"Yes? What is it?"

"I need to speak to your husband right now."

"What's going on?" MacLean's voice came from inside the house.

Luke pointed toward Wolf, who was out of sight from the origin of Mrs. MacLean's voice up on the deck. "My partner and I need to speak to Sheriff MacLean right now."

Luke looked up with imploring eyes, then ducked and sprinted toward Wolf.

Wolf frowned. "What the hell was that?"

"Who is that down there?" MacLean's voice echoed through the night. "Patterson? What the hell's going on?"

There was a swoosh and a clack as the sliding glass door slammed shut.

Luke held a finger to her lips.

Faint footsteps boomed inside the house. They were rapid. Angry.

Luke pulled her pistol. "You take the back door, I'll take the front."

Wolf got up and collapsed to a knee.

"Oh God, are you serious?"

He put a hand on the ground and held himself up from folding completely.

"Just stay there." Luke stood and listened, and then there was a noise and she sprinted away toward the front of the house.

"Freeze." That word and the sound of a dog barking was the last thing Wolf heard, and then his face hit the cold lawn.

CHAPTER 31

A PUTRID RAG slapped Wolf in the face and he opened his eyes.

Before he could tell what had happened, the rag slapped him again, this time on the cheek.

The smell was overpowering.

Then the moist rag swirled against his eye and he flinched back.

"Jeepers," a female said. "Come here."

Wolf sat up and opened his eyes. A leather sofa creaked as he perched himself on an elbow.

Luke sat forward in a chair a few feet away, her eyes wide and concerned. "Hey, Wolf. Wake up."

He leaned back when his head felt light. The leather underneath him grumbled as he slid forward on his butt.

Panting with a happy smile, a golden retriever stood next to his legs, thumping its tail on the carpeted floor.

"There he is."

Wolf followed the sound of the deep male voice and straightened at the sight of MacLean tied to a wooden chair with countless wraps of twine. Behind the captive man loomed an elk head. The tongue protruded from its open mouth as if in mid-call.

"No, down here," MacLean said. "Christ, he thinks the elk is talking to him."

"Wolf." Luke snapped her fingers. "You all right?"

He nodded. "Yeah. What happened?"

MacLean laughed. "What happened? Ha!"

An older lady with basset-hound blue eyes and a disheveled head of silver-blonde hair sat staring at Wolf on a leather high-backed chair. She was unrestrained, but her gaze was defiant as if she were being held against her will.

And then it all came back to him. They were at MacLean's.

"Aaaaand there he is," MacLean drawled.

Luke stood and motioned with her pistol to the woman. "We need to get him water."

The woman stood up and slinked away, eyeing Luke over her shoulder as they both left the room.

MacLean stared at Wolf, his goatee dancing as he chomped his lips.

Wolf stood and stretched his limbs. The stuffed fish clock on the wall said 5:30, and the faint light outside the window and mist-covered meadow told him it was morning.

There was a dark-wood desk in the corner by the window. One of the walls was shelved from floor to ceiling, filled with worn books—mostly mysteries and horror—and behind MacLean was a trophy wall, where three dead animal heads peered down among the brass plaques and picture frames.

It smelled of stale cigar smoke, cleaning agents, and dog. MacLean's manly office.

"I'm gonna have to take a piss pretty soon."

Wolf ignored him.

MacLean's wife came in holding a glass of water, averting her eyes as she relayed it to Wolf.

"Your name's Bonnie, right?"

She nibbled on a fingernail.

"Don't you dare talk to my wife." MacLean jerked against the restraints.

Wolf sucked down the entire glass. "Thanks."

MacLean's wife took the empty glass and headed for the doorway, but Luke stopped her and motioned her back to the chair.

The dog panted and thumped its tail.

"Okay, now that we're all here," MacLean said, "you wanna tell us what the hell is going on? You going to kill us, or what?"

Wolf's face soured. "No, I'm not going to kill you."

"Is that what you tell everyone before you kill them?"

"What are you talking about?"

"Nothing." MacLean swallowed and looked at his wife, who began to cry.

Luke shook her head. "They keep acting like this."

"Like what?" MacLean glared at Wolf. "Like Wolf's killing a bunch of people and running a drug racket in Rocky Points?"

Luke held up her hands.

Wolf pulled the Beretta from his waist, cocked the hammer back, and put it on MacLean's forehead.

MacLean clenched his eyes.

Wolf remembered the streak of blood on Sarah's pale hand as it hung lifelessly out of the BMW door. He felt the drizzle against his face as if he were there again. In his peripheral vision, he saw Sarah staring into nothing, her electric-blue eyes unplugged.

"Wolf." Luke put a gentle hand on his shoulder.

Wolf aimed the Beretta at the ceiling, uncocked the hammer, and tucked it back in the waist of his pants.

MacLean cracked an eyelid, then opened both eyes. Then the twine creaked as he sagged.

"Please," Bonnie MacLean said. "Please don't hurt him."

Wolf shook his head. "No promises, Mrs. MacLean. I'll need some answers from your husband before I decide on that. But first, and most importantly, he needs to stop saying that I killed my wife."

The dog panted and looked between them with arched eyebrows.

Wolf held MacLean's gaze. "You're behind faking those pictures with Gail Olson that made my deputy look like he was, or is, part of a drug racket."

MacLean smiled incredulously. "What?"

"You wanted my whole department to look like one big drug racket. Then you gave the pictures to Agents Smith and Tedescu. That's right. I know all about the two agents. You did all that so you could make us look bad and you could win the election."

MacLean shook his head. "Bullshit."

"Did you know you were married to that kind of guy, Bonnie?" Wolf asked.

MacLean leaned his head back.

"Did you really do that, Will?" Bonnie MacLean asked. "You ... framed this man's department?"

"What? Honey, no, I didn't. This man is a psycho."

She narrowed her eyes, studying her husband's face.

The dog stopped wagging its tail and stared at him.

"I swear!" MacLean popped his eyes. "This is insane. This guy is a dangerous criminal, honey. Just stay quiet. Let me deal with him, all right?"

"Stay quiet, my ass. Did you use pictures to blackmail this man into dropping out of the race? Is that why he dropped out of the race? Is that how we won?"

MacLean ignored his wife and nodded at Luke. "Agent Luke, you—"

"Answer the question, Will."

"Well, yes and no. Honey, you have no idea who this guy is. He's an honest to God drug lord, corrupt to the bone. I had proof that he was, so I used it."

Wolf took a step toward him. "Proof? Fake proof that you created."

"No, proof brought to me by the FBI. I didn't take those pictures." He looked at Luke. "She did, the FBI did. How is it Wolf has you duped like this? It's all him and his deputies, not me. Wait a minute, I get it. You're in on it, too. That's what's going on."

"I'm in on this? Listen, old man, you—"

"Stop. Shut up, both of you." Wolf rubbed his temples. "The video interview with Gail Olson proved you were behind the photos with Gail and Rachette. And when I showed you that proof, you figured out that Baine and I had copies of that interview. You stole them both. You stole my copy from my house, and Baine's from his desk. And now it's no coincidence that the FBI has never seen that interview. It's no coincidence that they think you're someone you're not."

"What interview?" Bonnie MacLean asked.

MacLean rolled his eyes. "First of all, I didn't steal that video from you or from Baine's desk. I have no clue what you're talking about. And, second, that video proves you and your deputy were behind—"

"Oh for Christ's sake." Luke launched up from her chair and pointed her pistol at MacLean. "Do you have this video?"

MacLean nodded.

"Then let's watch it, before I shoot every person in this room and then myself."

The dog barked and resumed tail-thumping.

"Fine by me. Over there in the wall safe behind the desk."

CHAPTER 32

THE VIDEO PLAYER on MacLean's desktop computer showed a split screen—one side with Deputy Baine sitting at an interrogation table, the other with Gail Olson sitting opposite him. Tiny numbers in the corner of each image ticked off in unison.

Wolf had seen the video before, but the last time had been just after his fall, which hardly counted for a conscious state.

He remembered Gail Olson being stronger. Now, on the screen, he noticed that makeup streamed from her eyes and her hands shook as she waited for Baine to speak. It was as if Wolf were watching it for the first time all over again.

"Ms. Olson, can you please state your name for the record." Baine's voice sounded as if he was speaking into an aluminum can.

She cleared her throat and sniffed. "Gail Olson."

"And Ms. Olson, can you please tell me what these are?" Baine pushed some pictures in front of her.

She lowered her eyes but was otherwise unmoved. "Pictures of me and Deputy Tom Rachette of the Sluice County Sheriff's Department."

"And what are you doing in this photo here?"

Gail leaned forward and then sat straight. "I'm handing him a backpack."

"What's in the backpack?"

"A few pieces of clothing and ... two pounds of marijuana."

Baine whooped. "Two pounds of marijuana?"

"Yes," she said in a low voice.

"Can you please speak up so the recorder can hear you?" Baine tapped the microphone on the desk and the computer speakers thumped.

"Yes." Gail sniffed and glared at Baine.

Baine leaned close to the picture. "Did Deputy Tom Rachette of the Sluice County Sheriff's Department know what was in this bag when you handed it to him?"

"No."

"What's that?"

"No."

"Aha." Baine stood up, scraping the chair back.

Gail Olson leaned back.

"Why did you do this? Were you using Deputy Rachette as a runner for these drugs without his knowledge?"

"Yes."

"Thank you. That was good volume on that answer. I appreciate it." Baine paced behind his chair, showing a shot of his torso only. "And you knew this man, Tom Rachette, before you handed him this bag of drugs, correct?"

She nodded. "Yes."

"Did you know he was a deputy of the Sluice County Sheriff's Department?"

"Yes, I did."

"Then again, I have to ask, Ms. Olson. Why? Why would

you so brazenly test your luck and target a Sluice County deputy sheriff? What could you possibly gain in using this man to run drugs for you? Why not choose some other random shmoe?"

She swallowed.

Baine sprung forward and slapped the table, and his angry face filled his side of the split screen. "I asked you a question."

Gail Olson closed her eyes. "I w-was put up to it. They—"

"Put up to it? What does that mean?"

"I was told to"—she looked up at Baine—"get to know Deputy Tom Rachette, and then ask to meet him at that exact spot. At that exact time."

"This exact spot in the photos, at the time of the photos," Baine said.

She nodded. "Yes."

"By whom? Who told you to do this?"

Gail Olson's eyes welled up.

Baine sat down and folded his arms. "Let me be more specific. Did Sheriff Will MacLean of the Byron County Sheriff's Department put you up to this?"

"Pssh, this is BS," MacLean said from his chair.

"Be quiet." Luke pointed her pistol at him.

"... was. Yes," Gail Olson said on the screen.

"What did she just say?" Luke asked.

"She said yes," Wolf said.

"Why did you do this for him?" Baine asked.

"Because he ..." Again, Gail Olson looked up at Baine, this time narrowing her eyes.

"Come on, honey. Spit it out."

"Because he paid me."

"How much? One thousand? Two thousand?"

"Yes."

"Which?"

"Two thousand."

Baine placed his hands flat on the desk. "And what else? That's pretty risky for just a couple thousand dollars. There has to be more."

She kept silent.

"That's it?"

She held up her hands. "And he ... expunged my record." She acted like she was pulling the words out of thin air.

Baine frowned. "Really? He did that, too?"

"Yes."

Baine stood up again and paced behind his chair. "Intriguing. He must have had some inside help for that. Do you know anything about how he did that?"

"I don't know? He said he would expunge my record, and pay me two thousand for the photo shoot, and so I did it. End of story."

Picking up a remote control from the table, Baine pushed a button and the video went blank.

Wolf leaned back on the leather couch.

Bonnie was giving her tied-up husband the evil eye.

"Not exactly the most professional interview I've ever seen," Luke said.

"I asked Baine to get the facts," Wolf said. "I wasn't looking to bust MacLean. I just wanted ammo to fight back against his blackmail attempt. I wanted Rachette and my deputies in the new Sheriff's Department, and that's what I used this video for. I knew Rachette wasn't running drugs and that MacLean was behind the whole thing somehow. I just needed the proof for the careers of my deputies. Forget actual charges against this rat."

MacLean shook his head.

"But, like I said, he ended up nabbing all other copies of this interview."

"And you had a copy, too?" Luke asked.

Wolf nodded.

"Where?"

"In my desk, in my office at home."

Luke raised an eyebrow. "The FBI would've found it. We didn't."

Wolf nodded. "Like I said, this guy had already nabbed it."

"And how would I have gotten that?" MacLean asked. "By breaking into your house while you were sitting there right in the middle of the living room in that hospital bed of yours?"

Wolf shrugged. "You knew how bad I was after that fall. You could have walked in during the middle of the night and searched the whole place without me knowing."

MacLean dropped his head. "Okay, let me know when it's my turn."

Luke looked at Wolf and shrugged.

Wolf stood up and went to the window. "Fine. Explain away."

"I hope you can explain," Bonnie said, "or you'll be looking for a new wife by the end of the day."

MacLean ignored her and glared at Luke. "Like I said, you guys brought me those photos."

Luke said nothing.

"Special Agent Smith came into my office one day and told us he'd been working undercover up in Rocky Points. He started talking about the county merger and you and me running against each other. He gave me those photos and said that I was free to do whatever I wanted with them. Naturally, I asked him what he meant, and exactly what I was looking at. He said it was what it looked like, that a Sluice County deputy was running drugs with the girl who'd been the biggest drug bust in Ashland in ten years. He told me they were watching your department closely and had reason to believe you were at the helm of it all."

Wolf said nothing.

MacLean shifted. "Can you loosen these ropes? I can't feel my left arm."

Nobody moved.

MacLean cleared his throat. "So, yes, I brought those photos to you."

"Blackmailed me."

"Look at it from my point of view. As far as I know, you're a drug dealer, running millions of dollars' worth of drugs through your Sheriff's Department. You're the scum of the earth. Hell yeah, I took those photos and ran with them. I warned you to step off or I'd expose you for what you really were."

Wolf narrowed his eyes. "But you took the pictures."

"I did not take the pictures. I just told you, Agent Smith brought me those photos. How else do you want me to say it, in Spanish?"

"But I told you to stop running the illegal investigation in my county and you admitted you had a guy undercover who took the photos."

"I was lying about that ... but I never said I took the photos. I never said he did, either. I was careful with my words."

"Slimy bastard," Wolf said.

"You slimy bastard. You're the one running drugs through your Sheriff's Department. I was thinking on the fly. I couldn't say the FBI gave them to me—that wasn't part of the deal."

Wolf wished MacLean was untied so he could see his body language.

"Then when I gave you those photos of Rachette and Gail Olson, you stonewalled me," MacLean said. "You were cool as ice, and the evidence was right there, staring you in the face. Hell, I'd gotten the photos from the FBI, and you were just pretending that I was a rat trying to screw you over. Just like you're doing now.

"I have to admit I knew you as too good a man to believe the photos, but when I saw how cool you were about the whole thing, how unfazed, I kind of got the creeps. And then, bam. Agent Smith and your ex-wife are dead, found shot up in a car. I put out the feelers and heard they were dating one another. So I thought, holy crap, who is this guy, Wolf? And you *still* hadn't dropped out of the race for sheriff.

"Then the FBI came to talk to me, right after your ex-wife and Agent Smith were found, but it was confusing as all hell. It's like I was talking to a completely different FBI. They had the same pictures, with Rachette and Gail Olson in them, and they started asking if I'd ever met the girl. I said no, which was the truth. But I knew they were talking with Rachette about those pictures—hell he was in them—so I had to fess up that I'd used them. Used them with your encouragement, that is." He pointed his chin at Luke.

Luke cleared her throat. "I think the important thing to realize here is that Agent Smith was a scumbag, and that you were, in actuality, talking to two different FBIs—one represented by a corrupt agent who dangled a carrot in front of your greedy face, and then, afterwards, one real FBI comprising special agents who abide by the law. That is, if you're even telling the truth about all this."

MacLean darted his eyes around the room.

"Continue," Wolf said.

MacLean closed his eyes. "Like I said, the FBI confused me. I had no clue what to think. They were looking at me like you're looking at me, like I was blackmailing you to get out of the race. But it was the FBI's idea in the first place, and I told them that. ASAC Frye told me they hadn't signed off on that, and that they didn't sign off on that type of thing. I said, no shit?"

MacLean shook his head. "Then I just kept wondering what Agent Smith was playing at by misleading me, and then he shows up dead."

Wolf watched two crows hopping outside. "Keep going."

"That day when we met at your house, you said, *I'm out. I'm officially out of the race, as soon as you fulfill your end of the bargain.* Then you presented me with that Gail Olson interview tape and your demands to hire your deputies. After that, I was wondering what the hell I'd just walked into. I was wondering if I was now the dummy man up front while you ran this drug ring with your list of corrupt deputies on the inside. I was wondering if you were somehow working with Agent Smith, and you'd offed him. Then I started wondering if you and he were setting me up from the beginning—dangling these photos in front of me."

MacLean was telling the truth, Wolf decided. At least a version of it he truly believed.

"And let's talk about that video," MacLean said. "If you look at that video from my point of view, it looks like your deputy is strong-arming her into saying whatever the hell he wants her to. She's crying at the beginning of the interview, for Christ's sake. Who knows what they were discussing before the cameras started rolling. Probably something like, *Say that MacLean was behind this whole thing or else.*"

Wolf walked behind MacLean's desk. The chair was missing and Wolf realized that MacLean was sitting on it. Pulling open the center drawer, he found a pair of scissors and walked to MacLean's rear.

"I showed Baine the photos of Rachette and Gail Olson, and I told him my suspicions that you were behind the pictures." Wolf cut the twine. "I told him to confirm my suspicions. Baine followed orders, my orders, to a T. I haven't seen that interview for some time, and when I saw it the first time my brain was spending more effort blocking out pain than noticing Gail's behavior."

The loose twine fell from MacLean and he massaged his wrists. "Okay. What does that mean?"

Wolf walked to the mouse and clicked on the media player on MacLean's computer. He found the spot of the video and let it play.

"I w-was put up to it. They—"

"Put up to it? What does that mean?"

Wolf clicked stop. "She was about to say 'they' something, and Baine cut her off." Wolf clicked the play button again.

"I was told to"—Gail looked up at Baine—*"get to know Deputy Tom Rachette, and then ask to meet him at that exact spot. At that exact time."*

"This exact spot in the photos, at the time of the photos?"

"Yes."

"By who? Who told you to do this?"

Wolf paused the video again. "She was about to fess up to the truth. She was distraught about it. Scared. Now I'm going to push the play button again. This time don't say a word." Wolf eyed MacLean and hit play.

"Let me be more specific. Did Sheriff Will MacLean of the Byron County Sheriff's Department put you up to this?" Baine asked her.

Gail Olson's eyes darted right, then left, and then she looked up at her interrogator. But as she did so, the fear disappeared. *"It was. Yes."*

Wolf clicked the stop button. They all looked at him.

"She was going to tell Baine that 'they' put her up to the pictures. That 'they' made her do it. And Baine cut her off and asked her whether MacLean had put her up to it, and then she said yes."

MacLean's eyes went wide. "Yes, I saw that."

"She was relieved to tell Baine it was you. At first she thought Baine knew the real truth, and she thought she was going to have to say it on camera. Baine *was* strong-arming her. He'd told her she didn't need a lawyer, because it wasn't an official investigation." Wolf shrugged. "He might have threatened her. That's probably why she was so upset at the beginning of the interview. Like I said, Baine can be a pretty persuasive guy. I'm not proud of it. It's just the truth."

"Yes," MacLean said. "I knew this interview was fishy. Baine steered her into saying what he wanted, and she jumped at the chance, because the alternative was ... what?"

"The alternative was to face the guys who really made her do it. The same guys who shot and killed a lawyer and his family a couple of days ago in Denver. The same guys who ambushed us yesterday, and the same guys who killed my ex-wife."

The room descended into silence again save the panting dog.

MacLean cleared his throat. "And ... who is that?"

"We've been calling them the Ghost Cartel," Luke said.

MacLean blinked. "I've never had a run-in with any cartels

other than a Mexican one a couple years ago. The Ghost Cartel? Never heard of them."

Wolf stared at him.

"What?"

"I think you've unknowingly been working hand in hand with them for years."

MacLean blew a puff of air past his lips.

"Who else in your department knew about those photos of Rachette and Gail Olson?"

"Lancaster, that was it. He was with me in the meeting with Agent Smith."

Wolf nodded.

"Wait." MacLean's face turned red and he looked like he'd been punched in the face.

"And the video? Who else saw the video?"

MacLean's eyes widened. "It was him. Lancaster was the only other person to see that video of Baine and Gail Olson. He's working with the cartel."

Wolf nodded. "And there's one more thing. You told me you had pictures of me, taken the night of the murders, of me and the suspect in the Cold Lake murders. Of us going into my house, and then both of us leaving the next day."

MacLean closed his eyes and nodded.

"Let me guess. Lancaster took those photos. He was in Rocky Points that night and he took them."

MacLean's mouth fell open. "Oh, Wolf, I'm sorry. It was him. He killed Sarah. It was him."

"Those pictures would've been a nice thing to show the FBI to give me an alibi for that night."

MacLean made a pained face. "I know. And when I brought them up to Lancaster, he told me the pictures were gone."

Wolf stared at him. "And it never crossed your mind that Lancaster had killed my wife that night and that he was getting rid of the photos to destroy evidence that he was in town that night? The evidence that he'd killed her?"

The room went silent.

MacLean's mouth fell open. "Wolf, you have to believe me. Our plan was to use the photos to make sure you were out of the race for sheriff. But you dropped out."

"And you never thought about Lancaster being the real killer, and all this slipped your mind until now?" Luke asked. "Yeah, right."

MacLean closed his eyes. "I told you, I thought about the pictures. But ... what can I say? I trusted Lancaster's judgment about not showing the photos to the FBI. I swear it never crossed my mind that Lancaster was responsible. I just thought the photos made it look like, or at least brought up the possibility that, we had something to do with the deaths, so it was a good idea to get rid of them. I swear, I had no idea Lancaster was *actually* involved. But now ... now I'll kill the man next time I see him."

Wolf swallowed his anger, and decided he almost pitied the sheriff for being so naïve. So gullible. Because he saw that MacLean was telling the truth, and more importantly he saw that MacLean genuinely felt regret.

MacLean never paused to think much outside the terms of his political aspirations. If he had, perhaps the entire situation would be different. Perhaps Sarah would even be alive. But Wolf knew he would be misplacing blame if he put it on MacLean. The man was human, with flaws. Others had exploited those flaws and were responsible for all this. It was these other men who Wolf needed to let his anger burn hot for.

"So what's next?" Luke asked.

"We need to get Margaret Hitchens and her sister out of jail."

CHAPTER 33

RACHETTE PICKED a grain of coffee out of his teeth and squinted against the campfire smoke.

Burton, Jack, Wilson, and Munford sat or stood around the fire, sipping their own coffees in silence. The Stellar's jays and popping wood provided the soundtrack of the morning, which would otherwise have been peaceful had they not known they were going into battle.

Rachette had never felt this before. He'd never been in the military and felt the certainty of mayhem and upcoming death. Sure, he'd been shot four times and there'd been ripping pain that he hoped he'd never have to feel again, but that had all been in the heat of the moment. He'd never had time to sit and meditate on the fact that he was going to kill or be killed at this time, on this day.

It was like they were soldiers sitting in the cargo plane, waiting to jump. Like a duel was scheduled for high noon.

Eyeing the others over the rim of his coffee cup, he was surprised at the composure of every single one of them, including Jack.

Most surprisingly Jack, he thought. Or maybe not. He was Wolf's son, after all, and Rachette had never seen a man more composed under pressure than Dave Wolf.

"He'll call soon," Burton said, apparently reading Rachette's thoughts.

Rachette looked up and nodded. "I hope so."

Munford smiled at Rachette through the billowing smoke.

Rachette wanted to gaze at her, to smile and walk over and give her a hug, but he also wanted to keep his dignity. He wanted to know what this woman was thinking about when she looked at him. She was the only Byron deputy here, and Byron was the enemy.

And what if she could be trusted? What next? Was he supposed to ask her out on a date? Is that the vibe she was giving him? Then he'd have to talk to her over dinner, shove his foot in his mouth a few times, then drop her off at her house in awkward silence, and then work with her at the department with her snickering about him with other women, probably with other men, too.

"We've got activity down here." Nate's voice scratched through Burton's Motorola radio. Nate and Fabian had taken up surveillance posts at the intersection of the private house drive and the county road a quarter-mile away.

Everyone stood and grasped their firearms. Coffee cups tumbled onto the ground. They stared at Burton with held breath.

"What's happening?" Burton asked.

"A convoy of FBI vehicles."

They could hear the rumble of tires all the way from the campfire.

"There's five of them. They just drove by, heading east."

Burton frowned. "Copy that."

"They're gone."

They looked at one another.

Burton made a show of looking at his cell phone. His facial expression said, *Come on, Wolf. Let us know what's going on.*

CHAPTER 34

WOLF HOVERED his finger over the plunger of MacLean's desk phone.

"Please." MacLean shook his head. "I think we've established we're on the same side, haven't we?"

Wolf kept still.

MacLean pressed the phone receiver to his ear and straightened. "Deputy Jackson, this is Sheriff MacLean. I need to speak to the booked-in cell F ... I don't care ... now. On the phone ... just do it or I'll get someone down there who will."

MacLean sighed, as if it had been painful to talk to one of his deputies that way.

Wolf pushed the speaker-phone button and they waited.

Six minutes passed and a tired-sounding Margaret Hitchens came on. "Hello?"

"Margaret, it's Sheriff MacLean."

She kept silent.

Wolf suppressed a smile. Margaret had hated MacLean with a passion ever since the picture-blackmailing tactic he'd pulled. She still blamed MacLean for Wolf not being sheriff.

MacLean cleared his throat. "I have someone here with me who wants to talk to you. Please don't say his name. Got that?"

"Hey, Margaret. It's me, Dave."

"Da ... hi. What?" She lowered her voice. "What's going on? Are you ... are they no longer—"

"We need to get access to Sarah's real-estate transaction records. How do we do that?"

"You and I already looked at them. I thought you said nothing stood out."

"That was then."

Bonnie stepped near the phone and spoke up. "Margaret, it's Bonnie MacLean. I've been telling them they just need to get into your intranet. If you give me the username and password, I'll navigate everything for them."

Margaret blew into the phone and it sounded like the county building had exploded on the other end. "And have you snooping around my figures?"

"Margaret," Wolf said.

"You can go into the office, grab all her files. I have them all there. Just ask Jeb."

"I can't. I'm still on the run."

"And you're with MacLean?"

Wolf rubbed his temples. "Margaret."

She exhaled into the phone. "All right, fine. Margothegreat."

"Excuse me?"

"Username is Margothegreat, no spaces. Password is"—she hesitated—"Booboo45."

Bonnie smirked and jotted down the information on a pad of paper. "Thanks, Margaret," she said in a sing-song voice.

"When am I getting out of here?"

"We're working on it," Wolf said.

"Make sure that bitch doesn't snoop around any more than—"

"Bye bye, Margo." Bonnie reached over and pressed the phone plunger and settled in behind the computer.

Fingers flying on the keyboard, she pulled up a website, logged in, and after a few seconds had Sarah's profile on screen.

Wolf, MacLean, and Luke crowded behind her and watched her navigate.

"What time frame are we looking at?" Bonnie asked.

Wolf stared at Sarah's headshot in the upper corner of the screen.

"Wolf?" Luke asked.

"I think we should start from the beginning. I mean, how many transactions can she have since she started three years ago?"

"One hundred and eighty-four." Bonnie whistled. "Christ, that's like five deals a month. I would've liked to have this girl on my team." She covered her mouth. "Oh my God, I'm sorry, David. I'm such a heel talking about her like that."

"Let's just start from the beginning."

She clicked the mouse and a list from three years ago came up. She scrolled down slowly, and, just like the last time he'd seen the list, nothing seemed unusual.

They seemed to all be single-family homes, purchased by individuals. Once in a while there were batches of properties labeled with the same date, purchased by the same person or business entity.

"There." Luke pointed at the bottom of the screen.

Scrolling into view came five properties in a row, all purchased by the same company.

"WCB Incorporated," Luke said. "WCB. Weren't those the initials on the insurance card in that guy's truck?"

Wolf nodded. "Yeah, WCB Holdings, I think."

"Quite a coincidence."

"Yes it is."

Wolf leaned forward. "These properties are all to the south. They were in Byron County before the merger. Is that normal? For an agent to go out of the county to sell homes to someone like that?"

Bonnie shrugged. "If she's good, she goes where the sale takes her."

"Is there a way to look at those houses?" Wolf asked.

She nodded and opened another internet browser tab. "I'll just look up the MLS numbers on Google." She cut and pasted the first number and then clicked the result.

A website listing of a house came up.

"What a dump," MacLean said.

And it was. A low house that measured 2,340 square feet according to the statistics listed, its white siding was stained with streaks of brown, the roof sagging in the middle, two holes gaping. Windows were punched out, and a pair of breasts were scrawled in spray paint on the garage door, which itself hung askew behind six-foot-high weeds. It looked like the kind of place a serial murderer went to hatch plans.

"Maybe they were interested in the land," Bonnie said. "Look here. Forty-one acres. But ... hmmm ... it's out in the middle of nowhere. There's no well. Electricity, but no well water? They'd have to haul in the water in truck loads. No gas service. Pretty useless piece of land, if you ask me. Way too remote. I'm sure the roads out there are a mess, too."

Wolf nodded. "And the other properties?"

She looked up the next one.

It was similar in every way: run-down, in the middle of nowhere, a big lot of land.

All five of them fit the same bill.

"Look for more transactions by this same company, please."

Bonnie scrolled fast, and they all watched the column, waiting for the initials WCB.

They appeared again near the top of the list.

"Here you go." Bonnie leaned back. "Two transactions, looks like five months ago. This last spring."

Wolf pointed. "But these two were in Sluice County."

She nodded. "Yeah, looks like they were." She looked up the MLS numbers on Google and once again the two properties were run-down, on large plots of land, and in the middle of nowhere.

"Let's pull back on that map," Wolf said.

Bonnie pulled back.

"Can you do directions from here?" Wolf said.

She pushed the directions button from their current location and pointed. "That one's just a few minutes from our house."

Wolf turned to MacLean.

MacLean leaned back. "What?"

"You have any guns in this house?"

MacLean raised his eyebrows. "No, I don't believe in that kind of thing."

"Get your guns."

MacLean left the room. "Do I have guns? Ha!"

CHAPTER 35

PATTERSON SIPPED her coffee and squinted against the sun blazing through the windshield.

Lancaster bounced in his seat as they drove from the asphalt to unpaved road, his mirrored glasses reflecting the mountainous landscape ahead.

They were traveling upward along the winding dirt road, past expensive homes built out of large tracts of forest, on the way to Dennis and Angela Muller's house.

Sarah's parents themselves were back in town from Vail because of the news that Jack had gone missing. They'd been brought into the station for questioning on the FBI's orders. At least that was the official reason. Patterson now knew they were being held for protection as much as anything else.

And now Patterson and Lancaster were out here playing a game of charades, though only she was aware of it. At least she hoped that was the case. She was acting like there was still a chance to find Jack Wolf, though she knew he was no longer missing.

Rachette, Wilson, Munford, Burton, and who knew who

258 / JEFF CARSON

else were with him. She was certain of that. Maybe even Wolf himself.

For the third time, she picked up her coffee from the cup holder and put her phone down in its place.

She needed to establish a pattern, showing Lancaster that this was going to be how she handled her phone today: leaving it out in the open repeatedly.

Once again, she picked it up and pushed the button, as if anxious to see whether any news had come in since the last time she'd looked at it. Seconds ago.

Lancaster kept his mirror shades forward, but she knew he was looking. He was an observant man. Hopefully just not so observant that he suspected she was pulling off an act.

She swallowed another bitter sip of coffee. The third strong cup was not helping her nerves any. At least the caffeine-induced fidgeting was helping her play the part of concerned family friend of Jack Wolf, wondering where the hell he'd gone missing to.

She had to calm down.

She was thinking about it too much. She thought about her mother, and wondered how her night's sleep had been on a hard jail-cell cot. Poor Mom. This was a woman who used two Thermarest pads underneath her sleeping bag when she went camping. Those jail-cell cots were like concrete.

She wished she could tell her to not worry, that they were keeping her there for her own safety now.

Lancaster braked and pulled to the side of the dirt road.

"What's going on?" Her heart leaped and she looked down at her phone. Still nothing.

He skidded to a stop and pulled out his own cell phone. Careful to keep it angled away from her, he stepped out of the SUV and walked to the rear, the phone to his cheek.

Turning an ear, she listened hard, but only heard the grumblings of his deep voice.

Keeping one eye out the window, she pressed the button and woke the screen to make sure she hadn't missed a text.

Damn it. She opened the window and poured out the rest of her coffee.

Lancaster got in without a word and drove.

"Who was that?"

"A friend."

Patterson raised an eyebrow. "You have friends?"

She put her phone down in the cup holder again and resumed her silent brooding.

CHAPTER 36

"STOP HERE." Wolf studied the map printout. "It's going to be within view after that corner up there. Pull into the trees."

MacLean turned off the road and bounced through a dip, then revved the diesel engine as they climbed up a rise, slaloming between the trunks of ponderosa pines.

At the top of the rise Wolf, MacLean, and Luke got out.

The wind howled over the ridge, bringing on it the scent of pinesap and an unmistakable odor.

"If that's not the Mary Jane, then there's a family of skunks who got murdered on the other side of this hill," Luke said.

They walked to the top of the hill and ducked down. Below them on the valley floor was a house squatting in the trees, surrounded by a cluster of pickup trucks.

"Down," Wolf said.

He recognized the house from the listing on the computer earlier, but it looked to have been renovated on the outside. Four men with automatic rifles slung over their shoulders paced out front between six pickup trucks—all full-sized, all decked out with lift kits and roll bars with halogen lights mounted on top.

"Looks like we found our cartel," MacLean said, pressing his binoculars to his eyes. "M4 rifles on their shoulders and pistols on their hips."

He handed the binoculars to Wolf.

The image bobbed into view. Four men pacing out front. There was a water tank on stilts in the rear with an insulated pipe leading from it into the back of the house, and two trap doors on the ground with exhaust pipes that spewed blue smoke.

"Grow house," Wolf said. "Water comes in from that tank, and electricity from the generators in the ground out back."

Wolf pulled the binoculars away and ducked down.

"That's a solid motive for killing Sarah," Luke said gently. "If the cartel converted all those houses she sold them into grow houses, that means that, after all was said and done, she was a liability."

MacLean ducked down. "There's an SUV pulling up. Shit, it must have been right behind us on the way in." MacLean surveyed the hillside behind them.

Wolf watched as a black SUV pulled in front of the house and three men stepped out. "That was the SUV parked across the valley from my house."

"That's definitely not FBI," Luke said. "Too much after-market crap on it."

Three other men streamed out of the house to meet the new arrivals.

Wolf recognized the last man who exited the building. "It's our guy from the storage locker."

"What?" Luke reached out. "Give me those."

Wolf handed over the binoculars.

"These guys look pretty well armed," she said, handing them back. "I don't like this."

Wolf pulled the eyepieces back to his face, and he saw even more men streaming outside. "Ten of them. Could be more inside. Looks like our albino guy with the tattoo is the leader, the way everyone's acting toward him. I knew we should've killed him."

"Can I see?" MacLean asked.

Wolf ignored him. "He looks pissed." Albino was pointing at the driver of the SUV. His raised voice drifted up to them on the breeze.

Wolf raked the magnified image from man to man and then froze. For the first time, he noticed a German shepherd lying down. Its ears were perked and it was staring right at him.

"Everyone down."

A bark echoed up the hill just as they ducked. The dog started going crazy until a man yelled for it to shut up.

They slid backwards on their stomachs.

"Time to go anyway," Wolf said.

"Are we going to finally hear about this plan of yours?" Luke asked.

"Yes."

MacLean and Luke looked at each other.

"And is part of your plan informing the FBI about all of this?" MacLean asked.

"And then what?" Wolf opened the passenger door. "Sit in some interrogation room in Denver while these guys carry out whatever they've got planned? No. The safety of my son's not up for grabs. We'll turn ourselves in after these guys are neutralized."

Wolf climbed in the passenger side and closed the door.

MacLean and Luke followed in silence.

"Where to?" MacLean asked, climbing up behind the wheel.

"Back the way we came."

CHAPTER 37

"WOLF IS HERE," Fabian's voice said through Burton's radio. "Wolf is here."

Those who were sitting on their camp chairs stood. Those who were standing gravitated to Burton and his blaring radio.

Rachette's pulse jumped, because he knew action followed Wolf closely, and at the same time he felt the comfort of knowing that the quarterback was here.

Munford stepped close. "Holy crap, is that MacLean? What's going on?"

Rachette shook his head as he watched the big diesel pickup lumber toward them. "I have no idea."

They parked and Wolf, Luke, and MacLean stepped out.

"There he is," Burton's voice boomed.

Wolf smiled sheepishly and shook hands all around.

MacLean ignored the cold reception from Burton and stepped to Munford and Wilson. "Aren't you two supposed to be at work?"

Munford's face went red.

"Sorry, sir," Wilson said. "Duty called."

Rachette looked past MacLean to Wolf as he approached

Jack. They all knew Wolf and Jack's relationship had run up on rocky ground, and Jack's earlier comments had revealed just how unsteady things had become.

Silence descended as they watched the greeting from the corners of their eyes.

Munford turned to Rachette and smiled wide when Wolf and Jack embraced.

"Baine and Yates are here," Fabian's voice scratched through the radio.

A beat-up SUV rocked side to side up the road and parked. Baine and Yates stepped out and hesitated at the sight of MacLean.

"Christ," MacLean said, "is anyone even at the station today? Who's next? Are the cafeteria workers coming too?"

Baine and Yates looked like they'd been caught stealing, then relaxed when MacLean shook his head and smiled. "You Wolf boys are popular."

"All right, everyone gather around, please." Wolf raised his arms.

They walked to Wolf while Burton and Jack slipped away to Burton's truck.

"Where are they going?" Baine asked.

"They're getting out of harm's way."

Baine frowned. "Somewhere safer than here?"

"The abandoned firehouse, where there's not going to be a shootout," Rachette said. "Now shut up."

"The group of individuals who killed my wife are just to the east of us right now. About eleven miles down that road." Wolf pointed at the back of Burton's vehicle as it drove away. "They're heavily armed. But so are we. And if we play this right, we won't fire a single shot, and you guys will be bringing in a whole bunch of cartel members along with me into the station."

"Not a bad day's work," Wilson said with a smile.

"Sir," Yates said, "the FBI went mobile this morning. Something big is going down for them."

Wolf paused. "What do you mean?"

Yates looked at Baine.

"They just flew out of the station," Baine said with a shrug.

Wolf looked at each of them in turn. "Then we don't worry about them. Ordinarily, we would be involving the FBI, but Special Agent Luke here has some inside information about their investigation, and I'm afraid we don't have time for lengthy discussions with them. The timing is perfect right now, and we have to move. If anyone feels too nervous to continue, please feel free to leave right now."

Wolf glanced at Munford.

She stood like a steel tower. Nobody else moved a muscle.

Wolf nodded. "The plan is simple."

CHAPTER 38

Patterson and Lancaster stood on the front porch of the Muller residence and rang the doorbell again.

Patterson peered inside the window next to the front door. The morning light hitting the other side of the house illuminated within, and there was no sign of movement inside Sarah's parents' house.

Still no answer.

She exhaled, feeling lethargic as her caffeine buzz wore off and the lack of sleep from the night before began to take its toll.

"He's not here, either. Let's try back in town, I guess."

Lancaster stepped off the front porch and she followed.

When her cell phone vibrated in her pocket she almost grunted with surprise. Slipping it out, she checked the screen.

Hello, Patty.

She'd been activated.

Howdy. She typed into the phone, and then waited to press send.

She checked her watch. It was 8:49:32.

They reached the car and Lancaster got into the driver's

seat at 8:49:40. She pressed the send button and watched the progress bar.

Come on, come on.

"You coming?" Lancaster asked.

She stood outside her open door and looked back toward the house, as if she was thinking about something.

Glancing down at the phone again, she saw the message had gone out. Her watch said 8:49:46.

One minute and counting.

Despite her electrified body, she climbed in and sighed, lazily setting the phone in the center console.

Lancaster started the engine and shifted into drive.

"You know what?" she said. "Ah, I feel like an idiot, but I have to pee so bad." She pushed open the door. "I'm going to go around the back of their house. No one's home. They won't care."

With no show of emotion whatsoever, Lancaster shifted into park and put both hands on his thighs.

"So ... I'll be back."

Leaving the phone, she stepped out and walked away down the driveway. With a discreet glance, she saw that her watch said 8:50:07.

At 8:50:46, exactly one minute after her reply had gone out, her phone was going to chime as a message lit up her screen. The center console of the SUV would vibrate, and Lancaster's eye would be drawn to a message that, like a huge sheet of fly paper, would ensnare him and his co-conspirators.

She stopped dead in her tracks, realizing she'd left her phone in silent mode.

Oh my God.

With shaky steps, she continued walking.

It would still vibrate. It would still catch his attention.

She stepped around the side of the house and out of sight of the squad SUV.

"Damn it," she hissed, clenching her fists.

She took a deep breath. There was nothing she could do about it now. What was she going to do? Sprint back there, open the door, flip the switch, and then leave the phone and walk away again?

Ten seconds to go.

Idiot!

Her heart hammered and the blood rushed in her ears. Realizing she actually had to pee, she relieved herself, which helped her kill more time, and then she stood at the side of the house for another few seconds for good measure.

At 8:52:15, just around suspiciously-long-pee time, she took a hard breath to steel her mind and marched back around the corner to the idling SUV.

She kept her eyes glued to the ground, and then halfway there she peeked up and saw Lancaster was on the phone inside.

Was it working? She stopped and tied her shoe, giving Lancaster a little more time.

A few moments later, she climbed back inside just as Lancaster ended his call.

"All right, all better now."

He shifted into drive and turned around.

Feigning disinterest, she picked up her phone and gave it a nonchalant glance.

When the screen woke from sleep mode she read the words.

Hey, don't worry. Me, Burton, Wilson, and Munford have Jack at 1483 Star Ridge Road. Keep it quiet until further notice. Come after work if you want. Still no sign of Wolf here. Keep us posted."

It was all there, clear as day. She'd set her phone so that the entire message would appear onscreen as it came in, even if the phone was locked.

The message had been from *Thomas Rachette*, a contact she had added last night for the cell-phone number she'd been given. The real McCoy contact in her phone was *Tom Rachette*.

She looked over at Lancaster.

He was a statue.

She told herself he must have seen. A person's phone sitting right in front of you, vibrates, you look at the screen and read it ... it was human nature.

It was probably how most cheating husbands and wives got nabbed by their significant others these days.

Lancaster drove in typical silence, revealing nothing with his World Series of Poker Champion face.

She smiled inwardly. Because he had been on the phone.

He'd seen it. He'd relayed the message to his murdering cartel cronies, and they were on their way to getting taken down by half the Denver FBI field office.

Now she just had to lure this freak back to the station, where they were waiting to take him down, too. Where she'd be free from the creepy interior of this SUV once and for all.

"Hey, I was—"

Her phone vibrated in her hand, cutting her off.

It was an incoming call from *Tom Rachette*.

She stared dumbfounded, reading the real McCoy's contact name a second and third time as the phone vibrated.

Silencing the call, she flipped the screen down and looked out the window.

"Aren't you going to answer it?" Lancaster said. There was a hint of a smirk on his lips.

Had he read who the call was from as she sat staring at it like an idiot?

With a red face and alarm bells drowning out her thoughts, she pressed the green button.

"Hello?"

"Hey, don't say my name, but it's me, Wolf."

Patterson's heart leapt and she took a deep breath. "Mmhmm."

Had Lancaster seen the subtle difference in the names? Had he seen anything at all?

"... my instructions exactly, okay?"

Patterson nodded.

"Patterson? Are you there?"

"Yes," she said in an annoyed tone. "Go ahead."

"Good. Now when I hang up, I want you to act distraught, and then really worried, and then tell Lancaster that it was me."

Patterson kept silent.

"When I hang up, he's going to ask who this was. Be cagey, and then admit that it was me, and that you know where I am. Tell him I'm with Jack and Rachette, and you want to go meet us. Say you're worried. He'll refuse and say that the official channels need to be notified, and he'll make the phone calls. Let him, because he's going to send some men to come eliminate us, and he can't be anywhere near when it happens. The address is 138 Wildflower Road. We're texting you the address now."

Wolf paused, and Patterson's phone vibrated against her ear. She checked and the address was there.

"Are you still there?"

"Mmhmm." Patterson changed phone hands and glanced at Lancaster. He definitely seemed interested.

"Tell him the address, show it to him, and then let him call the shots from there. Lancaster is dangerous, Patterson. He's working for a drug cartel from inside the Sheriff's Department and has for years in Byron County. You're going to lure the cartel to us and we're going to take them down. We're waiting here and we're prepared to do it."

"Good plan." She sighed loud like she was bored with the conversation. "Not necessary, but good plan."

"What? Patterson, do you copy? Do you need me to repeat?"

"No." She scratched absently at her pant leg, as if she were a teen having a conversation with her friend.

"We're counting on you," Wolf said. "Please text us back to confirm it's in motion. Can you do this?"

Patterson nodded. "Listen, Dad, I have to go. Just get her out, all right?"

"Good girl." Wolf hung up.

She pocketed her phone and gazed out the window, resisting the urge to scream out the window.

They had virtually the exact same plan! And they'd be surprised when it was a complete dud, but they'd be pleasantly surprised, and they'd all have a laugh in a couple of hours, after the FBI was done doing the dirty work.

"Who was that?" Lancaster asked.

"My dad. He's trying to get my mom out. I'm afraid he's going to try dynamite pretty soon. Listen, do you mind if we go back to the station so I can see them?"

Lancaster nodded.

Patterson leaned back. "Thanks."

Game. Set. Match.

CHAPTER 39

WOLF HUNG up and stared at the phone for a second.

"What's up?" Rachette asked.

He shook his head, recalling the single strange words Patterson had said—*Good plan. Not necessary, but good plan.* What had that meant?

"What? What?" Rachette was wide eyed, looking like he was going to strangle him.

"Nothing. Let's get ready, people. Let's put the trucks in the trees around back except for MacLean's and Baine's, which will stay where they are. Everyone into cover positions."

Baine wiped his forehead. "Shit."

Rachette slapped him on the shoulder. "Don't worry. I bet we won't even fire a shot. And what are you worried about? I'm the bullet magnet here."

"Speaking of," Munford said, "you going to be able to hit anything?"

Rachette glared at her and then smiled.

Wolf had trouble figuring out whether she was kidding or not.

"No, I mean I have to take a shit," Baine said. "I'm not feeling so good."

Rachette removed his hand from his shoulder. "Yeah. Okay, man."

Wolf watched Baine slink away into the trees, knowing exactly what his fellow deputy was feeling. It was pre-game jitters, and they were multiplied by ten when losing the game meant dying.

He remembered how he'd felt on his first mission as an army ranger. He'd vomited right in front of the entire squad. They'd even called him Puke for a few weeks after that.

Wolf pushed the radio button and put it to his lips. "Nate, you copy?"

"Go ahead."

"We're on."

"Got it. We're on."

Wolf clipped the radio to his belt and turned to Luke.

Luke stood tall and still, her hand resting on the stock of the M4 Fabian had given her earlier.

"You know how to fire that thing?" Wolf asked.

She blinked in response.

Baine came out of the trees, looking better, and came over to Wolf.

"You okay?" Wolf asked.

Baine wiped his forehead. "I've felt better."

Luke eyed him up and down and stepped back.

"All right, everyone. Let's go over this again."

Wolf outlined their plan to let the cartel get close and attack, going over various scenarios and what they would do in response.

There was no way to predict the cartel's exact movements. Would they stop down the road and come in on foot? Would they drive all the way to the front of the house and come out with guns blazing?

It was going to take good play calling on the fly from Wolf, and quick reactions from everyone else.

Morale was high after Wolf's third rendition of the basic plan. Now they just had to wait.

He checked his watch: 9:01. It had been eleven minutes since he'd talked to Patterson.

"What do you think?" MacLean stepped close.

Wolf closed his eyes against the sun's warmth. "I think Patterson will be in touch any minute now."

He shifted onto his left foot, and his right leg throbbed. Looking down at Rachette's phone, he wondered whether Patterson was having trouble getting back in touch. Maybe the wheels were already in motion but she had no way of contacting them. Cell service coverage was minimal in many areas around the Chautauqua Valley.

"How are you holding up?" MacLean asked.

Wolf nodded. "All right, let's get into position."

CHAPTER 40

By 9:13 A.M. there was still no response from Patterson and Wolf's blood pressure was escalating.

Baine swiped at something invisible. "Damn spiders are everywhere."

They both squatted behind a rotting pile of firewood a few paces off the east end of the house. The wood sat underneath a sagging lean-to structure made of bleached timber.

Off to their right Rachette and Munford huddled next to one another alongside the house, taking refuge behind two piles of scrap wood.

"They're quite the couple," Baine said with a smirk.

Wolf watched as Rachette's lips moved and Munford's stretched in a nervous smile.

"I wonder what her angle is," Baine said.

"What do you mean?"

Baine shrugged. "Mmm. I don't know. Beautiful girl like that going after Rachette? Kind of reminds me of Gail Olson all over again."

Wolf kept silent. He'd been thinking the same thing, but was never going to say it.

"She's the only Byron person here."

Wolf had gone through these same thoughts in his own mind and had already pulled Rachette aside, telling him to keep a close eye on her when the action started, and that's all that could be done.

"We have approaching vehicles," Nate's voice came through the radio.

Baine perked up. "Pattterson hasn't even called and they're showing up?"

Wolf held up a hand to Baine and raised the radio. "What do they look like?"

"They just came onto the straightaway. The lead is a black pickup truck with KC lights on top. It's kicking up a lot of dust, but I think there are three pickups in line behind it. Same type, different colors."

"All right! They're coming in. Everyone out of sight and wait for my signal!"

Wolf's pulse thumped in his neck.

Baine leaned on one knee and stared past Wolf down the dirt road.

They had a small gap in the trees through which they had a view all the way down the quarter-mile driveway to the end, where the county road passed by.

Right here they could see what the cartel's first moves would be, whether they pulled in and stopped, letting out the men to come in on foot, or whether they decided to drive up.

"All right. Keep me posted, Nate. You ready?"

"Damn right," his voice scratched.

Wolf smiled, thinking about one high-school game when Nate had the assignment of blocking the most dangerous man on the other team—a lightning-quick linebacker who later went on to play in the NFL. Repeatedly, Nate had gotten smothered, just barely slowing the big man enough to give Wolf time to let his desperate passes fly before getting leveled himself. Every time in the huddle before the next play, Wolf would ask him, *You got number seventy-eight?* and Nate would straighten his sod-covered helmet and say, *Damn right.*

"They're two hundred yards out."

A bead of sweat slid down Wolf's cheek. The droning insects suddenly stopped and a low rumble filled the silence.

"They're ... not slowing," Nate said.

Wolf dared not blink as he watched the county road below.

The rumble grew louder and a black pickup truck flitted by, then a white pickup, then two more pickups, and then there was nothing but a cloud of dust.

"They just went by. I'm looking ... no brake lights. They're not stopping."

Wolf stood up. "What the ..."

"What's going on?" Baine asked, coming up alongside him.

"What happened?" Rachette asked from the side of the house.

"They drove right by!" Baine answered.

Wolf held the phone in his hand and stared at it. There was still nothing from Patterson. He brought her phone number up on the screen.

"Wait a minute," Nate said, his voice urgent in the radio. "We've got more vehicles coming. Stand by."

Wolf pocketed the phone and walked to the woodpile again. "Everyone hold your positions!"

"What the hell is going on?" Nate said. "It's FBI."

"What? Are you sure?" Wolf gripped the radio tight.

"It's the same unmarked Crown Vics that've been crawling all over town the last few days, I'm sure." Nate sounded like he was standing in a waterfall. "Looks like they're going after the cartel. They're keeping their distance, that's for sure ... geez, there's seven, eight vehicles. I saw light bars inside the rear windows. Definitely FBI ... they're gone."

Wolf stood and put the radio on his belt.

"What do we do?" Baine asked.

Wolf felt a vibration in his jeans pocket, pulled out the second phone he carried, and took in the caller's ID—the white-skinned, tattooed guy from the storage locker.

He pressed the button and put it to his ear.

"Is this Wolf?"

The background noise was loud.

"Who's this?" Wolf asked.

"I said, is this Wolf?"

"Yes."

"Good. I just wanted to let you know we're on our way to get your son."

Wolf held his breath.

"I'll be in touch. Keep the phone on."

The phone went dead.

Already at a full run, Wolf pocketed the phone and opened Baine's truck door. Sitting behind the wheel, he reached up, finding the jingling keys still in the ignition, and fired it up.

Baine jumped in the passenger seat. "What's going on?"

"I'm not sure."

Wolf reversed, turned the truck around, and jammed the brakes as Luke jumped in front of him.

She ran to the back door and dove into the back seat. "What the heck is going on?" she asked. "Was that the Bureau trailing them?"

Wolf nodded. "Yep."

"What are they up to?" Baine asked.

Wolf stomped the accelerator, leaving Nate in a fresh cloud of dust as he turned onto the county road.

CHAPTER 41

POPE HUNG up and smiled to himself.

Pulling out the map he'd printed off their satellite internet-enabled computer twenty minutes earlier, he placed a finger on the turnoff they'd just passed, then followed the road to the turn-off they needed.

He leaned toward the windshield. "There's a gradual turn left, and then we're taking the next right turn after that."

Johnson was going too fast.

"Right, right!"

The truck careened sideways as he jammed the brakes, and they skidded past, missing the turn.

"Idiot!"

The train of trucks jammed their brakes behind them, and Pope heard sliding tires and then a pop of fender slamming into fender.

Pope bared his teeth. "Go."

Johnson swallowed and leaned toward the windshield. Chalky dust came in through the cracked windows and it was impossible to see, but Johnson pressed the gas anyway, knowing he'd incur Pope's wrath if he didn't.

The truck lurched and bounced as it passed through the drainage dip, and Pope held tight onto the roof bar. Through his flexed arm, he released the murderous rage he felt for the man next to him, threatening to rip the plastic handle clean off.

"Sorry, boss," Johnson said as they revved up onto the road and made their way in the right direction.

He glanced in the rear-view and shook his head, watching two men climb back in the trucks, shaking fists at one another, like they were a traveling circus.

Leaning back, he visualized murdering this Wolf guy one more time. Then he imagined murdering the numbnuts in charge of the FBI for losing Wolf in the first place.

Pope shut his eyes and elbowed his window as hard as he could, exploding the glass into a thousand pieces. It showered onto his arm and lap.

Checking the damage he'd done to his arm, he wiped a dollop of blood onto his pants and looked over at Johnson.

Johnson stared unblinking out the windshield.

"Don't worry, Johnson. When we get Wolf's kid, Wolf will come running. And then we're back in the clear."

But Pope was lying and they both knew it. Too many people were now involved, all lining up to help out this Wolf guy. He'd underestimated this man's resources. This had the potential to be a loud and messy situation. Biblical violence.

He closed his eyes and took deep breaths, feeling the crisp mountain air fluttering against his skin from the blown-out window.

Then again, not necessarily. He opened his eyes. If he got the kid, they could separate Wolf from whomever else he was with, and then just make him and his kid disappear completely. Or maybe stage a murder-suicide. A distraught father unable to cope with the sticky web of reality he'd spun around himself.

The framing of Wolf could still stand up. All the blame could still be pointed in Wolf's direction.

Pope exhaled, lamenting the FBI and their incompetence.

He wished he could smash the window again, or kill Johnson.

For a long moment, he stared at Johnson and visualized shooting him in the throat, and it made him feel better when Johnson broke into a fresh sweat.

Pope brushed off the map and put his finger on the dashed line representing their county road. "It's going to be a left after this straightaway."

Johnson let off the gas so fast it was a flinch, and Pope smiled to himself.

Checking the side-view mirror, he swept a chunk of glass outside and saw the line of trucks bringing up the rear, all within a few car lengths of them and choking on dust.

Just as he leaned back his mind registered a glint in the distance and he reached out in the wind and gripped the mirror.

"Slow down."

Johnson let off the gas.

Pope counted the trucks.

"We're being followed." The grill of the Dodge pickup riding their ass swung into view.

He pulled out his phone. There was no service.

"Damn." Checking the map again, he pulled out his pistol and laid it on his leg. "Punch it. Get to that left turn, then pull over."

Johnson mashed the accelerator and the truck jumped forward. The trucks behind them disappeared, but before long the chrome grill behind them emerged in the storm of dust, the men behind desperately keeping close as they'd been ordered to.

"Don't miss the turn this time." Pope pointed his pistol forward. "It's coming up."

They reached the end of the straightaway and the road gently curved right. Beyond that, the left turn was clear as day.

Johnson braked with plenty of space to slow this time and turned.

"Pull over."

Pope was out of the truck before they'd stopped. He took higher ground in the trees to see who was following them.

The other trucks pulled behind and parked, and everyone looked up at him in silence behind the windows.

He gave the cut-engine sign, and the forest plunged into silence.

Eyes stinging as the dust coated his eyeballs, he squinted and focused on the turn in the road ahead.

With stomach-sinking horror, he watched as a line of FBI vehicles came skidding around the corner.

CHAPTER 42

Wolf leaned onto the steering wheel.

"This is definitely the way?" Luke asked for the third time.

"Yes," Baine said, "for the last time, this is the way."

"But it doesn't make any sense. How would they know?" Luke leaned up next to Wolf and pointed out the windshield. "I saw a flash. Did you see that?"

Wolf nodded, letting off the gas. They'd been driving in a perpetual trail of dust for over a mile now, and it had dissipated enough to show a long straightaway, so Wolf had pushed the engine of Baine's old pickup truck to the max.

The needle dropped down fast from eighty miles per hour.

"Turn!" Baine yelled as he pressed himself back in the seat.

Wolf jammed the brakes and tried to control the skid as the rear end drifted left.

The dust was thick now.

There were three metallic pops on the hood, and the windshield became a white web of cracks.

"Gunshots!" Luke yelled.

Still skidding, Wolf cranked the wheel the other way to correct for the initial spin, and felt the truck swing opposite.

Outside the passenger window, a maroon sedan parked in the middle of the road came up fast.

"Hang on!"

The bed of the truck slammed into the back of the sedan with a crunch and the window next to Baine shattered on impact, spraying glass inside the cab.

Wolf reached for Baine and pulled him close just as Baine dove at him to escape the brunt of the impact.

They rocked to a stop and the truck stalled out.

Wolf straightened and saw Luke upside down in the back seat.

"Are you guys all right?"

Baine grunted. "Yeah."

Luke squirmed and kicked, and then righted herself. She had a stream of blood down her face, but looked alert. "I'm all right."

Only then did it dawn on Wolf that outside it had been a constant rat-tat-tat of automatic gunfire interspersed with popping pistols.

A man in a suit and flak jacket poked his head through Baine's window. "Are you folks all right? We need to get you ..." He stared at Luke in the back seat. "Luke."

"Benjamin."

"Are you all right? We've been looking for you guys for days."

Luke slid to the back door and tried to open it. "No shit."

Wolf got out and opened the driver's-side rear door and Luke slid out.

Baine climbed out after them and they ducked behind the wrecked truck next to Agent Benjamin.

Bullets smacked into the side of Baine's truck and they ducked low.

Benjamin crawled next to Luke. "No, I mean we've been trying to get hold of you. Haven't you checked your email?"

Wolf racked back the slide on the Beretta and watched the conversation out of his peripheral vision.

"My email?" Luke checked her pistol. "No."

Benjamin fired at a man in the trees dressed in camouflage pants and a football jersey, carrying an assault rifle.

The guy dropped without knowing what had hit him.

"What?" Luke asked. "An email?"

Benjamin nodded at Wolf and Baine. "Agent Benjamin," he said, introducing himself.

"Baine."

A window above them exploded and a bullet ricocheted off the dirt, cutting Wolf off from introducing himself.

"Why were you guys on their tail?" Luke asked.

"A sting gone bad. We followed them and they stopped and opened fire on us." Benjamin pointed. "At least most of them. One truck drove away up the road as we came up. They turned on us and started firing. It's like they were covering the one guy as he escaped, the coward."

Wolf ducked and ran behind the maroon Crown Vic, and then raised the Beretta as he passed through into the open.

A cartel member was standing behind the hood of a truck, letting rip a string of auto fire in another direction. Wolf fired two rounds into the man's side, dropping him, and then continued on to the next FBI vehicle.

The agent cranked his head, gave Wolf a double take, and then aimed at Wolf.

Wolf recognized the man as Agent Frye, the small wiry man from his interrogation months ago.

Frye dropped his aim as Wolf slid next to him.

"You, what are you doing here?" Frye asked.

"I need a car, now."

Frye fired twice into the trees after a fleeing cartel member. "Kind of bad timing for you to finally show up, Wolf."

"My son is a mile up that road."

Frye ducked down and put his back against his door. "What?"

"Up that road. My son is up there. I think that truck that left is going after him."

Frye shook his head. "Shit. There's still four or five cartel men taking cover between those trucks."

"Give me your keys."

Luke, Baine, and Benjamin slid next to them like base runners coming into third.

Wolf held out his hand. "Now!"

Frye handed the keys over. "I'll be shooting from the rear."

Without another word, Frye opened the back door, climbed in, and closed it.

"Lay down some cover fire," Wolf said as he climbed behind the wheel.

Luke, Baine, and Agent Benjamin nodded with wide eyes.

With knees jammed against the steering-wheel column and his head tilted to avoid the ceiling, Wolf shut the door, put the key in the ignition, and pressed the gas.

The V8 engine revved at the slightest touch and he silently apologized to Baine, Luke and Benjamin as he spat dirt all over them.

Wolf watched in the rear-view as Frye rose to his knees on the back seat. There was a loud pop inside the car as Frye shot out the rear window, and then his gun roared.

Wolf mashed the accelerator and shot out the passenger window, then continued to fire as they sped past the line of cartel pickup trucks.

The engine screamed and bullets slapped into the side of the Caprice. He squinted as shrapnel hit his bare arms and face. Holding his breath, he waited for a deformed piece of lead to enter his body. Certainly with so many bullets hitting the car he was going to take at least one bullet. He knew what it would feel like. It would sting and then be unimaginably hot. But it would be a pain that could not compare to losing Jack.

He pressed the accelerator hard into the floor, but the engine was already performing to its potential, pushing him back into the seat.

The sputtering fire of the automatic rifles was a blur outside, and then they were through.

CHAPTER 43

POPE HAD ALWAYS KNOWN he would die in battle. From the day he'd taken Gabe's advice and joined the marines, he'd known that being a soldier was the life for him.

Had his youth counselor from the Denver YMCA all those years ago lived longer, he'd have probably been unsurprised by Pope's dismissal from the marines and his rise to the top of the biggest illegal drug-smuggling operation the Rocky Mountains had ever known.

Pope had always been a leader, even back in the days of wandering the streets of north Denver. He'd always been a commander, a fighter who was willing to do the dirty work. When you were abandoned by your parents, that's what you had to do. Nobody else was going to look out for you. Nobody else was going to tell you that you had what it took to be great. You had to take greatness and wring it by its neck, and then shove it in your pocket.

The air howling through the passenger window dried the tears from his cheeks as he sped at seventy miles per hour up the dirt road.

He was at the end and he knew it. And he also knew he

would die just as he'd lived—with greatness. But to do so, he'd have to take it. He'd have to make it happen.

Everyone was going to die today. It was going to be something people talked about in awed whispers for generations.

As he approached the crest of a hill, he hugged the right side of the road because, though cataclysmic and memorable, a fiery head-on collision would be a trivial way to end it all after coming so far.

After coming so far? Where exactly had he come to? What had he been fighting and killing all these people for?

With that thought, he drifted back into the center of the road as he topped the hill, leaving his seat as the tires left the road.

There was no oncoming vehicle on the other side. No crash to end his miserable, pointless life. Only a straight downhill cut through the pine trees and a clearing at the bottom. In the clearing, on the right side of the road, stood a dilapidated building. The twisting wooden fire tower told him this was his destination.

So be it. Everyone would die.

He let the truck continue at breakneck speed for another few seconds and then pumped the brake.

The rear swayed from side to side as the wheels skidded, and the building came up fast. With expert precision, he slid sideways and then stopped alongside the building in a puff of dust.

Quickly he scanned the rear field behind the firehouse and saw a man looking in his direction.

Just as the truck rocked to a stop he jammed it in park and got out, not bothering to waste the extra second to turn off the engine.

The man in the field was the fat ass ex-sheriff, raising a

pistol and looking shocked by Pope's sudden appearance. He was out in the wide open, standing like a moron in the clearing with the cover of trees at least a football field away from him.

With his own pistol raised, Pope chose to run at the man diagonally, straight out in the open rather than taking cover behind the fire-tower stairs.

Pop-pop-pop. Bullets whizzed over Pope's head—close, but no cigar. Pope jammed a foot into the soft dirt and crouched to one knee, and then with trophy-winning accuracy and speed he shot the man twice in the chest, dropping him to the ground.

As the shots echoed down the valley, he heard pebbles crunch underneath a shoe directly behind him. He'd run around the back of the building and into an ambush from behind.

But Pope's name was on a plaque at Camp Pendleton, and as he twisted and locked the pistol sight on the kid's chest, he fired, knowing the kid didn't stand a chance.

CHAPTER 44

PATTERSON WAS as quiet as Lancaster on the outside, but was screaming on the inside.

They were almost there. Just a single block on Main Street and they were going to be in the parking lot of the station, where, if all was going according to plan, three special agents were waiting to take Lancaster into custody—crouching unseen in the parking lot and ready to move just before they entered the building.

Counting her, that was four against one, and she liked those odds.

But they first needed to get there without incident.

As the SUV bounced into the lot and Lancaster swung into a parking spot, she took a steely breath.

Hopping out and walking to the rear of the SUV, she almost collided with a Byron deputy she recognized as Prough.

Prough looked like he'd just finished running a hundred-yard dash with a tiger chasing him.

He stopped right in front of Patterson and gulped air. "You heard?"

Patterson cringed and looked around the parking lot. There was no sign of FBI agents.

"Some huge FBI sting up on Star Ridge Road gone wrong. Turned into a chase, and there's a whole bunch of shots ..."

Patterson looked at Lancaster.

Behind those mirrored sunglasses there was a twitch of his eyebrows, and that was enough for Patterson.

Like the crack of a whip she drew her pistol and leveled it on Lancaster. "Freeze!"

Prough went silent and stumbled backwards, catching a heel and landing on his ass on the asphalt.

She ignored the deputy, keeping her unblinking gaze on those mirrored shades. "Put your hands in the air right now."

Lancaster put his hands out and took a step back. "Whoa, Deputy. What's going on?" His voice had a high timbre she'd never heard before. Desperation. She realized he was playing to Prough.

And it worked. Prough got up, drew his own weapon, and pointed it at Patterson. "Drop your weapon, Patterson! Drop it!"

Patterson shook her head.

"Fire!" Lancaster yelled, like a quarterback trying to draw the defense offside.

Patterson flinched but kept her pistol level. "Prough, don't listen to him!"

"Fire, Prough! That's an order!"

"Stand down! Stand down!" Three FBI jacketed men weaved toward them through the cars, pistols drawn and aimed at Lancaster.

"Stand down, Deputy," the first agent said, reaching Prough. "Male deputy, stand down, now."

Prough swallowed and eyed the agents, and then lowered his weapon. "What the heck?"

With a draw so fast it was a blur, Lancaster raised his pistol and began firing. Two of the FBI agents toppled backward onto the asphalt.

Without hesitation, Patterson aimed her gun and squeezed the trigger, punching a hole in Lancaster's chest. Then she shot again, and then again.

As her hearing became muffled, she watched Lancaster's body convulse and spew blood as the other FBI agent emptied his clip into him.

Holstering her weapon, she rushed to the first agent on the ground. He was grunting and howling in pain. The other man clenched his chest, rolling from side to side, and then a loud inhale broke his silence.

With a flood of relief, she realized they were both been wearing flak jackets and, by the looks of it, were just catching their wind. They may have had a few broken ribs each, but they would live.

"Are you two okay?"

After another few seconds they got to their knees and looked at Lancaster's corpse.

Patterson ignored the carnage and stepped up to the agent who had fired. "What happened up on Star Ridge Road?"

CHAPTER 45

HAVING sat in disuse for twenty-five years, the firehouse was a weeded-over one-story, oversized garage with broken-out windows. The structure sagged under its own weight, and the four-story tower behind it had been roped off in case local kids decided to climb its brittle wooden stairs.

The building itself was a poor place for shelter, or cover from a gun-wielding madman, but the entire property was surrounded by thick forest on all sides.

As Wolf drove nearer, he saw the black pickup truck parked alongside the house and reminded himself just how well covered Burton and Jack would've been.

But would they have been expecting danger from a lone visitor? Would they have been drawn out into the open?

Wolf jammed the brakes and put the car in park. As it slid to a full stop, he jumped out the door with his gun raised.

Frye spilled out of the back and strode next to him, covering the left side while Wolf took right.

The pickup-truck door was wide open and engine still running, making it impossible to hear anything but the metallic rumbling of the diesel motor.

Wolf aimed inside, then reached in and twisted the key.

They froze in the silence.

"Jack!"

The suspense was too much. He marched around the side of the house with his pistol raised.

"Wait," Frye hissed, taking cover at the corner.

Wolf skidded to a stop, taking aim at the back of a man holding a pistol, then lowered his weapon when he realized it was Jack's lanky form. At his son's feet lay a muscular, white-skinned body covered in blood.

"Jack."

Jack twisted around and fell onto one knee as he raised his pistol.

"It's me, Dad!"

Jack's gun clattered to the ground. He blinked and tears fell down his cheeks.

"I shot him. He missed me and I shot him. He's not dead. I didn't kill him."

Frye stepped up and kicked a pistol lying on the ground into the dry grass.

Wolf pulled his son into a hug, and he had to grip hard to keep standing as relief flooded through him.

The man on the ground coughed.

"Clayton Pope," Frye said. "Known to be one of the highest-ranking men in the Colorado Ghost Cartel."

Blood pumped from a hole near Pope's heart. His tattooed arm was slathered in red, making the sick rendition of the Pope drawn on it look even worse.

"Where's Burton?" Wolf asked.

Jack pointed to the field. "He's shot. The guy shot him, so I had to shoot. I had to."

Frye ran into the field toward Burton and knelt next to

him. "He's alive! Shot in the right shoulder. Could have caught the lung."

Frye ripped off his own button-up shirt and began dressing the wound.

Burton squirmed and grunted while Frye called for an ambulance on his cell phone.

"He'll be all right," Frye said. "You'll be all right."

Wolf stepped to Burton and knelt down. "Hey, old man. You all right?"

Burton nodded with clenched eyes and teeth. "Jack got him?"

"Yes."

Burton nodded and let out a breath, clearly relieved.

"We've got a helicopter coming up for you. Just sit back and relax," Frye said.

"Shit, I don't need a helicopter."

"We'll take the ride, and then worry about if you needed it or not."

Jack stood frozen behind them, staring at a bullet hole in the side of the run-down building.

Wolf walked over and stood over Pope.

"Did I kill him?" Jack asked with a cracking voice. "Shit ... did I kill him?"

Pope looked up at Wolf and smiled. His chest gurgled repeatedly as he laughed, his red teeth gleaming in the sun.

"No. You didn't."

Wolf aimed at the man's head and pulled the trigger.

CHAPTER 46

WOLF TUCKED the gun in the rear of his pants and stepped away from the dead drug-lord.

Frye was standing next to Burton now, his hand lowering from his shoulder holster.

"He was reaching for his gun," Wolf said.

Frye knelt back down next to Burton. "I'll need to take that weapon, Wolf."

For the first time, Wolf noticed the absolute silence beyond Jack's labored breathing and Burton's grunts. "I think the shooting is over back there."

Wolf walked back to Burton and knelt down. "Thank you, Hal. You kept my son safe."

Burton's lips moved.

"Lean back and relax." Frye said. Then he stood and dialed a number on his phone. "What's going on up there? Okay ... casualties? Dang it ... all right. We've got a civilian with a gunshot wound. Medevac is on its way."

Jack stood motionless, staring at Pope's dead body.

Wolf put an arm around his shoulder and led him away.

"You think he was the one who killed Mom?"

"I think he was the one who gave the order."

"We've got one dead agent, three shot." Frye pocketed his phone and closed his eyes.

"Who was it?" Wolf asked, dreading the answer.

"Benjamin."

Wolf nodded, feeling guilt-ridden relief.

Frye opened his eyes and nodded. "Luke's been shot, too."

Wolf jogged away toward the shot-up Crown Vic.

"I need your weapon, Wolf!"

"So do I."

Wolf parked the sputtering sedan nose to nose with the first shot-up cartel pickup truck and got out. Two legs stuck out from beneath it, lying in a fresh stream of blood.

Sirens blared in the distance and the first in a line of SBCSD vehicles crunched to a stop on the county road.

Wolf jogged past the pickup trucks, swerving around dead cartel members along the way.

"Freeze!" an agent yelled, and suddenly there were ten guns trained on Wolf.

Wolf froze and held up his hands.

"All clear!" another agent said. "Hold your fire!"

Wolf waited until each and every pistol had been lowered, then walked toward a group of agents clustered around someone on the ground. He held his breath as he saw the gray sweatpants, then upped his pace when he noticed they were soaked in blood.

"Stand back," an agent said, his arms outstretched to the others.

"Luke."

She opened her eyes and Wolf was immediately relieved at her healthy appearance.

She looked more annoyed by the wound than in pain. "Are you all right? Is Jack all right?"

Wolf nodded. "Yes, he's fine."

"Stand back," the agent said again.

He tried to glimpse the severity of Luke's wounds as he backed away. The agent was pressing a towel on her thigh. Other than that, she looked scratched up from the earlier car crash. Thigh wounds in the right spot, however, could be fatal.

"I'll be all right," Luke said with tears in her eyes. "They got Benjamin." She nodded toward a body next to a vehicle down the line. An FBI jacket was draped over the torso and face of a man lying in red mud.

Wolf nodded. "Stay put and let them do their thing."

An ambulance stutter-honked and approached between the growing congregation of feds and Sheriff's-Department vehicles arriving on scene.

"I'll see you soon." Wolf peered through the dust and rushing men and women, and spotted Patterson climbing out of a vehicle in the distance.

"Is Jack all right?" Rachette appeared out of nowhere next to him.

"Yeah, he's fine. Burton's been shot. They're sending up medevac to him."

"What was that?" Patterson asked as she reached them both.

"Jack's all right," Rachette said. "Burton's been shot."

"How bad?" Patterson asked.

"He'll live," Wolf said.

"Lancaster's dead. Shot ..." Patterson swallowed the rest of her sentence.

302 / JEFF CARSON

Munford and MacLean walked up, and then Baine, Rachette, and Wilson. Everyone was wide eyed, taking in the mayhem.

"What the hell did the feds do?" MacLean said in a low voice. "We had them coming right into our hands, and they screwed it all up."

Wolf nodded. "The cartel must have seen them on their tail and decided to run. They knew they'd be trapped if they came to the cabin."

"No," Patterson said. "The cartel wasn't even thinking about going to where you were, because I never told them. I never told Lancaster."

"What?" Rachette squared off with her. "After all that, you—"

"The FBI already had a plan in place," she said. "It made no sense to put you guys in danger.

"Sir, the FBI got an email from Luke's partner—a guy named Agent Tedescu. It explained that Lancaster was working hand in hand with the cartel from inside MacLean's department. There's too much to explain now, but, basically, from the moment they got the email, they knew you were innocent. But they couldn't get in contact with either of you."

"What?" MacLean blurted. "When did they get that email? I never heard anything about that."

"The day after Wolf and Luke escaped. After the Gunnison sighting."

"They didn't tell me that." MacLean's face was red.

"They didn't tell you, or us, anything because they suspected you were involved."

MacLean shook his head and petted his goatee.

"They involved me because I was partnered with Lancaster. I gave him some false information and then lured him into the station so they could take him down. But he's dead." Patterson's eyes frosted over. "He shot two FBI agents in their flak jackets, and ... he's dead."

"Wait a minute," Rachette said. "What was this plan of theirs?"

Patterson shrugged. "Basically the same as yours. They knew the cartel had gone after Wolf and Luke, because they found the shot-up truck with their prints inside, and they knew the cartel would jump at the chance to use Jack as leverage to get to Wolf. The FBI sent me a text message that looked like it was from you, and gave a bogus address up in the mountains to lure the cartel in."

"Where?" Rachette pressed her. "What address?"

"I don't remember the number." She pulled out her phone. "Up on Star Ridge Road. And then you guys, no more than a few minutes later, called me and had pretty much the same plan."

"Star Ridge Road," Rachette said with a sour face. "That's a turn off the same county road we were on. But the cartel somehow got spooked by the feds, didn't take the turn, and then decided to drive right to where Jack and Burton were? That doesn't make much sense."

The truth hit Wolf like a punch in the nose. He closed his eyes and mouth to contain the scream welling up from within.

He opened his eyes. "I was just with Frye. He said that half the agents were waiting at a farmhouse on Star Ridge, and the other half were following in vehicles. They were going to pinch the cartel in at the farmhouse, but Frye thinks the following vehicles got too close. The cartel was just running. It was dumb luck the route they were taking was toward Jack."

Rachette exchanged a glance with Wilson. "You think?"

"Baine," Wolf walked away from them, "I need you to take

me back to Burton's wife's cabin. Jack left a few things we need."

"Wait," Rachette protested.

"Uh ... sir?" Baine stood in his spot in their circle. "My truck is wasted."

Wolf stopped. "Oh, yeah. Patterson, give me your keys."

Patterson stood with a confused look.

"Come on, damn it!"

She dug them out and flung them as fast as she could.

He caught them and pointed. "Luke's shot—go see to her. Baine, let's go." He tossed the keys to Baine. "You're driving. I'm in no shape to."

Baine fumbled the keys and then followed after him.

"Hey, can I get my phone back?" Rachette asked.

"No, I still need it."

Wolf walked away from confused grumbling and climbed into the passenger seat of Patterson's squad SUV.

As he settled into the leather cushion, he pulled out Rachette's phone and set it on his leg. Then he pulled out Pope's phone and set it on the other.

Baine crammed in behind the wheel. "Jesus, we've got a midget on the force, and her name is Patterson." He slid back the seat and eyed the devices on Wolf's lap. "What's with the phones?"

"I have to make a call. Drive."

Baine cleared his throat and drove.

CHAPTER 47

PATTERSON STOOD STILL, watching the SUV rumble away in a cloud of dust.

A helicopter thumped overhead, pulling her attention to the sky.

"Medevac on the way to pick up Burton," Rachette said, massaging his shoulder.

Patterson stopped a passing FBI agent. "Hey, what happened, exactly?"

The agent looked annoyed. "These cartel guys pulled out automatic rifles and shot us to shit, that's what happened."

"Yeah, but—"

"Hey, we lost an agent in the firefight and we have another two down." He pointed back toward the ambulance. "So if I may, please?" He walked away.

Patterson watched as Luke was stretchered into the ambulance. For a second she considered running to speak to her, but that would only cause more delay and confusion. Luke was shot, but she was in good hands.

"Did they see you following them or what?" Rachette asked another nearby agent.

"Who?"

"The cartel. You guys had a trap set up, right? And we hear they passed it by."

The agent faced off with Rachette. "There's no way we were made. I was the lead car following them, and we were a half-mile behind. A half-mile filled with dust. No way they would have seen us."

"That's not what it looked like to me. You guys were right on their ass."

The agent stepped up to Rachette. "What are you trying to say?"

MacLean stepped between them. "Hey, Agent, I'm Sheriff MacLean with the SBCSD. And I think my deputy has a good question."

"With all due respect, sir, I don't think he does. I think he's trying to say we screwed up. That all this is our fault."

Patterson turned away from Luke and stepped toward the ensuing argument.

Another few agents saw what was going on and moved near.

"Hey, hey." MacLean held up his hands. "We're not causing trouble. Answer my deputy's question, son. Were you guys made? You say you were a half-mile behind. But we saw you following closer than that when you passed us."

The agent refocused on the question. "We were half a mile out, and we were going to close in when they turned into the farmhouse. That was the plan. Only we got word that they never turned, so on ASAC Frye's command we closed the gap. Agent Frye and other agents left the farmhouse and caught up with us. We were trying to get a game plan on the fly of how to take them down. We knew from previous surveillance that they were armed to the teeth." He shook his head. "Frye was telling us to hang back just as these guys pulled off on this road and opened fire on us. Is that what you wanted to know?"

MacLean was lost in thought. "Thank you."

The agent shook his head and walked away.

Patterson watched MacLean. His lips were chomping and his eyes were glazed over.

"Sir, what do you think?"

He held up a finger. "I think if you're working with the cartel you stay away from the action. You don't get involved in it. You don't get caught up in a firefight. If you did that, you'd be worried about allegiances in the heat of the moment. Your fellow agents would see." He looked up and faced the trail of dust Wolf and Baine had left behind. "Your fellow deputies would see."

Patterson went rigid. "What are you saying?" She looked around the circle and stopped at Munford. "Wait. Was she with you guys that whole time?"

"Whoa, easy," Rachette said. "She's not working with the cartel."

"You sure about that, Rachette?" Patterson beamed a look at Munford. "Your track record of reading women's not too good."

Munford stood frozen.

"Hey." Rachette stepped in front of Patterson and put both hands up. "Back off—"

Patterson shoved both of Rachette's hands away. "Don't touch me."

"Hey, guys, cool it!" Wilson was transfixed on something. "Where's MacLean going?"

MacLean's truck fired up and showered rocks into the line of SBCSD vehicles as it sped away.

She turned around and quickly realized her mistake. "Shit.

Let's go!"

CHAPTER 48

SCROLLING THROUGH ONE CELL PHONE, Wolf steadied the other on his lap as they bounced down the dirt road.

"Who're you calling?" Baine asked for the second time.

Wolf ignored him.

"What ... is that your phone?"

Wolf found the phone number in Rachette's cell and memorized it. "Just making a call."

Baine almost ran off the road and cranked the wheel. "Dang it."

Wolf eyed him. "What's wrong? Gotta take another shit?"

Baine wiped his forehead and rubbed his hand on his pants, like he was trying to start a fire with his palm.

Pocketing Rachette's phone, Wolf began searching one by one through the contacts in Pope's.

"The trouble with these damn cell phones," Wolf said, "is that you never remember a number any more. I can remember five of my childhood friends' phone numbers to this day, and not one of my deputy's. Kind of messed up, huh?"

Baine let out a noise—something between a gasp and a laugh.

"Ah, here we go."

Wolf held up Pope's phone and made a production of pushing his index finger on the screen.

Baine looked over with an uncomprehending frown.

Wolf nodded. "The call." Waiting patiently, he looked at the screen. "Ah, roaming. It might take a few seconds, I guess." He put it to his ear and heard nothing, and then there was a patchy ring.

Baine's face fell.

Wolf dropped the still ringing phone on the floor and pointed the Beretta at Baine.

"I can see the gerbils running in that tiny brain of yours. You're wondering if you can pretend your way out of this. Like the phone in your pocket isn't vibrating. Like I didn't just figure out that you were programmed as number eight in the cell phone of a drug-cartel member."

Baine sagged and started to pant like an overheated dog. "I had to. They were going to kill my sister and her family if I didn't do what they said."

"I don't believe that for a second. We're the Sheriff's Department. We're stacked with some good firepower ourselves, Deputy Baine. What I do believe is that they sweetened the deal with money."

Baine swallowed and gripped the steering wheel with ten wriggling fingers.

"I was wondering how someone breaks into your locked desk without you knowing to steal that interview tape, then also manages to erase the file off YouTube that you emailed me that first night."

Baine shook his head. "I had to, sir. I had—"

"Don't call me sir. You have no allegiance to me."

Baine's breathing stilled and so did his hands. Glancing

down at Wolf's lap, he jerked the wheel to the left and straightened his arms.

The truck revved high and then tilted left as it flew off the steep shoulder, and they sailed into a cluster of lodge pole pines.

Wolf floated in his seat. He put both legs on the dash-board, dropped the gun, and tried to get a handhold on some-thing before the impact.

But it all happened too fast.

His entire world was an explosion of glass, the crunch of metal, a white powdery airbag punching into the side of his head, and then he was weightless. Perhaps dead.

Then came a symphony of springs popping, shafts crack-ing, aluminum bending, and liquids sloshing as he connected hard with the plastic and leather of the interior.

And then it was over.

Dust and airbag powder stung his corneas as he blinked. It was impossible to see through the cloud of debris, so he closed his eyes and tried to feel his limbs one by one. He was conscious, but other than that he could feel no specific sensation.

With sudden ferocity, his head spun, and with a gasp he opened his eyes.

The dust had settled somewhat, and he saw that everything was upside down. He was on the roof, he realized, lying on his back, and he was staring at Baine, who hung upside down, still strapped in his seat, a deflated airbag, streaked in red, hanging from the steering wheel in front of him.

Baine convulsed, and then jolted awake, and blood erupted from his nostrils like twin geysers.

With a new sense of urgency, Wolf began to move. His right leg was completely numb. Looking down, he saw the bend in his thigh and knew his healing femur fracture had snapped in two.

His arms were painted in warm blood from scrapes and lacerations from the glass, but otherwise free of broken bones and moved well enough.

Baine unclipped himself and landed on Wolf's leg.

Wolf howled in pain—proof that his broken appendage had plenty of feeling left in it after all.

With labored, gurgling breaths, Baine righted himself, with no regard to how much suffering he put Wolf through as he rolled on top of him.

"I had no choice." Baine's face was inches from his, his teeth oozing strings of red saliva while his nose poured hot blood onto Wolf's neck.

Wolf locked eyes with Baine's maniacal gaze and kept silent. With slow movements, he began to grope for a weapon along the rooftop underneath him, hoping against all odds that he would find the cold steel of the Beretta among the pebble-sized shards of glass.

"No choice." Spittle flung out between Baine's teeth onto Wolf's closed mouth.

Baine snapped out of his rage and eyed a seatbelt strap hanging down near Wolf's head.

"Should have worn your seatbelt, Wolf."

Wolf grabbed the loose strap and wrapped it once around Baine's neck, then grabbed both ends and pulled as hard as he could.

Baine's eyes bulged, and he tried to pry his fingers underneath.

With all the strength he could muster, Wolf grunted and pulled harder.

Sagging onto Wolf, Baine's face turned lobster red as he

gagged and squirmed. Then he thrashed, his knees slamming into Wolf's thigh, sending fire-hose pulses of pain through his body.

Baine saw the effect, so he started running in place on his knees.

"Ahhh!" Wolf leaned up as hard as he could, connecting a head-butt against Baine's nose. Then another. Then another.

Baine sagged to Wolf's side, and Wolf steered him onto his back on the felt covered roof. He pulled himself on top of Baine, his grip on the seatbelt strap relentless, but the pain in his leg was almost too much to bear.

Baine's face turned bright red and his puffy lips began moving, pleading.

Wolf let up the slack and Baine sucked in a desperate breath.

"Tell me everything." Wolf's own voice was muffled behind a growing symphony of ringing bells.

"I had to, Wolf. You have to believe me."

"Was it you? Did you kill Sarah?"

"No. Please. I'll tell you everything. I can't breathe."

Wolf released a little more pressure. A veil of black started to creep in from the edges of his vision.

"It was Lancaster. He did it. I've just been reporting to these guys. Just keeping them informed. That's it. It was that big white-skinned guy, Pope. He came to me a couple of months before the election. Told me I'd be working for them from now on, or he'd kill my sister and her family."

Wolf shook his head, trying to shake the darkness away.

"I love them, Wolf."

Wolf tightened his grip, and the darkness seemed to recede. "I loved my family, too. I loved Sarah."

"It was ... Lancaster."

"You knew he'd killed Sarah and you let him live? You could have told me from day one. You bastard, we could have taken them down."

"I was scared—" Baine made some choking noises and his eyes rolled.

Wolf let up again on his grip. "You deserve to die," he said between desperate breaths. The darkness was taking hold again, and his vision tilted.

Baine's eyes widened, and then relaxed. "I almost got strangled just like this for that taped interview with Gail Olson. I thought I was doing what the cartel wanted, keeping you in power so I could be their inside man in the new department. I didn't know that Lancaster was already in place and they wanted MacLean to win the election."

Baine was stalling, letting Wolf slip further and further into the darkness, and there was nothing Wolf could do about it. He felt his grip slackening on the vinyl straps. His arms began to shake and go numb.

Baine held still and talked faster. "Man, that Pope guy was pissed. I had to go back and get rid of that video. That was when Lancaster and I became acquainted. He said he'd get rid of MacLean's copy. Said I was lucky to be alive, and I couldn't screw up again or else my sister and her family were dead."

Wolf shook his head. "Shut up."

"But I guess he couldn't get rid of MacLean's video copy. The sheriff put it in a wall safe in his house or something. I got rid of your copy. Remember when I was there that day at your house? I just pretended to put it back in your desk. You were messed up on pain pills. And that Scotch you were drinking."

Wolf's arm shook, almost giving way. "Shut up." He pulled on the belt.

Baine's head rose fast.

His head thumped, like a bowling ball had hit him in the nose, and he collapsed onto Baine's chest. His ears were filled with a thousand bells chiming at once.

He felt himself being rolled over by Baine's strong hands. Blinking rapidly, his vision wavered like he was bobbing in fifty-foot seas.

Baine straddled him and pressed the seatbelt across his neck. "I had no choice, Wolf. I had no choice about all this. And you should have worn your seatbelt."

Wolf let out a hacking noise as the strap dug harder into his neck. He felt and heard a crunch in his throat. Trying to suck in a breath, his diaphragm convulsed.

And then, mercifully, Baine let up on his grip.

Wolf's lungs wheezed as he gasped for air, and it was the most painful yet relieving thing he'd ever felt.

"You know, your wife made those noises after I shot her in the chest that first time." Baine's red teeth glimmered.

Wolf's eyes went wide and he punched the side of Baine's head as hard as he could.

Baine ignored the feeble gesture and pressed again on the strap, cutting off the air once more.

"God damn, she was so beautiful. You really messed up with her, didn't you? David Wolf, otherwise the perfect boy scout, a worthless screw-up like the rest of us when it comes to women."

Baine's cheeks shook as he pressed as hard as he could.

Wolf's face felt like it was going to explode.

"Allow me," a voice came from somewhere else, and then the barrel of a pistol pressed against Baine's forehead.

There was a boom and scorching heat, then choking gunpowder smoke, and then nothing but darkness. Ringing bells, and darkness.

CHAPTER 49

A PAIR of monarch butterflies floated near her perfect face, flapping against the warm wind as if striving to stay near. Her smile was too bright to look at directly. Wolf had to squint so hard that his surroundings became an overexposed wash of light, but he was content to lean back and close his eyes, knowing she lay on his shoulder, her straw hair tickling him softly as it blew on the freshening breeze.

Cracking his eyes, he saw vivid blue orbs filling his vision. "You gonna wake up?"

He smiled and nodded.

"Wolf."

He blinked.

"Hey."

He searched for the voice and found it in a wheelchair next to him.

"How the hell do you pee?" Luke leaned forward and lifted Wolf's bed sheet.

The blue-wrapped plaster encased his entire right leg, crotch area, waist, and part of his left thigh. A bar connected them both to keep them immobile for the time being.

According to the doctor, he'd be stuck in this peeing-dog position for two weeks before some of the cast came off.

"I was wondering why my leg was so warm." He grabbed a
sip of water from the bottle next to him.

She laughed. "You were dreaming about Sarah."

Reality came back to him: beeping machines, a button for
pain medication, a button for his bed, crappy daytime
television.

"I was?"

She nodded. "You said her name."

He leaned back and closed his eyes. "I need more meds."

"They got me on Percocet. Good stuff."

He nodded and cracked an eye. "How are you feeling?"

She looked down at her leg, which was in a cast and jutting
out in pike position.

"I don't think I can even get in that position," he said, "and
they put a cast on you like that?"

"You said that joke yesterday."

He laughed and winced as pain spread underneath his cast.
"I need more meds."

"I wanted to come by, read you this email before I get out."

"The all-this-was-for-nothing email? I don't know if I want
to hear it."

They stared at one another for a second, both knowing
that he was lying. He wanted to hear it, and he owed Luke
everything for what she had done for him.

This Agent Tedescu email he'd been hearing so much about
supposedly explained Wolf's innocence, but if he and Luke had
simply turned themselves in and let the FBI go about its business of taking down the cartel, Sarah's justice would've been
left in the hands of lawyers. High-priced cartel lawyers like the
ones who had gotten Gail Olson off for possession of twenty-

two pounds of marijuana and over one hundred thousand dollars, reduced it to nothing, and then turned it into a counter-suit against the Ashland Police Department.

Witnesses would've been murdered.

Sooner or later, it would've ended the way it had.

"Let's hear it," Wolf said.

Luke cleared her throat and read off the screen of her phone.

Dear Agent Frye,

This message is to you, who I feel I owe more to than our SAC, who we both know I've never gotten along with since Farmington, and to the agents of the Denver field office of the FBI. When you are done reading this and acting as you feel fit, please share this with them.

I am sending this email to explain the conduct of myself and Special Agent Paul Smith in the last three years.

I'm pretty certain I'm being hunted and that my days are numbered. In fact, I'm sure I'm on my final day of life and I need to clear my conscience, and make sure the Bureau knows that my wife and children knew absolutely nothing about what Agent Smith and I have done.

I have given Special Agent Kristen Luke the location and access to a storage locker in which we have placed physical evidence that will prove the existence of the Ghost Cartel. In case the information in that storage locker is not self-explanatory, or if the information is gone because the Ghost Cartel has beaten Special Agent Luke to it, which is a very real possibility, I want to explain everything. Lives are at stake.

In case it is in dispute, let me make it perfectly clear that Special Agent Luke knows nothing about what we have done. She has been a solid, respectable partner who has been dedicated to upholding the oath she took when she joined the Bureau.

Agent Smith and I have known about the existence of the Ghost Cartel—the players, the members, the exact methods of operation—for over three years.

Two years ago, Agent Smith figured out that a corporation named WCB Holdings had purchased some rural properties in Byron County. Upon further investigation, and with the help of a real-estate agent named Sarah Muller from Rocky Points, Colorado, we found WCB Holdings to be a shell company for the Ghost Cartel.

Smith and I staked out and took extensive pictures of these properties, proving they were illegal marijuana grow facilities. We followed their business activities for months, documenting and taking pictures of the operation, which included the smuggling of vast amounts of marijuana from Colorado to other western states including California, Nevada, Idaho, and New Mexico, all funneled through Ashland Moving and Storage, located in Ashland, Colorado.

Just recently, we learned that the Ghost Cartel had again approached Sarah Muller, once more under the guise of WCB Holdings, to purchase two more properties, this time north, just outside of Rocky Points, Colorado.

This is where I tell you about my and Agent Smith's illegal activities. I'll spare you the long story explaining the whys, and say only that the humiliation we had to endure after the Farmington raid went south, and the aftermath, and the demotion, and the split-up, and how we were treated as less than agents from that point on, was too much for us to bear. We were changed. We were broken, and we broke our oaths. I cannot speak for Agent Smith, but I'm not proud of it.

After we compiled a detailed case file against the Ghost Cartel, instead of bringing it to our superiors, we took a copy of the entire file to the cartel itself. We made it clear that, upon our deaths, we had a mechanism in place to inform the Bureau about everything if harm should come to us. Our silence cost them a fee, and we've been collecting that fee for the last few years. I won't discuss the exact amount, but know that my wife was not aware of this payment or its source. She was under the impression that I'd inherited money from my late father's estate.

As we all know, three and a half months ago Agent Smith was murdered, along with the real-estate agent in Rocky Points, Colorado. This has to do directly with the new properties purchased by the cartel outside of Rocky Points, the fact that Smith and I learned about them, and the political race for sheriff of the newly merged Sluice and Byron Counties.

Agent Smith and I realized that the cartel was expanding northward into the former Sluice County—expanding its operations as the size of the county expanded. Agent Smith approached the cartel and told them we required more money since we would be keeping this new information quiet. As Smith put it, as their operation grew, so our fee needed to grow.

They acquiesced, and began paying us more money. I was increasingly frightened by the prospect, but Agent Smith was not. He did not have a family to worry about. He seemed to be living his true calling, acting the extortionist to dangerous men.

Agent Smith, as we all know, ended up dead in a sedan with the real-estate agent in question. The reason is clear enough. The reason I was spared for all this time is not, but I was told that Smith's death was not a sanctioned move inside the cartel. I'm not sure what this means, other than there could be a power struggle happening within the cartel itself. Perhaps a breakout faction of the cartel murdered Agent Smith, fed up with his brazen moves. Perhaps this faction has won an inside battle, and that is why they are going after me right now.

As far as the former sheriff of Sluice County goes, he is innocent of all wrong-doings, no matter how it will look by the end of the day. I know this because Agent Smith and I were given those photos of Gail Olson making a drug swap with the Sluice County deputy. Gail Olson worked for the cartel and, as far as we could gather, the cartel made her set up the Sluice County deputy named Rachette, and they took the photos of her making the drugs hand-off.

We were given those photos because we were told that if we were to be paid more money, we needed to start pulling more weight in the cartel's affairs.

We started working with a man named Clayton Pope, whose profile is included in the storage unit, but easy enough to gather yourself. It was clear to me that Pope did not like us, and I'm pretty certain he is the one after me today.

Back to the point, Pope ordered Smith and I to put the pictures into play to make the Sluice County Sheriff's Department look bad, and help MacLean and the employees of the Byron County Sheriff's Department retain power in the merged county going forward.

Why? Because the cartel has a mole or moles inside the Byron County Sheriff's Department, and they want to keep them there as the county expands. We suspect that the man named Lancaster is a mole. His attitude spurred us to look into his financials, and he is clearly taking payments. After a thorough investigation into MacLean and his financials, it's clear that the sheriff is unaware of the infiltration inside his department.

All of the information Agent Smith and I have compiled on the Ghost Cartel and proof of what I've said in this email can be found at the Trout Creek Moving and Storage facility in Gunnison, Colorado —Unit #62.

I'm afraid that time is short on retrieving this information, however. Jeffrey Lethbridge was the lawyer we secretly tasked to pass on the information to the Bureau upon our death. Somehow the cartel found out his identity, and the nature of our relationship with him, and he and his entire family have been executed this morning. Furthermore, his copy of the storage key has been taken.

I have given my copy of the storage-unit key to Kristen Luke in the hope that she can beat them to the contents inside.

I'm not proud of what Agent Smith and I have done. But I hope in the end that this email and the information we've compiled can help bring down these evil men.

By the end of today, I know I'll have suffered a fate that I deserve. We messed with the bull and got the horns.

Please, sir, I implore you, make sure my family does not suffer the same fate as I have.

Sincerely,

Terrence Tedescu, Former Special Agent

Wolf took a sip of water. "What I don't get is that this email came in to Frye that night we were camped out in the woods, right?"

She nodded. "Yep."

"So why weren't Frye and the FBI waiting for us at the storage unit the next day?"

"Because I didn't get the email until later that day." Frye's voice came from the doorway. "I was driving all around the mountains, chasing your ass, and the poor excuse for cell service you guys have up here didn't deliver Tedescu's email to my phone until a day later. After we'd already missed you at Gunnison."

Luke wheeled back from Wolf's bed and swiveled to face her boss.

"That, and it eventually came to my personal email address, and I'm not in the habit of scouring my personal emails on my phone when I'm chasing a perp. So I didn't see the email in time. And then once I had seen it, you guys had already disabled your phones and weren't answering our calls." Frye walked in uninvited and gazed out the hospital-room window. "Nice view."

Wolf followed his eyes to the western peaks, which were darkened in afternoon shadow.

"What day is it?" Wolf asked.

"It's Tuesday," Luke said. "Four days after."

Wolf remembered the gun poking in the truck window and pressing against Baine's head. He recalled the sound, light, and heat. And the voice.

"MacLean saved me," Wolf said.

Luke nodded. "He followed you and Baine in his truck, saw you guys wrecked in the trees."

Frye cleared his throat. "According to Sheriff MacLean, he heard Deputy Baine confess to murdering your ex-wife."

Wolf's eyes glazed over as he remembered his final moments of consciousness that day. "Yes. He did."

Luke exhaled. "Tedescu said nothing about Baine in his email."

"Like Tedescu said, the cartel was expanding." Frye walked to Wolf's bed and looked him in the eye. "Right into your department."

Wolf shook his head. If there was one deputy in his department who had the personality to cross to the dark side, it was Baine.

"I need to ask you."

"No."

"You haven't heard my question yet."

"You're going to ask if I suspect that any other deputies might have been working with the cartel. And my answer's no."

Frye stared silently and then nodded. "We raided seven

grow houses and the moving and storage company down south."

"And?"

Frye shook his head. "Huge operation. We seized over a thousand plants, and we're not done weighing the product yet, but it's going to be a lot. We brought in twenty-one suspects, and most of them are singing. We'll bring in more today. Ashland Moving and Storage had a fleet of ten rental trucks with false bottoms. That's how they moved the product from here to their final destination."

"And why frame me and leave me alive? That's what I want to know." Wolf closed his eyes. "Why not just plant the gun and shoot me in the head from three hundred yards and get it all done with? Or better yet, come kill me and make it look like suicide?"

Luke shrugged. "First an FBI agent killed, then a real-estate agent, then a drug runner, then a former sheriff? Would have brought some serious suspicion."

Wolf thought about Jack. Had he visited him this time in the hospital?

"I was a wreck back then. I could've killed myself."

"They were going to take you down in the county jail once you were mixed in with the general population," Frye said. "One of the men we took in, Luther Garcia, knew the whole plan. He says our Pope guy took control of the cartel just a few days ago. It was Pope's idea to eliminate the Smith and Tedescu blackmail issue and to set you up. The whole plan was killing two birds with one stone, eliminating the blackmail problem and putting their inside man into the sheriff's office."

"And they had to eliminate Sarah, too," Wolf said.

"Yes."

Wolf shook his head. "What if I'd got a good lawyer and stayed out of jail?"

"The charges would've stuck. The bail would've been astronomical." Frye nodded. "We would've made sure of that given the nature of the crime. You would've spent at least a few nights in general population. Needless to say, now we're looking into corruption in Quad County. It's a damn mess."

They sat in contemplative silence.

"But," Frye said, clapping his hands, "you can thank your girlfriend here for defying orders, and the late Agent Tedescu for being a scumbag disgrace to the Bureau with a conscience. I've got a busy rest of the day. Feel better, Mr. Wolf."

Frye left without saying another word.

Luke stared after him, then wheeled forward and banged her foot against the bed. "Ah, crap."

"I'm sensing he's a little bitter," Wolf said. "You going to be in trouble after all?"

She shrugged. "No. He's just passive-aggressive by nature." She turned around and bent her head back at an awkward angle. Lips pursed, she stared at Wolf. "Give me a kiss."

Wolf smiled and leaned over.

They squirmed and grunted, and managed to peck each other, connecting more teeth than lips.

She wheeled away. "I'm getting out. I'll see you later." She stopped at the door and turned on squeaky wheels. "I'll send Jack in."

His body stiffened as he watched her leave, a knowing, sympathetic smile on her face. "Luke."

She stopped and reversed into view.

"Thanks," he said. "Sarah says thanks, too."

She lowered her eyes and wheeled through the door.

CHAPTER 50

WOLF STARED at the doorway for what felt like an eternity.

Shadows accompanied with sounds passed by—medical personnel murmuring about patients, squeaky-wheeled gurneys, footsteps, and a lone cough—but Jack would not come.

Maybe he'd assumed too much about the state of his and Jack's relationship.

Wolf had found the man who'd killed Sarah, and though he'd been unable to dole out the justice himself, justice had been served. But it remained as Jack had said it: Wolf had failed Sarah that night. He'd ignored her phone call and voice message and gone out drinking. He'd ignored her pleas for help, ultimately landing in bed with a deranged psychotic instead of taking care of his family.

Lowering his eyes, he stared at the sheets through a blur of tears.

"Dad?"

He blinked and wiped his cheeks.

"Can I come in?"

He nodded. "Yes."

Jack walked in hesitantly, studying every nook and cranny of the room like he suspected they were on some hidden-camera television show. He put his hands in the back pockets of his jeans and stopped at the foot of the bed.

His green eyes were ringed red.

"I'm sorry," Jack said.

"About what?"

"Doubting you."

Wolf swallowed. "I'm sorry, too. I'm so sorry."

Jack rounded the side of the bed. "It's not your fault."

The tears welled up again. This time Wolf let them pool and stream down his cheeks.

Jack collapsed onto him and cried into his shoulder.

The cast twisted under the weight of his son and pressed into the tender bone of his femur. With clenched eyes and teeth, Wolf hugged Jack as hard as he could, feeling none of the pain.

CHAPTER 51

Two Months Later ...

"About time you showed up." MacLean stood up, a shadow among the gleaming glass and wood of his office.

Wolf shuffled his crutches and shook his hand. "Good to see you, MacLean. Nice view."

The floor-to-ceiling windows framed the western skyline, from the low hills of Cave Creek to the north, to Rocky Points Ski Resort to the south, and all the blazing white peaks in between.

"Yeah, isn't this a beauty office? Sit, sit. Cold as crap out there, huh?"

He lowered himself gently into the chair, and shifted until the pain dissipated enough to sag his entire weight down.

"Geez, you okay?"

"I'll live."

"I sure hope so. We need you here in the department." MacLean opened a folder and pushed a stapled stack of papers forward.

Wolf eyed the Sluice–Byron County official seal on the top of the page. "Cutting right to the chase, huh?"

MacLean bridged his fingers. "It's what I do."

"You haven't come to visit me," Wolf said. "Not once."

"I couldn't. Been busy. You're one to talk."

Wolf nodded. "I wanted to wait until I could come in under my own power, without the help of wheels."

"I'm glad to see you're up and around."

A metallic crash came from somewhere outside the office, like someone had dropped a metal bowl or platter.

MacLean stood up and looked through the glass wall. "I take it you've heard about the Christmas party we're having at lunch today. Not gonna be much. Just some food everyone brought in. Hope you'll be joining us."

Wolf cleared his throat. "I haven't had a chance to say thanks for saving my life."

"You want coffee?" MacLean walked to his door. "I'm going to get coffee."

Wolf stared at him for a moment. "Yeah, sure. Black."

MacLean left and walked past the windows, and a few moments later Patterson poked her head in.

"Hey, welcome back," she said with a smile.

He smiled back and nodded.

"Come say hi when you're done. We're in the squad room." She left.

He shifted onto his left butt cheek, cringing at the dull ache in his other leg.

"Here you go." MacLean entered and handed him a steaming Styrofoam cup.

"Thanks."

"So?" MacLean sat with a sigh. "What do you think?"

"About what?"

"Shit, you haven't even looked at the contract?" MacLean picked up the packet of paper from the desk.

"No, sorry."

MacLean smiled and sipped his coffee. "You're such a bastard. I put a lot of time and thought into this offer. And you don't even look at it?"

Wolf sipped his cup.

MacLean walked to his windows and gazed out. "I have a dinner scheduled with Senator Chama this evening in Ashland, a gala I have to attend this Saturday night, a council meeting on Monday, discussing the budget allocations of the upcoming year, and, oh yeah, I'm going skiing with Margaret Hitchens and a colleague of hers who's some sort of big-wig in a real-estate development firm. Guy's no idiot, knows I'm a voting member of the council when it comes to most county projects so he wants to meet me and make sure he takes me to the Antler Creek Lodge for lunch."

Wolf watched a pair of deputies walk by the office windows.

MacLean slapped down the packet of papers. "And as I can see by the way your eyes glaze over when I talk about that kind of stuff, ruling you out for my undersheriff position was the right move. Naturally, my undersheriff will be expected to attend many of these social events with me. I'd rather have that man be *all there*, if you will. Check me if I'm on the wrong track, here."

Wolf shrugged. "Sounds logical to me so far."

"I also have some nut-job walking around town flashing his private parts to women, and I've got a string of car robberies in the parking lots at Rocky Points Ski Resort. It seems my deputies can't find their own buttholes on this, and I'm going to get reamed for it all at the council meeting on Monday if I don't make some progress. So, for the love of all things good and cuddly, sign the damn papers, take your ten percent raise and head up my detective bureau already."

Wolf took the packet of papers and studied them.

"I've offered undersheriff to Wilson. He's refusing to make a decision until he knows if you want it or not."

"I think we're clear on that."

"I'll let him know today. You think he's a good choice?"

"I do. Wilson is a fine man."

MacLean put both hands on the desk. "So? You're killing me with suspense here. Head detective? You're basically second in command laterally with Wilson, but don't tell him I said that. Or the county council."

"This says I start tomorrow." Wolf poked at a page.

MacLean shrugged. "Coming in here a few days a week will give you something to do while you heal."

Wolf tossed the packet back onto MacLean's desk. "Twenty percent."

MacLean leaned his head back and laughed. "You kiddin' me? This is a ten percent raise from your previous salary as sheriff. As *sheriff*." He pushed the packet forward. "Come on, let's go, Wolf. I can't bring that demand to the county council. I'm already feeling more heat from them than a blow-torch. Sign the papers."

Wolf scooted forward and teetered up onto his good leg. "I happen to know the new budget figures you're working with, Will. You won't get heat for securing a high-value employee by giving him an offer he can't refuse. Not with that budget. I'll see you later." Gathering his crutches, he hobbled to the door.

"Come on." MacLean stood and shook his head. "Well, I guess that's the way it is. I really can't be paying my head detective that much. I'll just have to start looking elsewhere. I have an eye on a good man from my old department."

Wolf paused and looked over his shoulder. "Just a heads-up about Chama before your dinner tonight. He came to me with a USB drive before the election. I never saw what was on the drive, but he all but told me it was a video of you caught in some sort of risky business, if you know what I mean."

MacLean's face went whiter than the peaks behind him.

Wolf planted the crutches. "Oh, and they're related."

MacLean blinked rapidly. "What?"

"Your flasher and the car thefts."

"What? How?"

"Only the flasher's not really showing his genitalia to women, is he?"

MacLean tilted his head. "How did you know that? Oh, right. One of your loyal minions out in the squad room."

"No, it wasn't. There was a guy in our middle school, Matthew David. He used to walk down the hallway with his ... uh ... pants down and his genitalia tucked back with his legs together in a way that made him look like a girl? Anyway ... used to waddle down the hall, chasing girls like this, shouting at them. He did that, I don't know, fifteen, twenty times a year for two years in sixth and seventh grades. Everyone called him Tuck."

MacLean laughed. "You're kidding me right now."

Wolf shook his head. "He was developmentally challenged. Whatever was wrong with him, he couldn't help himself. Couldn't stop. They eventually kicked him out of school, and he was home-schooled by his mother for his high-school years. Ever since, his mother seemed to keep his urges reigned in, or at least kept them in the privacy of their home."

"So it's him."

"And he had another quirk. He used to break into lockers, teachers' desks, and offices and steal things."

MacLean set down his coffee, spilling some on the top of the desk.

"Not just anything, though. Only eyeglasses. Reading glasses. Sunglasses. Yesterday's paper said the Sheriff's Department was not divulging what was stolen out of the cars, but I take it by the look on your face that it was eyeglasses and sunglasses. Busted-out windows, cars rummaged through, all for that one specific item in each instance."

"My God, you're right. So what? This guy's having some sort of relapse?"

"His mother died nine days ago. That was also in the papers. Obituary section. There's been no mention of the flasher yet, so I hadn't had the opportunity to make the connection until just now. His older brother still lives in town, but clearly he isn't too excited about the role of caretaker he's inherited. His name's Bill David. Lives on Central and 4th.

"And you'd better be quick about whatever you're going to do, and delicate about it, because two of the eleven council members know the whole story of Matthew David as well as I do. And they weren't the ones likely to call him Tuck growing up. In fact, one of them felt the school had been cruel to kick him out, and he used to visit Matthew all the time at home. Good thing the paper hadn't picked up on the flasher yet, otherwise half the town would've had the whole thing solved before you."

MacLean made a fist. "Not one deputy knew about this guy."

Wolf shrugged. "They're all too young, or transplants from elsewhere."

"Which council member was it that used to visit him?"

Wolf smiled and walked out. "Twenty percent."

"Okay, okay, okay." MacLean strode next to him. "Twenty percent it is. You're killing me." He laughed and flourished the contract. "Here."

MacLean flipped to the page that dealt with salary, crossed out the number with his platinum pen, added twenty percent, and then handed it to Wolf.

Wolf studied it for a few seconds, and then shook MacLean's hand. "Thanks, Sheriff. It's going to be a pleasure working with you."

Wolf pressed the contract against the wall and signed it, and then found another line, crossed it out, and wrote in something else.

"What's this?"

Wolf left, crutches creaking in rhythm down the polished hallway.

"Wait a minute. This says you're starting a month from now. Over a month."

Wolf smiled.

"And which freakin' council member?"

He slowed to a stop. "Trust me, you'll look better if you don't know. Just be nice to Matthew David."

MacLean lifted a finger. "You said *he* earlier. It's a man."

Wolf left.

"What are you going to do for another month?"

"Heal."

MacLean made a disgusted noise and his shoes clicked away behind him. "You're killing me."

CHAPTER 52

"THERE HE IS," Patterson said as Wolf entered the squad room.

Wolf stopped outside the circle of deputies that included Patterson, Rachette, Wilson, and Munford.

"Hey." Rachette lifted a cup of coffee and took a large bite of donut, leaving a chunk of blue icing on his lip.

Wolf gave a round of handshakes and noted that Rachette stood shoulder to shoulder with Munford, and she seemed to welcome the closer-than-normal proximity, despite the food dangling from his face.

"Congratulations on undersheriff," he said to Wilson.

Wilson's mouth fell open. "Really?"

"I told MacLean he made a good choice and you're the perfect man for the job."

"Thank you, sir."

"You're the sir, now."

"Wait a minute," Patterson said. "What are you going to do?"

"I still can't handle being on my feet for very long. Jack and

I are heading down to Arizona with his grandparents for the holidays. I think I'll sit by the pool, work on my tan."

Patterson blinked. "No, I mean about working here. At the department."

"I'll be heading up the detective bureau when I return."

Patterson sagged with relief.

"You have your detectives picked yet?" Rachette failed to hide the eagerness in his voice.

Wolf nodded. "I've had the job for about forty seconds but, yeah, I have a couple of them picked out already."

"I hope one of them is me," Rachette said.

"And me," Patterson said.

"And me." Munford stood straight.

Wolf nodded and eyed them in turn. "I'll see you guys in a month. We'll talk then."

Patterson smiled wide with sparkling eyes. "I'm so ... so ..."

"Oh, no," Rachette said. "Here we go. Easy, fruitcake."

"Hey, Thomas." Munford slapped Rachette in the shoulder. "Watch it."

Rachette looked at Munford. "Yeah, okay, you're right. Sorry."

"And wipe the frosting off your lip," Munford said. "You look like you just blew a Smurf."

Rachette and Munford exploded in laughter as he wiped his mouth with a napkin.

Everyone else waited in silence as Rachette and Munford finished their laughing fit.

"Well, I have to go," Munford said with a red face. "I'll see you when you get back, sir. I look forward to working with you."

A snap echoed off the walls as Rachette backhanded her behind.

"Ah, geez!" Munford's face went red and she giggled uncontrollably as she walked out of the room.

Rachette smiled wide and bounced his eyebrows.

Patterson rubbed her eyes. "Ugh. You know when two dogs start sniffing each other's butts and everyone kind of just stops and watches it happen?"

"Whatever. You're just jealous."

She stood with closed eyes, clearly practicing breathing techniques to calm herself.

"How's Burton doing?" Wilson asked.

"He's fine," Wolf said. "Wound's healing nicely. He raves about how he's lost forty pounds in two months."

"So that's the secret?" Wilson asked, patting his ample belly. "Just get shot?"

They laughed, and underneath the vaulted ceilings of the brand-new squad room, with floor-to-ceiling windows that framed snow-covered mountains carpeted with pine forests, Wolf felt a calm that had eluded him for over five months. And, he realized as he looked at his watch, it had nothing to do with the contract he'd just signed. It had nothing to do with the certainty of his future as a cop being re-chiseled in stone.

"I'll see you guys in a month."

CHAPTER 53

WOLF AND JACK stood in silence underneath the cloudless December sky. The air stung their nostrils with each inhale, and froze their exhales into plumes of smoke.

Here lies Sarah S. Muller. A Beloved Mother, Daughter, and Wife.

Ex-wife, Wolf thought, but knew the headstone needed no editing. The text had been deliberately written that way months ago, chosen by Sarah's parents, and it didn't bother him in the least.

"You know, I told Grandma and Grandpa to write the headstone that way," Jack said.

The truth stunned Wolf. He adjusted his numbed right hand perched on Jack's shoulder and cleared his throat. "I like it."

Jack sniffed and exhaled through wet lips. "Do you?"

"Yeah, I do. That's how I remember Mom."

A tear dripped off Wolf's chin, adding to the frozen glaze of tears already on his jacket. It was the truth. He'd never once been comfortable referring to Sarah as his ex-wife, knowing in his heart that one day they were going to pick up where they'd left off all those years ago.

SMOKED OUT / 339

The truth was that he and Sarah had never been separated, but at the same time had never given life together a chance. After they'd said their vows, Wolf had joined the army and left her high and dry. When he returned, she was a changed woman, and they'd struggled with and ultimately given up on their relationship.

He had to reach back all the way to high school and college years to find a snippet of memory of when they were a normal and happy couple.

After that, they had split into two entities, destined to drift in the same system on different but crossing orbits—only passing close to one another in fleeting moments, the gaps between way too long.

And what were they orbiting? This boy, this young man at Wolf's side.

"What are you thinking about?" Jack asked.

Wolf looked at him and wiped a cheek. "You."

"What are we going to do?" Jack asked.

He was taken aback by the question, but managed to keep a strong face. "We're going to carry on, but we're never going to forget the great person your mother was. She'll always be with us. She'll be there to talk to when we want, or when we need. She'll always be in our hearts.

"And you're going to come live with me if you want, or you're going to live with your grandparents if you want. And whether you want it or not I'm always going to be there for you."

Jack looked down and fresh tears spattered onto his jacket. With a nod, he sniffed and then laughed.

"What?"

"I feel sorry for Mom."

"Why?"

"She's gotta sit here with your dad and John. They're going to annoy the crap out of her."

Wolf laughed and blew a bubble out of his nose. Then they laughed even harder.

———

Ten minutes later, with the aid of his son, Wolf hobbled down the ice-laden pathway into the parking lot.

Jack stopped next to the driver's-side door. "Are you sure?"

"Yeah, I'm sure." Wolf tossed the crutches next to the bags in the truck bed. "My leg hurts too much when I do it."

"But it's like a twelve-hour drive to Arizona, isn't it?"

"If you keep your foot on the gas." Wolf climbed into the passenger seat.

Jack shuffled in behind the wheel and with wide eyes remembered to put on his seatbelt. "Am I allowed to do this with a learner's permit?" He adjusted the rearview mirror. "And between states?"

Wolf leaned back and exhaled. "How the hell would I know?"

With spinning tires, they lurched backwards out of the parking spot.

Jack jammed the brake and shifted the stick into neutral. "I want to live with you, okay?"

Wolf nodded, unable to hide the wave of happiness passing through him. "Sounds good."

He cringed as the gears scraped and the engine revved to blood-pounding volume. Then Jack let off the clutch in a smooth motion, just as Wolf had taught him the day before, and they were trundling back down Hilltop Road, on their way to the desert southwest, and to warmer weather.

"How was that?" Jack asked over the climbing pitch of the engine.

"That was better. You're getting the hang of it."

"I hope the truck holds up." Jack mercifully shifted into second gear and they rocked back and forth. "All right. Now just another twelve hours."

Wolf smiled and leaned back, blocking out any thought of the endless stretch of highway that awaited them, not to mention the weather they would face on the way.

"One mile at a time," he said. "One mile at a time."

ACKNOWLEDGMENTS

Thank you for reading Smoked Out. I hope you enjoyed the story, and if you did, thank you for taking a few moments to leave a review. As an independent author, exposure is everything. If you'd consider leaving a review and helping me with that exposure, I'd greatly appreciate it.

I love interacting with readers so please feel free to email me at jeff@jeffcarson.co so I can thank you personally. Otherwise, thanks for your support via other means, such as sharing the books with your friends/family/book clubs/the weird guy who wears tight women's yoga pants while picking his kids up at the school, or anyone else you think might be interested in reading the David Wolf series. Thanks again for spending time in Wolf's world.

Would you like to know about future David Wolf books the moment they are published? You can visit my blog and sign up for the New Release Newsletter at this link – http://www.jeffcarson.co/p/newsletter.html.

As a gift for signing up you'll receive a complimentary copy of Gut Decision—A David Wolf Short Story, which is a harrowing tale that takes place years ago during David Wolf's first days in the Sluice County Sheriff's Department.

THE GIRL STOOD at the side of the dirt road, rooting around inside her trunk. As she looked up at Wolf's approaching vehicle, he recognized her immediately.

She must have recognized him too, because her first reaction was to step back and drop her jaw.

Skidding to a halt, Wolf rolled down his window just as a cloud of dust engulfed them both.

"Hi, Cassidy," he said, peering through the choking dirt.

"Hi, Mr. Wolf."

Her pristine red German sedan was tilted to the rear passenger side.

"Flat tire?"

"Yes," she said, waving a slender hand in front of her face.

"Sorry." He squinted as a hot blast of air came in the window. "Let me pull over. I'll give you a hand."

"Okay, thanks," she said with a mixture of relief and what sounded like dread in her voice.

He pulled behind her car and shut off the engine. As he stepped out onto the shoulder, the weeds snapped and crunched under his old leather work boot, flushing out some grasshoppers that scattered like popping popcorn. Their cracking wings and the burbling Chautauqua River below on the opposite side of the road were the only sounds.

It was only 9 a.m. and the early August sun was cooking the back of his neck.

The wind cleared the dust and Cassidy Frost stood with her hands in the pockets of her frayed jean shorts, which were barely more than a bikini bottom in Wolf's estimation.

He knew Cassidy Frost, had known her well for the past seven months, because she was dating his fifteen-year-old son, Jack. She was just older than Jack, two months into her sixteenth year, and with a driver's license; and since Jack was living with Wolf, and still without a driver's license, Cassidy had been burning a lot of gas, driving up and down this road lately.

But today? He hadn't expected to see her today.

Her eyes were wild-looking, adrenaline still pumping through her veins from the tire, and she stutter-stepped forward with an outstretched hand.

He nodded and took her thin, dainty hand, which tensed into a firm shake.

She really was quite beautiful. Her large blue eyes always reminded Wolf of his late ex-wife, Sarah. And then there was the straw-blonde hair streaming across her face. The resemblance was uncanny, and he knew it was more than coincidence that Jack was drawn to this girl who looked like his mother.

Skid marks had gouged the gravel just a few yards from where she'd pulled over. It was clear she'd been traveling just above unsafe speed when the blowout had happened, and now the adrenaline-powered look in her eye made sense.

"You all right?"

She nodded.

"You have a spare, right?"

"Yeah, it's in the trunk."

He walked to the open trunk. Inside, a piece of carpeted plastic had been pulled away, revealing a thin spare tire and a cheap, insufficient-looking jack. Next to the compartment, a sleeping bag was pushed into the corner, and next to that was a duffle bag, dusty with a piece of pine bark clinging to the fabric.

Pretending not to see those two items, he pulled out the tire and jack.

"I was trying to call for help,"—she held out her phone —"but there's no service here."

"There's never any service all the way down this road until you hit our house."

He wondered where Cassidy's tent was.

"I'm going to help you do this, all right?" he said. "Every sixteen-year-old needs to learn how to change a tire."

She smiled sheepishly and put her phone in her back pocket. "I know. My dad keeps saying the same thing."

Wolf helped her set up the jack, remove the tire, and put on the spare. She was a quick study, asking intelligent questions, all in all diving into the whole thing with a commendable attitude.

But his mind reeled as he watched the sixteen-year-old girl tighten the last lug nut.

Just a sleeping bag and a duffle bag. Where was her tent?

"Mr. Wolf?"

"Yeah?"

"I ... was asking, what next?"

"Oh, yeah." He showed her how to lower the car safely and stow the damaged tire and jack—once again playing the unobservant idiot with the camping gear as he pushed down the trunk with a thump.

"Take it into Mitch's tire shop as soon as you can," he said, keeping his hand on the warm paint of the trunk.

They stared at one another for a few seconds.

"And, Cassidy?"

Cassidy swallowed. Her face dropped and her lip quivered involuntarily as she looked into Wolf's eyes. "Yes?"

"Were you camping with Jack last night?"

Her eyes welled up with astonishing speed.

"What's the matter?"

"You think I'm some sort of slut. I know it."

His mouth dropped open and his face went red hot.

"I see it. I know you do."

He felt like he was being punched repeatedly in the stomach. "Cassidy, I don't think that."

She was openly weeping now, tears splashing in the dust.

He reached out a stiff arm and patted her shoulder, unsure of what else to do. "No. I don't think that."

"I hope you're telling the truth." She looked up with desperate eyes and sniffed.

It was the truth. He often questioned where the second half of her outfits had gone, but he'd known a lot of sluts in his day, and Cassidy Frost was not one of them. Her parents were good people and he knew they were good parents, and she was a good kid. And if Jack and Cassidy were now ... ugh ... "I just saw your sleeping bag. Jack didn't tell me you were included in the group of his friends going camping."

Her eyes narrowed for a second and then she looked away, and Wolf knew at that moment there was no "group of his friends."

"Take the tire into Mitch's tire place. You know it?"

She nodded.

"Tell him I sent you. Or tell him your dad sent you, I guess. He knows your dad too. But get it taken care of. You don't want to get another flat tire and be stranded in the middle of nowhere with no way out."

She nodded and stared up at him, and then her lip started quivering again.

"That would suck," he said with a smile.

She burst into her own smile. "Yeah, it would."

He saw a perfect moment of escape so he backed away. "Okay. See you around. Drive careful. Drive slow."

"I will. Thanks, Mr. Wolf."

She wiped her nose and climbed in the car, started it, and drove away back toward town.

He watched her trail of dust disappear around the bend, and then sat behind the wheel with a sigh.

"What the hell ..." he murmured to himself as he fired up the engine.

He drove at a steady clip up the meandering Chautauqua River toward his house, seeing little of the road ahead of him. It was times like these that he missed Sarah the most. Not that he thought she would know what to do in this situation. In fact, he could picture Sarah's eyes darkening with a distant gaze, and her jaw screwing shut at the news that her son may have just spent the night with a girl.

He smiled at the thought as he drove up the hill to the headgate of his ranch. He missed having a partner, a teammate, to work these things through with. But she was gone. The problem was all his to bear now.

Nate Watson was at his house already, parked in front and standing on the circle drive next to the tall lanky figure of Jack. Jet, a retired German shepherd police dog that Jack had adopted six months ago, wandered next to the barn with his nose on the ground.

Wolf came to a stop behind Nate's full-sized pickup truck, which was branded with a Watson Geological Services Inc. decal that included a professional-looking logo.

"There he is," Nate said with a smile.

Jet lifted a leg against the barn and stared into the woods, and Jack waved and kicked at a weed.

"Sorry I'm late," Wolf said, closing his door. "I had to help a motorist with a flat tire. Hey, Jack. You're home early."

Jack nodded, offering no further explanation.

"I thought you weren't coming back from the trip until tomorrow morning. Heck, you made a big enough deal about it."

Jack shrugged, still averting his gaze. "Mitch Henderson drove, remember? His mom called and wanted him home for some emergency."

"Really? What emergency?"

"Psh, I don't know."

"I hope it's not serious."

His son shrugged and pointed into the distance. "Nate says you guys are cutting trees because there's a fire up north?"

Wolf nodded.

Jack squirmed under his gaze and took a theatrical breath. "Well, all right. I'm going to go inside."

Wolf nodded.

Jack loped away on his stick legs toward the house, picking up his camping gear on the way and dumping it by the kitchen door.

Nate Watson stepped forward and clamped his hand on Wolf's.

With each pump of his friend's hand, Wolf was reeled out of his dark mood. "Hey."

"What was that about?" Nate asked in a low voice.

Nate was a thick stump of a man. Standing at five foot seven, he was at least two hundred pounds, with a thick chest and an inverted delta-shaped torso, like the men Wolf had served with as an army ranger.

Nate's blond hair was shaved to the scalp nowadays, hidden under a sweated-out Colorado School of Mines hat—both ways of coping with the growing bald spot on the top of his head.

The two men had grown up playing football together. The field was where they had bonded, with Wolf at quarterback and Nate at running back, with Nate always there to block for Wolf, always there to throw a bail-out pass to when there were no other options.

Through the years, despite the occasional missed blocks and footballs that had hit him in the back of the helmet, Nate had always been the most reliable man Wolf had ever known. And true to undying form, Nate was here now.

"I just saw his girlfriend. She blew a tire down the road down and I helped her change it. He was camping with her, not his friends."

Nate nodded and gazed into the distance. "Yeah, I know. I was here when she dropped him off."

Wolf narrowed his eyes.

"I was going to tell you."

Like the other people Wolf chose to surround himself with, Nate was a reliable man, but he was also a man that liked to sugarcoat things. He also had the habit of omitting information if he deemed it would cause someone unneeded stress.

Wolf shook his head. "No, you weren't."

Nate ignored him and turned to the north. "So, you're freaked about this new fire, huh? I thought you and Jack already had a hundred feet of defensible space cleared around this joint."

A horrific smell swirled around them for a few seconds and then dispersed on the wind.

Nate wrinkled his nose. "What the hell is that?"

Jet sat a few yards away with a leather glove in his mouth. He dropped it and backed up, looking proud of his find.

Wolf bent over and picked it up. "I lost that glove months ago. Good job, boy."

Jet's tail swished and thumped on the crispy grass.

"That's cool that he finds things," Nate said, "but what's wrong with his ass?"

"Let me guess," Wolf raised his voice toward Jack, who was back outside, picking up his tent, "you forgot to give him the medicine before you went camping."

Jack stared at the sky in thought.

"Why don't you go get it?" Wolf said.

Jack looked at him.

"What?"

"I don't know where it is."

"Maybe Cassidy can give you a ride to refill the prescription today."

Jack nodded and disappeared back inside.

Six months ago, Wolf had gotten a call from a friend in the Vail Police Department asking whether he was interested in adopting a retired German shepherd police dog named Jet. Wolf had looked at the implications of taking in the dog, and knew he wouldn't have time to take care of it with his job, so he'd said no.

Overhearing Wolf talk about it the next day, Jack had told him categorically that he wanted it.

With Jack losing his mother almost a year ago, and the depression, anxiety, and anger that followed finally showing signs of lifting, there was no way Wolf was going to say no to his son. So he called his friend back and said yes.

When they'd driven up to meet the dog, Wolf had been impressed. Jet was massive, which had concerned him at first because, like other German shepherd police dogs, Jet had been taught various commands such as *Fass!,* which was German for attack. But the dog's demeanor had been calm and stoic, like a wise old man who'd seen plenty of battle and saw little that surprised him now.

During the visit, they'd learned of Jet's nine-year career with the Vail County Police Department as a tracking dog, busting countless smugglers and criminals along the I-70 corridor over the years. In the end, they'd been charmed by the dog and brought him home.

On many occasions since, Wolf had seen the animal's intelligence, and his bursts of impressive speed and strength. But Jet was quick to tire and getting on in age, there was no doubting that.

Along with fatigue and a passion for finding things that his human master might find useful or illegal, Jet had developed a bacterial overgrowth in his small intestine, common with German shepherds, and now, unless Jet kept up with a regimen of pills from the veterinarian, he tended to live up to his name —jetting hot air from his backside

Nate cleared his throat and slapped Wolf on the shoulder. "The fire?"

"Yeah. Have you heard about it?"

"The brush fire north of Cave Creek? I heard about it from you this morning."

"Right. Well, I had Jeff Adkins up here the other day and he was saying I should clear those trees on the southwest corner."

Jeff Adkins was the local fire chief and he had been doing house calls, making sure everyone was ready if and when a fire hit.

Nate put his hands on his hips and looked to the southwest. "They haven't been touched by the beetles."

"They haven't, but everything else out there has."

The forest to the south howled as a hot blast of wind blew through the trees.

It had been one of the driest summers on record, and after a hundred years of fire suppression coupled with the widespread pine-beetle infestation of the Rocky Mountains and Mountain West, huge tracts of forest that had once been green and thriving were now rust-colored, dead, and hollowed out by the voracious bugs.

At least half of the trees visible to the south and west of Wolf's property had been hit.

"And that fire to the north has you spooked, and you want to make sure you're prepared if some jackass tosses a cigarette butt out the window on Williams Pass," Nate said.

"You know me well, my friend."

While the acreage to the south and west was thick forest, the trees on the east mountainside behind Wolf's house had been charred and scarred from an explosion years ago, and now saplings grew where the new gaps had been made. As for the reconstruction of his house, it had been long, and Wolf had lived in a half-shell of a house with no running water through one cold winter. He'd likened the experience to living in a shallow cave and he wanted none of that again.

"There're seven to cut," Wolf said, pointing.

"Piece of cake." Nate picked up the plastic case at his feet. "I've got my Stihl. Yours probably won't start, so, you just want me to go ahead?"

Wolf ignored him and went to the barn to retrieve his own chainsaw, knowing full well that Nate was probably right and it was going to take some doing to get the finicky motor of his much older saw to turn over.

Jack came back outside staring at his phone, and stumbled at the bottom of the stairs.

Probably getting a text message from Cassidy explaining that their little jig was up, Wolf mused. Or one of the other million other things he did on that phone every day.

"Dad." Jack put the phone to his ear.

Wolf slowed to a stop at his son's excited tone.

"What's up?"

"Cassidy?" Jack held up a finger to Wolf. "Why? ... okay, okay." Jack stepped up and thrust the phone at Wolf. "It's Cassidy. She wants to talk to you."

Wolf raised both his hands like Jack had a pistol pointed at his face. "Jack, tell her we'll talk later. After you and I have a talk."

"Dad." Jack put the phone against his body and covered it with his other hand. "I've never heard her so freaked out. Something happened. She said something about how she couldn't call 911 on her phone."

He thrust the cell out again and Wolf took it.

"Hello?"

"Mr. Wolf! My—"

There was scratching and then silence.

"Cassidy?"

No answer.

Nate and Jack stared in mute curiosity.

"Cassidy? Can you hear me?" Wolf's curiosity was piqued. The few words he heard definitely sounded spooked.

"Mr. Wolf? Can you hear me?"

"Yes. What is it?"

"My dad's been shot. He's been shot. Can you hear me? I can't call 911 on my—"

Silence again.

"Is he hurt?"

No answer. Damn it. Damn the cell service. And what a question, Wolf thought. Of course he was hurt. He was shot.

"Cassidy? Is he okay?"

"No."

The simple answer, the clarity and desperation in her voice, made Wolf's insides sink.

"Go to the Sheriff's Station, Cassidy. Go there now."

Go to Amazon.com to get the next David Wolf Mystery and continue the adventure!

Made in the USA
Monee, IL
21 June 2020